PRAISE
FOR
EDIE ON THE GREEN SCREEN

"Lisick's languid prose has a magnetic pull to it (not dissimilar to the experience of watching a Noah Baumbach film)... It's pleasurable to tag along on Lisick's winding tour through the Bay Area... Lisick's stringent humor is what makes this tale worth reading..." —**Kirkus Reviews**

"At once an ode to a bygone San Francisco and its characters, who have been pushed to the edges by the city's new era, this novel is a glorious, multilayered midlife coming-of-age story..." —**Booklist**

"Beth Lisick's *Edie On The Green Screen* really hit my sweet spot: a darkly funny, honest, touching look at what it means to be an adult in the world today—and what happens when you can't quite figure it out. I inhaled this book." —**Jami Attenberg, author of *All This Could Be Yours***

"Beth Lisick possesses one of the most alive narrative voices I have ever heard, full of humor and truth and pathos and smarts. I heard her read a piece of this novel at its start and I have been haunted by the driving beauty and passion of it." —**Michelle Tea, author of *Against Memoir***

"Beth Lisick's writing is so vivid, so alert, intelligent and alive you feel ninety-eight percent smarter every moment that you read her—when you're not doubled over in helpless, delighted laughter. If Eve Babitz was living and writing in the Mission District today, this is who she'd be." —**Matthew Specktor, author of *American Dream Machine***

"Beth Lisick has proven time and time again to be the storytelling voice of our collective adolescence, of our dreaming in vast American suburbs, and our heading into cities, come what may. She's a rare voice in the age of quasi instant gratification like posts and tweets—a writer who waits until the time is right and the words are ready. *Edie on the Green Screen* is somehow both a howl and a murmur, bright and shadowy, funny and heart-worn. Here's that book we're all always hoping to find next, the one that feels like you're hanging out with a new friend—one who finishes telling you a story that leaves you sated but immediately hoping there's another, and another, and another."

—Dan Kennedy, host of *The Moth Podcast*

PRAISE FOR
YOKOHAMA THREEWAY

"Lisick is a clever poet and comedian with the skills to elicit laughter, tears, and (sometimes) cringes . . ." —**Bust Magazine**

"Lisick has decided to let us into her strange inner sanctum and it feels intimate and sweet. And though you'll be laughing, you won't be laughing at her but with her — a critical distinction and an incredibly difficult task in writing, one that Lisick accomplishes masterfully. So while you or I may never have the guts to share the sorts of stories that Lisick does, I promise you'll be grateful she did. Grateful and maybe a little shocked." —**Bitch Magazine**

"A strangely touching and engaging portrait of the artist as a young screwup."—**Booklist**

PRAISE FOR
HELPING ME HELP MYSELF

"Not only hilarious, but enlightening." —**People Magazine**

"Sweetly neurotic and funny." —**Los Angeles Times**

"A hilarious, knowing tale of a year of willing ridiculousness."
—**San Francisco Chronicle**

"A delightful, Plimptonesque exercise in immersive journalism exploring the strange world of 'self-help.' Funny, perceptive and surprisingly open-hearted under the cynicism." —**Kirkus Reviews**

PRAISE FOR
EVERYBODY INTO THE POOL

"The tales veer from razor sharp to hilarious, and it's a voice–both offbeat and upbeat, wised-up yet curiously wholesome."
—**Entertainment Weekly, "Top 10 Nonfiction Books of the Year"**

"Lisick is an accomplished storyteller. Darkly funny."
—**Kirkus Reviews**

Printed in the United States of America

First Edition

Distributed by Small Press Distribution in Berkeley, California.

Cover design: Gigi Little

Copyright ©2020 by Beth Lisick
Library of Congress Cataloging-in-Publication Data:

ISBN: 978-1-7333672-0-2
LCCN: 2019954224

to all my friends

1998

CLASSIC THAT I COULDN'T figure out how to get into the building once I finally found it. There wasn't a buzzer so I tried to yell up to the open window, but my voice was trashed. I kicked the door with my boot then used an open-palm approach in a series of no-bullshit slams. Nothing. I scanned the sidewalk for a decent rock to pitch. What a relief to know that when you've been invited to a nondescript location with no doorbell or any instructions on how to alert the occupants you've arrived, it's perfectly acceptable to bail.

Still, I lobbed one eepy last-ditch *hey!* up to the sky. My voice didn't carry.

Party croak. That's what I call the husky drinker/smoker's crackle I've had since I was a kid, though back then me and my best friend would try to bring it on by screaming at the top of our lungs in the apricot orchard in our neighborhood. I was always pleased with the result. Mild laryngitis: when you want people to think you've overdosed on fun. It wasn't lost on me that I had finally realized one of my childhood dreams. I had become a grown woman who no longer had to keep screaming into the void in order to prove to everyone that I'd been out having a really good time.

There was a phone booth at the corner gas station, which could have been useful if I had a number to call, but that thought was interrupted by a violent buzzing. At last. I shouldered into the heavy industrial door and was greeted by a fortyish redhead. The woman's hair was dyed gemstone bright, in order to assert her boldness about being a woman in her forties, I assumed. Her skin looked slick and epoxied, like an egg-washed pork bun or an expensive chunk of cheese. Must have been the result of some kind of fancy treatment or science-based cosmeceutical. Me, I didn't have many wrinkles yet, and I wasn't worried about it. I thought I could stay trapped as I was, in the warm amber glow of twenty-eight, like a cucaracha on a keychain, until nothing mattered anymore. The suspense was killing me.

"She's almost done with Stella," the redhead stage-whispered to me as we climbed the stairs, looking back in a not unsexy way. She had a pretty good ass in her bootcuts, which looked vintage. Real vintage, like early '70s, not this faux "vintage" all the bullshit chain stores were trying to pull off. She paused and looked back again. "I'm Tanya, by the way. I'm makeup."

She continued her march up the stairs, mules tapping against her heels, and I realized I probably should have stayed home. I was hungover, my nose was running, there was sleep in my eyes, my breath was all coffee and cigarettes. When she reached the top, it was probably my silence that made her think she had to explain.

"Your face. I mean I can do your face."

The ritual of a daily makeup practice was something I had begun with a passion at twelve and pulled the plug on by fourteen. I used to pile on a showgirl's ration of sparkly blue eyeshadow and heavy liner each morning, all tarted up for my big day of learning algebra and flirting with boys in the quad, Cheeto dust sticking to my heavily glossed lips, no doubt. And then one morning in Spanish class, Gina Hartnett and Lorna Collier disinvited me to a party in tandem, voices sing-songing in unison like psychopaths from a horror film, before returning to feathering blush on their sucked-in cheeks. I surveyed them from across the room and it hit me. Wearing makeup was telegraphing to the whole world that you were trying to improve upon yourself. All that ambition piled right onto your stupid face. So I gave it up. I might slap on a cheap lipstick if I were holding a tube, but I mostly found them/lost them again at the bar. I could never stomach using a purse. It's essentially like carrying your vagina around on the outside of your clothes. *Hi, I'm a lady and all my special things are right in this ladybag that I bring with me everywhere.* Nope.

I followed Tanya around a tight corner and then stopped at the doorjamb to take in the scene. The place had twenty-foot-high ceilings and a wall of windows facing Harrison Street, definitely the most professional photography studio I'd ever been in. Very sleek and moderne. Boho mofo chic. Clean Lines Dot Com. (That used to be a joke for a couple years, after the invention of the internet, to say *Dot Com* after literally anything. Hey, could you pass the ketchup.com? Ugh, I have the worst cramps.com. That girl rejecting my clothes for resale at the Buffalo Exchange? WantedToStrangleHer.com.)

Tanya popped open a tin of mints and offered it to me. "Well, I'm makeup *and* styling," she said. "Budget shoot. Stella didn't need me at all, though. She came totally camera-ready. Have you seen her films? Do you know her?"

Stella, currently being photographed, was Stella Onfire, an indie porn producer who got all sorts of attention for making DIY videos with real, non-surgically enhanced bodies in them. We'd never met, but I'd been to a few of her enormous parties, which were enjoyable enough displays of extreme exhibitionism among people who probably had mild psychological disorders. Stella was the kind of person who reveled in feeling overtly political by giving away sex toys, year after year, dong after dong. It was a never-ending dildo parade over there. I had no real problem with that, with the exception that it was getting very boring. San Francisco's sex nerd lifestylers caused me an unreasonable level of mental fatigue. We get it. You're a pervert. And guess what? So is practically everyone. Some people just keep a tighter lid on it because they understand that humans start getting less and less interesting once you've figured out what they want.

Tanya motioned me to step all the way in and take a look. Stella was so gorgeous. One of those Hellenistic goddesses with a forehead a mile wide and fierce manhands that should either be slapping the shit out of some well-deserving simp for money or directing traffic under the Arc de Triomphe. She could really work a photo shoot. She knew how to push and pull and suck and tilt and preen and lift; when to be the lady on the bow of a ship and when to collapse into a vulnerable heap, making her body fold onto itself like a magician's discarded cape. Abracadabra, now I'm a puddle of alabaster flesh. For a minute, it looked like she was one of the few people in the city who was making it through the '90s without a single tattoo, until she spread her legs and revealed some stick and poke script on her inner thigh. What relief I felt. The badassness, the blank slateness, of not having tattoos was my thing. It's what set me apart from almost everyone else in this scene, now that I had reached the top of the scene ladder, The Free Shit Level. Drinks, food, haircuts, bike repair, concerts. Handled. Simply by being around, by being an enthusiastic and constant presence in the city's underground art scene for ten years. So that's why I was at the studio in the first place, getting photographed for a spread in the alternative weekly paper. The It Issue, they were calling it. Only in San Francisco in the '90s could you be celebrated for doing next to nothing.

"What do you want to do?" Tanya asked.

"What do I want to do?" I felt stricken, too self-conscious to pose. "I guess I'm just getting my picture taken, so it doesn't really matter."

"Right," she said gently. "But do you want to do anything? Like, do you have a concept?"

My gaze went back to the action on the floor. The photographer was a beachy blonde babe in a long skirt and thick wool socks, her face obscured by an enormous Nikon, her body moving in a series of economical twists and pivots. The two of them had totally different energies, but were so compelling as a duo. Like John and Yoko. JFK and Jackie. Patti Smith and Robert Mapplethorpe. That guy who sold dope on my street corner and his ladyfriend Universe. They were giving and getting so much from each other that I could see their exchange of energy as a color, as pulsing lavender buttons. Which freaked me out. I was a native Californian and familiar with a wide spectrum of ethereal and esoteric pseudosciences, but I was allergic to anything New Age or granola-adjacent. I blinked to make the colors go away.

"See how she's doing all the pictures against that screen?" Tanya said. "That green screen will make it so they can fly anything into the background. Give everybody a different environment and play a little."

I'd never seen one before. "New technology. It's everywhere," I said in my gee-whiz voice. It was a phrase I'd found myself saying out loud almost every day. Someone at the bar was always telling me about their newest gadget or device, or the latest technology company that was going to *change the way we lived.*

"Check out this electronic calendar," one of my customers would say, holding up a rectangular piece of black plastic that fit in your palm and a little black stick that clipped onto it. A stylus. A stylin' stylus. "This thing is going to make paper and pencil obsolete!" And not even glancing down at it, I'd say right into their face, *New technology. It's everywhere* and walk off to fix another drink. I was incapable of engaging with it. It seemed like in the past few years the humans around me were becoming increasingly machine-like, all on their own, without making it worse by carrying around their little robot friends.

The photographer was getting frustrated with her camera. Every time she clicked, the image would pop up on this huge monitor on her desk. She said it was her first time working digitally and it was messing with her intuitive mojo. She didn't like seeing what she was doing while she was doing it. In between shots, she looked at the display and then try to shake it off.

"Just shut it down," she said to her assistant as he adjusted the screen. "I don't want to look at it, but if it's up there I can't not look."

Tanya popped a mint into her mouth and walked over. "I can help style you, depending on what you brought to wear. We can do makeup to fit with your look."

My look? I was wearing a version of what I wore every day. A T-shirt and jeans and boots, my stick-straight dirty blonde hair chin-length and unwashed. "That's all right. I already feel weird enough being here, so I better not do anything to make it weirder."

The stylist didn't get it. To her this was a wasted opportunity for giggles and glamor. She produced a pink feather boa and pair of oversized sunglasses from a leather tote and I replied with a soft hurling noise. Baby Boomers were the worst. No clue that it wasn't cool to call too much attention to yourself.

I made my walk extra slouchy as I moved across the room to the windows. "It's fine," I said to the street below. "I'll just look normal, thanks."

What a joker I was, acting like I was completely without artifice. Hardly. Everything I had on was quite purposefully old and a little fucked up. The T-shirt was from the boy's section at a thrift store, an old elementary school gym shirt that all the letters had faded from. As far as I knew, I might have been responsible for the entire trend of wearing shabby secondhand T-shirts. Thrifting with my friend in eighth grade, I came across one in the racks that said *Tarbottom Family Reunion, Grand Tetons 1982*, complete with tart, efficient caricatures of the Tarbottom family. It made me laugh so hard, I had to plunk down the ninety-nine cents and wear it to school the next day. Thus began my obsession with collecting shirts from other people's lives. Now, fifteen years later, it was possible to buy similar T-shirts from any of the giant retail stores where all of America shopped, emblazoned with fake clam shacks, summer camps, and surf clubs, intentionally distressed by child laborers in the Dominican Republic.

My jeans were Levi's that I'd taken from my high school

boyfriend back when everyone wore the same cut, 501s, before the phrase "boyfriend jeans" had been coined by new types of marketing geniuses. And then I had on my black motorcycle boots, the most expensive clothing purchase I'd ever made, from a motorcycle shop by the Oakland airport. The guy at the shop asked me what kind of bike I rode and I was forced to admit I arrived by bus.

"Looks like we got another poseur over here," he laughed as the woman rang me up.

"Don't listen to him," she said, handing me my change. "People like you keep us in business. Kids who want the look without the danger."

I scrunched my eyes tightly against the insult to keep it from infecting my soft tissue. I lived in a warehouse, I worked in a dive bar, I was on a first-name basis with all the junkies and homeless people on my block. I didn't even have a set of those straight, white teeth like all the other ex-suburban kids did. How could this woman not see how tough I was?

Tanya put some powder on me, to suck the shininess out, before I stepped out on the floor in front of the green screen and tried to be loose. If only I'd brought my flask.

"What did you win?" the photographer asked. "I should probably know this, but we're doing so many today."

I paused for a second to consider the possibilities of an intelligent answer, but there wasn't one. "I," I pressed my palms into my eyeballs, "am the It Pal."

"It Pal?"

"I know. They told me they had voted me It Girl, but then that was probably sexist which, okay, and if they had an It Girl, they'd have to have an It Boy, and there was something about it being gendered and they couldn't agree on who to vote for and it all sounds so dumb. Like high school, right? The weekly newspaper is anointing the citizens of our city with stupid titles and no one is taking to the streets about it. Where is the outrage?" I shook my fist in the air and added a dopey smile. I wanted her to like me.

An editor at the paper popped out from the sidelines to defend her publication, a once-independently owned enterprise that was now run by a national conglomerate, fighting against their failure to be what they wanted to be above all else: "edgy" and "local." The editor extended her hand, making things feel way more formal than they needed to.

"Our idea for the It Issue was to come up with categories that we've never had before and make it fresh," she said, running her hand through her shoulder-length waves. "That's why we have things like the It Pornographer, the It Tagger, and the It Vegan." The pleasure she took in saying these phrases made me squirm. She was trying so hard. Give her five years and she'd be living in Mill Valley, popping out kids, and feeling competitive about her workout.

"I think that's the thing," the photographer said, ignoring her, which pleased me immensely. "What you're doing right now. Keep not smiling if you want." She pointed the camera at me while I tried to look through her, or through the camera and then through her, through the brick wall of the studio and out onto the alley where there were people in wheelchairs with their heads taped up. An alley of hacking coughs and oozing gauze and cheap coffee and forties and a lot of freebase. South of Market was like triage at an outdoor hospital.

As the shutter clicked repeatedly, I realized I was having a "peak experience," a phrase I once heard a Jewish shaman named Vicki use referring to what could only be the beginning of one's decline. There I was, summoned to a photographer's warehouse on a wintry day to get my picture taken with the rest of the winners. It's clear to me now that I was going down.

2011

THIRTEEN YEARS AFTER I saw my face staring out blankly from the cover of the newspaper as San Francisco's It Pal, I was still living in the warehouse and working at the bar. If insanity is doing the same thing over and over and expecting different results, what's it called when you're doing the same thing over and over and you're expecting the same results, but you're just not getting them because everything around you is different? The old enemies, who we used to call "the dot-com people" had turned down the volume for a few years, but had recently come back stronger than ever as a more formidable army called "the tech industry."

But no matter how jaded I'd become, I still liked opening up the bar in the late afternoon and seeing how the light filtered in, lasering its rays through the cracks in the curtains and the door-frame, as if the sun was urgently trying to bust down the front wall and give me some good news. This was when the old friends, friends who hadn't fled to Los Angeles or Portland or the suburbs, popped in to say hello. On their way to yoga, coming back from the grocery store, out on a bike ride, buying plants at the nursery. Definitely not stopping in for a shot and a beer to kick off their evenings like they used to. There were still a few people my age or older who came in to drink at night, the ones who'd been here as long as I'd been, some longer. The regulars. I called myself a regular too, acknowledging that it had been my choice to show up for work these past two decades. Not to move or travel or go to school or learn a new skill, but to fully own and accept the power inherent in the act of holding it down, year after year after year.

So the wall phone rang and my brother Scott blurted it out right away. *She couldn't be revived.* I probably wouldn't have known how to tell him either, if the roles were reversed, if our aunt had chosen to contact me instead. All I could focus on was Scott's tone, how flagrantly proud he seemed that he was the point man, though neither of us had spoken to our mother in nearly nine months. We hadn't seen her since two springs ago when Scott came out from Boston with his family and I joined them for fried seafood at a cheesy tourist restaurant on Pier 39. My brother and his patrician wife Carolyn, all glowing with that pampered and moneyed sheen, while me and my mom remained slightly dour throughout, icy Bloody Marys within reach; her shivering and complaining about the cold. (Me, also cold but not saying a word, because I'm self-aware enough to know it's boring to complain about the weather.)

I told him I had to get off the phone. It wasn't busy yet and I had every excuse (Mother. Dead.) to peace out and leave work, to go off the rails or hide in the basement, but I stayed working, enraptured by my own stoicism.

At the beginning of the shift, the place was nearly empty. All the young tech workers were still in their tech boxes or on their tech commuter buses with faces fixed to their screens doing their tech jobs. My catch-all phrase for whatever it was they did was Petting The Glass. Everywhere I looked nowadays people were Petting The Glass.

I went outside for a cigarette and tried to remember what else Scott had said. That Ginny, our mom's sister and the inveterate Jesus person, would be driving up to San Jose from Fresno tomorrow and I should go meet her. To figure out what to do. To identify the body. Settle the details.

I'd thought of how this day would transpire many times over

the years, not from any underlying malice for my mother, but simply in grinding out one of my reality-based brain rehearsals. Who would I call if I got arrested? How would I defend myself against a rapist? What happens when my mother dies?

I looked over at Sally, a seamstress and singer, and Arthur, the antique dealer from next door, and thought more about being *a regular*. Being a regular seemed like an acceptance of your station. Maybe my mom should have done that. A fatal heart attack or runaway blood clot, the kind that knocks you flat out of nowhere, can be viewed as a blessing of sorts. Over and out. But when your heart explodes after years of referring to yourself as a wage slave, a cog, a paper pusher, and a drone? She might have been better off believing she was a trusty and dependable guard. An immovable force. A shield, like me. Bob-O had told me about the Paradox of the Immovable Force and the Unstoppable Object. The shield meets the sword and boom, they both become impossibilities. *My mother is dead*, I practiced saying a few times in my head. Finally, I had become the orphan I'd fashioned myself to be all these years.

I poured myself a pint glass full of black coffee and sliced lemons and limes for a while. Two young skaters came in to play pool in the back, probably weren't even twenty-one, and Tommy from the furniture store was having his customary afternoon Guinness. We all nodded and commenced ignoring each other. I used to be such a jabberjaw at work. I could endlessly gossip about who was fucking whom, getting kicked out of what apartment, or getting fired from the part-time job they hated anyway. Talk like that now seemed petty or mean. Over time, I'd watched as so many of these minor scandals landslid into full-on tragedies. Partiers became addicts, strippers felt ensnared, eccentrics were actually mentally ill, artists were homeless, and guitarists stopped talking about making the next record and started learning how to program computers or plumb.

Food was still a relatively safe topic. I engaged in a lot of "best al pastor taco" and "best slice" talk, but even that was becoming shrouded in a glum little cloud about how nobody could afford to eat at the new places opening up that were supposed to be so good and were overrun with interlopers. Like those coconut lime doughnuts on the corner. They were amazing, but four dollars apiece. An old-school doughnut still only cost seventy-five cents, if you could locate an old school doughnut shop left in the neighborhood. A real one with a formica counter and crusty old people and shitty coffee. My mom taught me to love bad diner coffee, but it seemed the value of having a cup of shitty coffee was lost now. It had meant so much over the years. It meant that I was broke, that I was struggling, that I had stuff to get done, that I had better things to worry about, better things to spend my money on. It meant that I was satisfied with simplicity, that what I wanted was inextricably tied back to what people had wanted for centuries. It was affordable, accessible comfort. The problem was, everything in this city was going the way of the cortado and the gourmet doughnut, and I was still a percolator and glazed old-fashioned type of person.

"Edie? The game?" Arthur was crabby, and his skin was blotched-up with gin blossoms, so he was starting to resemble a crab too. I handed over the remote so I didn't have to deal with him.

Of course I was cranky about the TV, though I didn't want to be one of those strident anti-TV blowhards. Apparently TV had gotten really good lately. That's one of the main things I heard people talking about next to IPOs and stock options and hooking up and food. But TV in a bar? It used to be that only sports bars had TVs. If you wanted to watch a game, you went to a certain kind of bar. And when the game was over, the TV would go off. Now almost every bar had one. We had held out here for years, a source of pride. Now I heard people talking about scheduling TV watching parties for shows I'd never heard of. Drugs and dragons and zombies and terrorism. A bar is supposed to be about sitting amongst strangers in a dark room. It's about being alone with other people. It's about the stories of the people sitting in the bar, not the stories the people in the bar watch on TV. I didn't understand why Harry, the owner of this place, spent so much time and energy on his perfect vintage furniture and pornographic paintings from the '70s and the old-fashioned jukebox full of thoughtfully curated songs if he was going to fuck up the whole vibe by putting two ugly and enormous flat screen TVs in each corner, semi-obscuring the mid-century modern hanging lamps he bought on the internet for three hundred dollars apiece. Eyes will always go to a screen and they will focus on boobs first and eyes second, I read that in *Psychology Today* when I had to go to the clinic for a urinary tract thing, but no one is actually paying attention to what's going on. Plus, much of the time, the sound is turned off because it's annoying to try to have a conversation with a TV blaring. So if you're smart enough to decide that your customers don't want to hear the audio on an ancient episode of *The Nanny*, you can guess they most likely won't miss it flickering with closed captioning either. When I was working, the TV stayed off. Except when Arthur came in because that was the law.

I fast-walked to the bathroom, feeling briefly like I was going to throw up. My chest heaved in a quick wave, but nothing came out. A convulsion. Punched by a ghost. Maybe my mom had just socked me one. For all sorts of trespasses perpetrated in my youth, but also for not being more upset right now. What had Scott said about cremation, a will? She didn't have shit except for the house.

I stuck my head in the sink and when I came out, Vince the UPS driver was sitting there with his buddy from Grass Valley, a dude who said he was psychic. There are certain things you see over and over when you work at a bar. Amateur palm readers and magicians, conspiracy theorists, romantics, sadsacks, clowns, liars, acrobats, exhibitionists, snobs, ringleaders, therapists, and people who try to teach you how to make new cocktails or slyly let you know how much money they have or pretend they're from England. Self-proclaimed psychics are high on the list.

So the friend, Trey, orders and says, "I'm going to have a pint and Vince is going to have another pint and then I'm going to tell you something about yourself, Carlotta P. Lasky."

I looked over at Vince who was busy checking out the neck tattoo of some elfin girl who just wandered in. The tattoo looked like an Egyptian necklace with turquoise flames shooting up towards her face.

"Vince!"

He swiveled back around on his stool.

"Is he all up in your grill already, Edie?"

"I know she calls herself Edie," Trey said. "But that's not her real name. I don't know what her real name is, but Carlotta P. Lasky is what I wanted to say, so forgive me father and so forth."

I gave him a look. Daggers lite.

The story wasn't that great, but one weekend after I moved here, I saw Warhol's *Ciao! Manhattan* and the Maysles brothers' documentary *Grey Gardens* back to back at The Roxie for five bucks. I came out of the theater with the new first name Edie. A bit of the tragic glamour of Sedgwick and the loopy charm of Bouvier Beale. My last name I came by honestly, taken from the street I grew up on, like the old "porn star name" trick back before it became the trope it is now. Edie Wunderlich. Not blowing anyone's hair back, and definitely not as memorable as my poor dead friend Moses Dick Washcloth.

On the other side of the bar, the skaters were eyeballs deep in their phones in a semi-stupor. I changed my mind about giving them money to keep the jukebox alive.

"You guys gotta go," I told them. "I don't care if you play pool, but you can't sit there drinking water and petting the glass all night. Out!" They shuffled off and I was disappointed they didn't put up a fight. Real punk rock of them.

I watched Vince and Trey in the mirror. They were cartoon-ish, like a pair of Muppets who were giving each other a fat pep talk. And then, right in the silence before a Roy Orbison song kicked in, Trey stood on his barstool, cupped his hands around his mouth, and said in a composed voice, "Excuse me, *Paula*."

And he was fucking right. Paula was the name my mother gave

me. Lasky wasn't quite right, but close enough, and Carlotta must have come out of his ass, but still. It was pretty impressive. I didn't reveal any of this to him, of course. Instead, I looked at him like he was drunk, which he was.

"I get better at this as I drink," he said.

"It's true," Vince said. "Until he starts getting worse."

"Beer really helps my intuitive powers." With this, he wiggled magic fingers around his lumpy bald skull.

"I'm like that with pool and bowling and sex," I said. "Alcohol seems to work as an aid, and you start thinking it's the most amazing drug ever. Until it stops working and then you lose your focus and realize you're just wasted and should have eaten dinner."

"Exactly," Trey said. "Let me tell you some more things about you."

"That's all right. There's nothing to tell."

Deirdre arrived. Any night that Deirdre came in was a goddamn blessing and there she was, holding the door open with her ass, which was an epic one, like a shelf. She had this party trick where she tossed her coat straight up in the air, pivoted sharply, and then caught it on her ass like it was hanging on a rack. No one ever got tired of her doing it because why would they? We didn't see each other nearly as much as we had in the '90s, but she was still my closest friend.

She waved me over and we walked out onto the sidewalk, both of us squinting into the fog. If the sun's right and the fog rolls in, the sky becomes bright silver and iridescent, like the inside of an abalone shell. Tinges of pink and blue. Pearly and bright. I knew I should probably tell her about my mom, but I needed to sit with it. There was nothing but time. I turned to light a smoke and she was leaning her head into an old Rambler station wagon. Was she talking to Judith Huntington? Hutchinson? Hutcherson? A bass player from a band that used to be pretty popular. She looked the same, jet black hair teased and sprayed into a messy beehive, perfectly tailored '60s capri pants, a pressed white blouse with a

Peter Pan collar, and an entire arm covered with Japanese-style tattoos. There was a baby on her boob.

"This is Ace." She tilted the boy's body to show off his face, his black onesie, his Mohawk. Someone most definitely went right ahead and put hair gel on a baby.

"You're still with Michael, right?" Deirdre asked her. "Little Acey there has his eyebrows. Eyebrow." Michael had once won an impromptu unibrow contest at the bar.

She fiddled with the sagging headliner on the old car, pushing the fabric up with her fingers and watching it drop. "We moved over the bridge about a year ago. It was lame at first, but now we're used to it. And the best part is that we park our car in our very own driveway."

"I can totally see you guys in the suburbs," I said, trying to sound supportive. "Like a throwback. Like make some deviled eggs and have a cocktail party on your flagstone patio."

"Yeah," she said. "We keep meaning to invite everyone over. It's too crazy now, but we will."

I had known her, not super close, but off and on for over twenty years and Judith absolutely knew what "too crazy" was. I offered to bring her a Shelley Shot, something an old bartender used to make. Tequila and lime juice. A gimlet but in a shot glass. Shelley left a long time ago, for Nashville or Austin or somewhere, but her drink lived on.

"I wish," Judith said, grabbing one of her giant boobs and shaking it like a fist.

A gust of wind blasted my ankles and I hopped up and down. I never went without socks, but the laundromat on my block had shut down last month because the landlord raised their rent too high, so washing my clothes was now an ordeal. Hence, no socks and inside-out underwear. Michael came back, wearing Bermuda shorts, holding two designer throw pillows. They were shaped like pills. One said PROZAC and the other, ZYRTEC.

"His and hers," I said.

"Oh, hey." He was talking to his shins. "It was a little warmer over there when we left."

"It's a great look," Deirdre said. "You've really got the suburban dad thing down."

Michael patted his belly and laughed, looking at the sidewalk. "I'm working on it."

It was painful to see him being embarrassed about gaining weight and moving to the suburbs. Are you supposed to *be cool* forever? What wasn't embarrassing about my own life, working at the same old bar and not doing shit?

I told them about the party last night.

"Man," Judith said. "I feel like I might have seen something about that, but everything is kind of a blur right now. That would have been fun. To see everybody. Was it fifteen years?"

"Twenty!" I said. "Twenty years! Kepler was deejaying and Harry ordered all this Korean food. Free drinks and everybody was here. Deirdre's new burlesque act totally slayed and then it turned into one of those super clowny nights on the dance floor." I didn't know why I was making it sound so memorable. In truth, I was bored and seeing most of those people made me depressed.

"It was okay," Deirdre said. "Solid seven."

"Well, yeah," I said. "Not really anything you haven't seen before."

"I can barely stay up past nine anymore," Judith said. "Were Juliet and Kyle there?"

Of course they were. Juliet and Kyle were one of those couples that made being in a long-term romantic partnership and having children seem simple and glamorous. They had started out in the '80s as record store owners and now made tons of money jumping from company to company. Consulting. Making products seem desirable by roping in young bands and filmmakers and having multinational corporations pay them with every artist's favorite form of currency: exposure. Supposedly they'd gotten a college student to be their live-in "intern" and had a free babysitter whenever they needed one. And, like most people who have the money to be away from their young children as often as possible, they were.

"Babe," Michael said. "We should really get going. We have that guy coming over to drop off the thing at seven."

"And the traffic is going to be such a nightmare. Someday they'll get it together."

The Bay Bridge had been under construction for years, since the earthquake in '89, making the already terrible bridge traffic all the worse. I thought you had to be nuts to live across the bridge, but the mass exodus to the East Bay had shifted into high gear.

Deirdre threw her arm around my shoulder and we went back inside and she asked the question I hoped she wouldn't. The question of didn't I have some sexual intrigue with Judith and Michael, that night at Ray's party.

Ray's party, ten years before, had become one of those things repeatedly referenced among about 400 art scene people who were now between the ages of forty and sixty. A legendary night. He lived in an old framing shop on Natoma Street, in one of those dirty, sleepy alleys, and any party there was thrown for a cast of hundreds. That was when you could decide to have a party at 8 p.m. on a Friday night and by eleven, it was crawling with people, all of whom heard about it from talking to someone else. You would run into friends getting a burrito or hanging out at a bar or walking down the street and word would get around. You'd call the landline of a group house and leave the info with whoever answered it. A band would be playing, another band would bring their gear, kegs were loaded in. There was pot, coke, speed, acid, mushrooms, pills. Free ecstasy, which was kind of a new thing. As it got late, it splintered off into some kind of orgy scene in one of the other rooms, and then a couple huge touring bands came through after their show at The Fillmore and the whole thing went balls to the wall. A crew of those gnarly fire-and-robot dudes were lighting shit off outside in the street and still nobody called the cops. After this party was described as epic, I started hearing a lot of people in the bar use that word. A surfer's word, a skater's word. Epic. An epic party. An epic ass. Now it was on a billboard across the street advertising online banking. *Make An Epic Fund Transfer, Bro!*

The thing everyone always talks about no matter what else they did that night was when Ricardo, Ray's boyfriend who made trippy paintings in which biblical characters wore Air Jordans and Gucci, invited his mom to come over in the morning. A cute old lady showed up at about 7 a.m. with a friend of hers and they cooked breakfast for everyone. Huevos rancheros and fresh tortillas. The mention of *Ray's party* made my body respond with a substantial cringe when I thought about Judith and Michael, which I tried to shake off by flopping my arms and legs around. A flounder shame dance.

"You did, didn't you? You did have sexual relations with that woman and man," she said.

I drew out my *no* for a long time while Deirdre looked at me like, *why lie?*

"...comment," I added to make it official.

A selective memory, or else flat-out denial, is an essential survival tool if you are going to spend your forties in the same place you spent your twenties. I supposed I could put up a false front with another popular coping mechanism: taking unflinching pride in my mistakes, bragging about them in a you-only-live-once way. Yet shame felt more natural.

Trey the psychic started in on Deirdre. "Miss Lady. You a friend of *Paula's?*"

Deirdre's expression gave the whole thing away. She was the only one who knew my real name.

"Psychic," I explained. "Vince's friend from when they were kids. He for real guessed it out of nowhere."

Trey was getting great pleasure from this victory.

"Your real name is Paula, Edie?" Vince was on his fifth beer and had entered puppy dog territory.

"I knew she was hiding something," Trey said. "In my brain,

I just thought, what's this woman's deal? And then I was, like, I know. She's a person behind a curtain."

Deirdre raised her glass to that.

"She's back there waiting for someone to pull a cord and open the curtain."

I set another pint down in front of Trey to encourage him to be less psychic.

Of course he was right and I hated that he was. I knew it was over. I'd been back here dancing and no one was ever going to pull the cord for me. I was doing nothing, had more or less been doing nothing my entire adult life because I was so busy doing everything there was to do. Everything and nothing at once. That's a real expression someone made up exactly for a situation like mine. And now that I realized it, and admitted that the city I moved to wasn't here anymore, or that I could no longer be the kind of person I was, every new day felt squished flat. The buoyancy and momentum of riding on a scene wave was gone.

There was a time when the bar and the people in it used to make me feel secret, like I had a clubhouse. For so long I thought ambition, industry, the daylight, the dayworkers, the sun itself, all of it, was *them*, the enemy. The darkness, the slow crawl, the crooked wind-up energy of night, was *us*. Our team. But that wasn't true anymore. As my team died out, moved up, moved on, morphed, I started to think I had been wrong all along. There was less and less proof that me and my team had been around at all.

I wondered if I could handle being on the side of the light, if I could stop thinking that light was so scary. There are people who live their whole lives in the light and they can't all be faking it with shit for brains and zero insides. I wondered about it for a while, an alternate universe where I did more than serve people drinks and hang out and go to shows, but I had trouble latching onto an image. Idea clouds flew in and out of my brain like weather patterns on a TV map, touching down and repeating a few times before being replaced by new ones. Finally the night grew dark and the new young people came and went. My knees began to hurt around nine, the pain coming earlier than it used to, and that was another secret. To admit it was to succumb. I popped a couple ibuprofen and washed them down with the coffee, thinking about arthritis. My mom had it. My grandma had it. I flattened my hands on the bar and checked out my knuckles. Slightly swollen. Little pink life preservers around my bony fingers. Surely the beginning of an autoimmune disease that would soon take over my life and I would start talking nonstop about inflammation.

Deirdre left around eleven for a sex date she made on her phone. Vince and Trey ended up in tears talking about a childhood friend of theirs who had recently died of cancer. I had a few expensive tequilas and got a little less surly with the customers. Drinkers stood three-deep at the bar while other bodies pushed past them through the bottleneck, weaving in and out of them like rainwater flowing past garbage in the sewer. At 1:45 a.m., Jay the barback turned on the lights, we kicked everybody out, and counted up the money in the basement. He went off with his girlfriend and then I set the alarm and locked the gate behind me for the millionth time. The first I'd done it since my mom was dead.

I walked down the sidewalk on 16th toward home. Its grime felt like my grime, transfused through the soles of my boots, up through my cracked heels, pulsing up my ankles to my lungs. I breathed it in, my legs swinging underneath me, rusty clappers in a bell. I passed a guy I knew, a true booze and pills guy, who had managed to stay sober for about a year. We didn't say anything, just gently slapped each other's palms as we passed. I had walked a few steps when I heard him call my name. I didn't want to get into a long thing, but I knew he was struggling. I turned around and looked into his eyes. He seemed sober.

"What's up, Chuck?"

"Just wandering around. I don't know where to hang out late at night anymore now that I don't drink and Hunt's is gone." The twenty-four-hour donut shop. "My housemates suck and I'm pissed I still have to live with other people. I'm an old man! I made the mistake of stopping into Bender's the other night like a fucking idiot. That's where I spent most of my time up until the end."

"Pretty gnarly in there, yeah?"

"So I felt like I could handle it and I had spent so much time and money, Jesus the money, and I at least wanted to drop in and say hi to Kent. Bartender. So all the guys are still there, still in their same spots, and I go in. I don't know what I expected, but they kind of look up and no one says anything. Whatever. They've got business to attend to. There's some new guy in my spot, on my old stool, and I swear it seemed like I was looking at a performance art installation of my life. I talk to Kent about nothing, I mean, what did we ever talk about? Chicks. Jobs. Anyway, I ran into him tonight and he says that after I walked out, the guys were like, 'Hey, who was that guy?' No one even recognized me. I spent the last six years of my life there, and most of my money, and they couldn't pick me out of a lineup."

There was a moment when I almost told him about my mom, but I stopped. His pain looked realer than mine felt.

"I'm sorry, man. I don't know what else to say. I'm so beat from working, so I'm going to give you a hug and keep moving, okay?"

"I get it. But you know what's funny? I realized that if you don't know who the worst drunk in your neighborhood bar is, it's probably you."

"That's good, man. That's sad and good and perfect. Night."

I FELT LIKE I was standing with my umbrella in the splash zone, waiting for the log ride to come down the flume. I knew I was supposed to get soaked, but it hadn't hit me yet.

Scott had been calling for over a week, leaving messages on the warehouse answering machine or talking to whomever picked up the phone at the bar. The sheer futility of that. Telling some kid in his twenties who was probably baked out of his gourd to remember something. I imagined those pink message notepads we used to have on the table next to the phone growing up. A Monopoly Man-looking guy was shouting into a bullhorn next to a speech bubble that said, "While You Were Out!"

His message was basically this: *You suck.*

I didn't go to meet my aunt the day after my mom died and he was pissed. In my defense, I tried to work it out, but by the time I was up and ready to get on a train, she said I'd be too late. She was thorny and religious and on some kind of intense schedule. She ended up dealing with the morgue and the ashes and the paperwork and the bills, tabling the idea of a memorial service for another time, which I deeply suspected would never come to pass. No one on their side of the family ever had services. Frivolous on every level, they thought.

The deal now was that I was supposed to do all the work to get the house ready to sell because I was closest and didn't have a "real job" or a family. If bartending wasn't a real job, then what was? Having a job that involved physical labor, moving your body, the exchange of cash for services, was the only kind of real job as far as I was concerned. What did Scott do? Work at a place that used too many different words for money: securities, funds, options, dividends, equity.

We were supposed to split the money from the house three ways after we paid back my aunt for everything she'd laid out. Who knew how much that place was worth, a three-bedroom tract house right in the heart of Silicon Valley? Maybe a million dollars, probably more. I thought we should sell it as is. Hell, they'll probably tear it down anyway, a rip-off Eichler that got a shit remodeling job in the '80s. My parents bought it in 1964 in a valley that was then full of orchards and nicknamed the Valley of Heart's Delight. That was before the silicon came. As if all hearts desired was plenty of fruit and easy freeway access.

I gave myself a challenge. Let me see if I could make that one phone call. If I could get through that, calling Scott back, I would have earned the right not to do anything else for the rest of the day.

He picked up right away. "Dude! What the fuck is your problem?"

"I know."

"What the everloving effing eff?"

"Kids walk in the room?"

"Listen. I don't know what's going on with you, and I'm sorry if you have a horrible disease and I'm being insensitive without knowing it, but I can't believe you didn't go to meet Aunt Ginny."

"I tried!"

"She said you called her at three p.m. sounding like you just woke up."

"I was ready to get on the train."

"Listen, the main thing I want you to do is call the realtor dude, okay?"

"I did already." I'd do it as soon as I hung up.

"No, you didn't. I just talked to him. One motherfucking second before you called, I was talking to Ken, the realtor. Kenneth Iwanaga, remember him? He went to our high school. Kenny. One of the five Asian dudes."

I felt obligated to correct him. "Scott, there were more than five Asian guys at our school."

"Yes, I know. One of the five *cool* Asian dudes is what I meant. So Ken told me, after I had to listen to a bunch of other where-are-they-now crap about the class of '85—who is gay, who is a millionaire, who died—that he hasn't heard from you and you are now disgusting me with your lies because you were never a liar."

I backed off. "Sorry, bay-bro." Baby brother.

"Don't bay-bro me now. And please don't become a liar, P.J." Paula Jane. "Your honesty is one of the few things you have going for you."

"And my hair. My hair still looks pretty good."

"Not sure. Can't sign off on that. It's probably thinning."

"You're the one with a bald spot."

"Ken is going to come by later this week and check the place out. I haven't been there in like five years so I have no idea what's going on. Is the key still there in the place? In the fake soup can?"

"There was never a key in a fake soup can."

"Yes, there was! The entire time we were growing up, there was one of those SkyMall fake cans and the key was inside it."

"No. Listen to me. No. There is a real can of Campbell's Tomato Soup, and if you lift up the can, the key is underneath it."

"Oh my god. You're right, Peej. It's just underneath the can, which makes the can sit crooked on the shelf. Could it be any more obvious? A Campbell's soup can from the '70s sitting off kilter on a shelf next to the door."

"Memory. It's a joker."

"Mom would have never spent money on one of those fake cans. Are there still rats in the garage? Raccoons?"

"Yeah, I think so. I mean, I haven't been there since I was there with you, but remember there was a bunch of chewed-up stuff. Lots of turds, so probably."

"You gotta deal with that, dude."

"This is exactly why I can't do this. There's just too much. It's too overwhelming."

"No, it's not. Overwhelming is a woman's word for being stressed out. Men would call it 'something I need to deal with' and a woman would call it a 'to-do list' and then write it out on some dumb flowered notepad from a stationery store. And then freak out over how it was making her feel inside. You're just lazy."

"I'm not lazy. I've had a job ever since I was twelve."

"You're mentally lazy. You don't want to strain your brain cell or do anything that jeopardizes your immediate comfort zone. In the past twenty-five years, your comfort zone has become an eight-block prison of bars, cafes, and clubs."

"And art galleries."

"Right. Art."

I knew I needed to fight back. It was the only way we would eventually start getting along. "Don't talk to me about my comfort zone, dude. Your comfort zone is the whole fucking world and you know what that makes you? An entitled jerk with no emotional range or empathy. You're not self-aware enough to realize sometimes you need to step back and not be comfortable everywhere."

"Good one. You know I love it when you call me entitled because by virtue of that word's definition, you're saying I can never understand what the hell you're referring to. It's one of those trick words and it's not fooling me. We have to get this done and in order to do it, you're going to have to dig a little deeper. There's enough money in the account to do a lot of the work and when we sell it we can pay off her debts and split the rest. Just pretend like you're fourteen again. Pretend you're the person who used to barge around through the world kicking ass and asserting your identity and getting your independence."

At some point I started to back down from any challenge that came up. Case in point. "I don't feel strongly about this, Scott."

"Remember when you were popular?"

"No." I had been very popular, but I didn't want to agree with him.

"Bullshit. You were on the cover of the newspaper. You were the It Thing or whatever it was. I came out with you that night and you knew every person at every place we went. Or they knew you. You were kind of wasted so you kept forgetting who a lot of people were."

"Free drinks."

"Right. We got free drinks everywhere. Do you still? Is that why you can't let go?"

"No, I don't get free drinks anymore because nobody young knows who the fuck I am. And it's fine."

"What happened to you?"

"I don't know. I used to be cute and I got old. I used to party every night and I got tired. I'm not doing anything that warrants any attention anyway. Back then all kinds of people were just getting picked up in the whirl. It's not like I'm going to go out and beg for it. It's like a merry-go-round. You get one big push and then you're dizzy and you jump off but the thing keeps spinning and you can't walk straight for a while. Now I'm in the part of my life where I've got about a minute before it comes to a complete stop and I fall down." I felt good about that answer. It was time for me to screw a celebratory cigarette into my mouth as a reward for finally picking up the phone and calling him.

"Gross, you're still smoking. I can hear it.'

"I'm down to a couple a day." Five or six.

"Just quit cold turkey. It's the only way to do it and you'll feel so much better. You probably already look so much older than the last time I saw you. Carolyn has been doing these laser treatments and her skin looks incredible."

"Yeah. Cold turkey. Laser treatments."

"You're not going to do anything, are you? You're going to keep coasting along, ever so slowly bottoming out. Like a pill addict who takes forever to get to the bottom. You're just on this sad, slow descent, dragging and dragging until I'm going to have to come out there and deal with everything."

"Will you?"

"What?"

"Come out here? Just for the weekend. Just so you can look at everything and we can decide what we have to do and then I promise I will become a responsible person and I will take care of it and we will sell the house for tons of money and you can buy your Cape Cod vacation house or whatever. Please?"

"Vacation house? We're not going to be able to buy a vacation house on a decent part of the Cape with what's left over. That's crazy. God, I wish you were a drug addict so there was an excuse for your behavior."

"I know. Me too. It's just an extreme lack of enthusiasm in most areas of life."

"What about the money? That's not an incentive? Every single day I read another article about real estate out there. It's not going to last forever. It's a bubble and we need to get out of there before it pops."

"What would I even do with money? I hate to travel. I hate to shop. I guess I'll need it when I'm really old to ride a dolphin or something."

"Yes, you will get old and you will need money. You could get health insurance and go to the doctor. I bet you haven't been to the doctor in years. Maybe you're dying. Maybe you have breast cancer like every third woman I know in the Bay Area."

It was true that I hadn't been to the doctor in years. I would go to the women's clinic every once in a while to get a pap test.

I'd never had a mammogram, but it seemed like my boobs were a manageable enough size that I'd be able to tell if something nefarious was growing in there? Every once in a while I got a cold and would stay bundled up in my sleeping loft until I felt better, but besides that, I was healthy. Working in the bar for so long had made my immune system bulletproof.

"What about getting out of that disgusting warehouse? I know you're tired of living with those people. You've been telling me that for years. You live in a bedroom you made out of nailing plywood together when you were twenty-five. Weren't you supposed to get evicted from that place years ago?"

"Yeah, but this lawyer helped us fight it. Pro bono. It's a temporary stay, but the guy really backed off after that."

"So you're just going to stick it out until they forcibly remove you. Of course you are. And then what?"

I flopped forward, folding myself in half, and shook out my hair.

"Paula, your bedroom window opens up into the inside of a liquor store."

I bolted up and caught myself in the mirror behind the bar. Look at that green, bulging vein in the middle of my forehead. It wasn't receding very fast. When did that happen? "It's not a liquor store, Scott. It's a market run by the very sweet Hamed family, that also happens to sell beer and wine. The grandma makes lentil soup. With the orange lentils! Ever had those? For three dollars. And that's three dollars for a twelve-ounce container." I took a breath and switched to my gentle special-occasion voice. "Will you please come out?"

"We're supposed to go to Connecticut this weekend and then next weekend is a wedding of somebody Carolyn works with."

"Okay, well, after that then."

"But it's a gay wedding, so maybe I can miss it."

"Nice."

"I don't know them very well, I mean."

"Of course you don't." I exhaled my smoke into his stupid ear and slowed way down. "Hey, dude? It would be a super big huge deal if you came out and helped me."

"I'll see what I can swing, but in the meantime you need to get down there and check it out so it's not too scary when Ken comes by." And then he said the same thing to me that I'd said to customers countless times when it was obvious they'd had too much.

"You need to go home."

AT ONE TIME, HOME was hundreds of apricot trees. On summer mornings me and my friend Josie would walk among them, the leaves forming canopies, branches hanging heavy with small golden bulbs. We worked in the orchard's old barn at long splintered tables, pulling up armloads of fruit from the bushels the pickers left, cutting out the pits, and setting them on trays to dry in the sun. We made ten cents a tray, same as the Mexicans and the Vietnamese, and if we worked steadily, we could make up to fifty dollars a week. But we hardly ever worked steadily. We would talk, next to nonstop, about anything we just found out about. The Clash, Koyaanisqatsi, oral sex, Ella Fitzgerald, burning zits off your back, apartheid, Keith Haring, where your meat comes from, AIDS. We would stretch out on grain sacks in the sun, tanning our bony bodies dark as the tree bark, or ride bikes to the frozen yogurt shop to watch the older kids kiss and fight. At the end of the day, we'd wind up back in the barn, fingers sticky with juice, apricots split and laid out in even rows, the late afternoon heat on our skin, listening to college radio. Where would we be without the radio station at the juco to crack open our worlds like eggs, to show us what else was hidden inside the small smooth universe we currently knew.

All praise the patois of the college radio deejay! The sheer relaxation of delivery, the shuffling of papers on the mic, the stall for lost liner notes, the humble struggle to remember or pronounce a difficult band name, the laugh following the record skip, the dead air of an ill-timed bathroom break, the droll ramble of the public service announcement, and the promise that the next song up was going to blow our minds. Discovering college radio meant that I said goodbye to my mom's AM radio of traffic and weather together "on the eights" or mellow gold songs about angels in the morning and piña coladas. The college deejays sounded like people I wanted to meet someday, laidback and in-the-know, hot with some fresh tip, ear to the ground, curious, nerdy, not ashamed.

I carried my pitting knife like I was a Latin Queen in Chicago instead of a suburban girl earning cash to buy jeans and records. It was a sharp switchblade with a handle carved from an olive tree that once belonged to my grandfather on my mom's side, the Polish one. I'd wear it on my belt, the weight of it informing my swagger, as I walked back home on the pristine black asphalt of the streets in the new housing developments. Green lawns, ranch houses with three-car garages, shiny black mailboxes with little red flags, heavy Spanish-style doors with brass hardware, fresh-ly-planted agapanthus in lavender and white, and obedient juniper stretching across the curbsides. All of this where acres of apricot and prune trees used to be.

I refused to take piano from the hollow-cheeked bunhead at the end of the cul-de-sac or play soccer in those balloony white shorts with my ponytail bobbing behind me like a punchline. Instead I practiced my scowl for the teenage boys who jumped fences between yards, sharpened my knife blade on the fine grit of a ceramic stone, and watched TV show after TV show while drinking generic orange soda and eating frozen French bread pizzas. I felt like an animal lying in wait. Something was out there and if I paid attention I would hear a signal calling for me.

Josie and I hatched a lot of plans in that barn. The best one that didn't come true was that we would move to the city and start our own line of apricot-based beauty products. Think of the low overhead with all those free apricots. We hoarded the pits and made our own makeshift lab, smashing the almond-shaped stones with hammers on the concrete pad, back where Josie's parents parked their camping trailer, and then we mixed the coarse dust with coconut oil from the pantry and vanilla beans swiped from the grocery store. We put them in jelly jars and went door to door selling it to our neighbors. The part we kept a secret was that we knew the pits were supposedly full of arsenic until roasted. We schemed about doing a tidy business as poisoners for hire on the side.

By our last year in high school, the adults in our lives were kind of like those in a cartoon; nearly absent, shoes going up into ankles and shins and then disappearing. Words coming out in a mushmouth garble. Assembled from parts. Josie's mom was a pair of high heels on linoleum, her stepdad was thick glasses behind a book and her real dad was a push-broom mustache with wheels instead of feet. My mom was a cigarette in a hand on the steering wheel or a lump in the bed. The only one who loomed large was my invisible dad. A tombstone on a brown lawn near the garlic fields of Gilroy. He split before I was born, circling back around to get my mom pregnant with my brother before leaving again. The marker on the grave said 1979.

My mom had always been more like a roommate, busy with a life that seem to only include her job working at the locksmith. She handled all the appointments and billing, and who knows what else from her creep boss. I don't know why she didn't ever try to escape and come up with something better, but Scott said once that maybe she was in love with him. Held captive by a mediocre man with a family of his own.

The night of our graduation, Josie and I went to Santa Cruz with a pack of other kids. She was heading out soon on a monster solo backpacking trip and I was at loose ends, not having technically graduated due to a failed science class I was supposed to retake that summer. When I heard a couple girls talking about driving up to San Francisco the next day to go shopping, I asked for a ride.

Early that morning, I tiptoed into my house and packed a duffel bag. Then I lay in my bed, fully dressed, waiting for my mom to go to work. The car was backing down the drive as I scribbled the note: *Moving to SF. I'll call soon.*

Those next hours passed so slowly, watching game shows and soap operas, eating an entire Sara Lee poundcake, looking out the window, waiting for those girls to arrive. They finally came to pick me up in one of their graduation presents, an aqua Suzuki Samurai, a Barbie car. We headed up the 280 and they went toward the shops on Haight and I disappeared into the fog bank of the Panhandle. Later that night, I met some cool people at a bonfire at Ocean Beach and crashed with them for a few days, leaving a message for my mom on the home machine when I knew she'd be at work. Within a few days, I'd found my own room off a flyer. I called back and left her my permanent phone number, the first in a long string of permanent phone numbers. She wrote them down on a piece of paper she had on the fridge for years, always scratching out the old one, but rarely calling the new one.

I TOOK A BUS to a train to another bus and got dropped off a mile from the house. Two and a half hours to do what would have taken less than an hour in a car. I walked down Highway 9, past the string of strip malls and low-slung stand-alone businesses. The pool supply shop and the Japanese market and the unisex hair salon my mom went to for forty years. Unisex. An equal opportunity word for cheap and terrible haircuts. There were a bunch of new places too. Chicken restaurants, tutoring centers, realty offices, a tae kwon do studio, a coffee place, a consignment store for women's designer apparel called Our Secret. (Yeah, your secret is that you paid too much for a tunic.) I turned the corner at the elementary school into my mom's neighborhood and realized I hadn't walked past another person the entire time. A few bikes, one jogger, but no walkers. Here were the quiet ranch houses, vaguely Spanish-style split levels, and Eichlers I'd grown up around. Most of the lawns were browning from the drought. The boxwood hedges were crispy. There were a few fancy cars in front of the modest homes, not like when I grew up and every family had a Honda, Toyota, or American-made station wagon. The Time Before Minivans. Now I saw Mercedeses, Jaguars, Lexuses, BMWs. Sedans and SUVs. I saw a brand new lime green Volkswagen Beetle on the street, the only car that wasn't tucked into a driveway, and I already knew it

belonged to a teenage girl visiting a friend's house after school. As I
passed the car, I saw the high school parking sticker on the bumper.
Bingo. I took a moment to congratulate myself on being right
about something. One thing I knew about myself: I was extremely
intuitive about things that were of no consequence at all.

There was the house. A flat brown rectangle with a hideous
island of ancient red lava rocks in front instead of a lawn. Over
the years, the rocks had been stolen by kids, pissed on by dogs, or
partially ground to dust, so there were big bald patches where the
industrial plastic groundcover peeked out. I pulled the shredded
piece of twine on the side gate and walked through. The same old
green garbage cans cracked in the heat and at least thirty or forty
clay planting pots that had been sitting fallow since my childhood
were collecting dirt near the fence.

I crossed the dead lawn in the backyard, clumps of brown grass
punctuated by dessicated cat and dog shit, and opened the door into
the garage. It was worse than I remembered. Old cans of paint were
stacked taller than me, a tangle of ancient bicycles and random parts
blocked the pathway to the door to the laundry room. There was
a partial croquet set and plastic tubs full of canned foods and evap-
orated bottled water and batteries. An earthquake supply kit that
probably got assembled after the big one in '89. I opened the refrigerator door and found a few cans of Coke and a box of white wine.
Fumbling over to the shelf near the water heater, I saw the soup can.
Campbell's Cream of Mushroom, label peeling off, key underneath.
Not tomato like I had remembered. How could I forget? Campbell's
Cream of Mushroom was a crucial ingredient in every recipe my
mom knew how to make from her *Casseroles n' Crocks* cookbook.

I opened the door and went for the keypad on the burglar
alarm, but it hadn't been turned on. Or maybe she had stopped
paying the bill? No matter. It was obvious that the place hadn't
been entered in weeks. God, it smelled gross. Rotten and forgotten. Dead and festering. The pungency of neglect. All decent
album titles for the right metal band.

I walked through all the rooms, trying hard not to imagine some disturbing image every time I opened a door, a lifelong habit. Every time I entered an empty room, I would think, "What would be the worst thing to see right now?" I'd envision a body dangling from a noose or walls splattered with massive amounts of blood or a pile of bodies with bugs crawling in and out of their orifices. But there was nothing violent or horrifying in any of the rooms. There were just beds and couches and chairs and towels and candles and books and plastic bags of yarn and an assortment of outdated electronics. Extension cords and candles and baskets of ancient potpourri.

I slid the door open to the closet in my old room. It was full of clothes: mixed fiber sweater sets, nubby sportcoats, pressed slacks folded on hangers. None of them had belonged to me except my prom outfit, still preserved in its dry-cleaning plastic. For my junior prom, I wore a white Chinese silk pantsuit that I'd bought in a tourist shop on Grant Street in San Francisco. How chic I imagined I was. How cool and punk rock with my dyed orange flat top hairdo and el cheapo outfit dancing to the B-52's at the Palo Alto Hills Golf Country Club. What else was I supposed to do? Wear a pretty dress from the mall like everyone else? It was your basic existential shit. When I observed the thing that most people were doing, I'd consciously take action to do something different. It was reflexive. I was afraid of being the same as them, I guess. Was the normal, regular thing actually so bad? I thought that if I could see what other people were doing, it was double air horns that I should do something different. By noticing something prevalent, it was my job to subvert it, not by doing something necessarily better, but just doing something that wasn't that. It was fairly normal teenage behavior, yet here I was, forty-five and still doing it. Being like this for so long had made simple acts, buying a pair of comfortable shoes or tolerating the music being played in most public spaces, extremely challenging.

I pulled the prom pantsuit out of the closet, suddenly

remembering how the pants, with their elastic waistband and simplistic cut, were especially unflattering to my broad hips. The suspicion pierced me: I wasn't any kind of artist or visionary or iconoclast. I never had been. I was never moving toward an individual and unique vision at all. I had spent my life merely reacting to the circumstances around me without a lot of thought as to why.

I sunk to the floor and noticed all the carpet had been replaced by a fake wood laminate. When we first moved in, it was shag. Royal blue with every five or so strands shorter, and white or light blue. It created topographical maps on the floor. Was there an industry term for this? Hi-lo? The carpet had come with a special tall, yellow rake. One of my childhood chores was Rake The Carpet.

I pawed up the wall and stood facing two framed photo collages, one for Scott and one for me. On top my mom had hand-lettered our names, Scott and Paula, but being hung directly underneath a skylight made the sun-bleached photos barely visible now. Our faces smiled like pale yellow ghosts, trapped inside the convex bubble frames. I removed them from the wall and stacked them in the closet.

Room by room I proceeded, opening the windows on their rusty aluminum hinges, looking in the closets, opening drawers. Not seeing blood, not seeing bodies. I stepped down into the living room with its twin sofas, upholstered in creamy rayon with green ferns, and matching curtains. This room had only been used for Christmas, or on the rare occasion that the neighbors unexpectedly stopped by and a guaranteed clutter-free place was needed to sit. There was a hi-fi sitting in the deep walnut cabinets, but no records. No more listening to the hi-fi on the hi-lo.

The pantry was bound to have bugs in it, so I didn't open the door. I couldn't look in the fridge either. Maybe next trip. The TV worked. Maybe I would take it back with me and start watching it. It could be a gateway, a bridge to understanding people better. But then I remembered that in order to watch it I would have to interact with some kind of corporate service provider and nixed that idea.

In the backyard it was eerie the way the swimming pool was perfectly maintained. A service automatically deducted from my mom's dwindling bank account. A leaf blower started up on the other side of the fence and I became startled. When I was growing up, no one had professional gardeners except for the Gomezes. They were the only Mexican family in the subdivision and my uncle visited once from Indiana and made a joke about it. It cracked him up to no end that the Mexicans had Chinese gardeners. Only in California, he said. My mom and her siblings came from the times of "ethnic humor." They were Polish and liked to make Polack jokes. Did you hear about the gay Polack? Slept with women. And something about new immigrants thinking hot dogs were dog dicks and a guy who didn't know that a suppository went up your ass. I couldn't remember the details, but they had laughed and laughed with obnoxious extended honks about all those dumb people from other places who now lived here and couldn't figure out how things worked. He had also died, sometime in the last seven to twelve years.

The gardeners moved on and it was so still except for the little robot machine crawling around the bottom eating the algae and swishing the leaves toward the filter. I yanked off a boot and put my toes in the water with my sock still on. It felt amazing. I sunk my whole foot in and watched the water ripple away from my shin and then decided, fuck it, and took off my other boot and dove in. Quick to the bottom before letting myself float for a while, my jeans heavy, my hoodie soaked, the weight of the keys clipped to my belt loop pulling me off-balance. I flipped over and scrunched my eyes against the sun and lay there, ears underwater. When my face began to dry out and sting, I embraced the challenge of peeling off my clothes and watching as they descended to the bottom. A disintegrating Styrofoam noodle floated by and I hugged it to my chest, pieces of it flaking off in my fingertips and all over my body. I did the dead man's float until I couldn't hold my breath anymore and then pulled myself out of the water like a primordial ooze creature. I fell asleep on the patio, face down, letting the pebbles make a mosaic on my skin.

I must have been asleep for a while and woke up thinking, *Is there vodka?* I went to the freezer in the garage, my soggy underwear sagging on my ass, and found a plastic bottle of cheap stuff. There was also a 9x11 glass casserole dish covered in foil. I brought them both inside and regarded the booze bottle sitting off-balance on the yellow-tiled counter. Why not. I rinsed out a coffee mug, splashed some in there, and called Deirdre. The machine picked up. Deirdre also enjoyed having her old-fashioned five-pound telephone and '80s answering machine and in the years we'd been friends, she had never once picked up. She screened everything. *Hi, this is Deirdre. You know what to do. Beep.*

"Hey, it's me. I'm down here in suburban paradise looking out at the pool and having a cocktail." I hoped my generous use of the word *cocktail* would catch Deirdre's attention enough that she would pick up. It worked.

"Hey! Is it sunny?"

"Of course, it's sunny. It's June."

"Gross. You know how I feel about the sun."

"I do. I wasn't saying you would love it here. What I was calling it was a paradise from the perspective of many other people who like the sun. What are you doing?"

"Buying a bra on my computer so I don't have to go outside. How are you feeling? Is it okay being there?"

"I want to defrost this casserole I found in her freezer. There's absolutely no telling when it was made, but it's triple-wrapped in Saran Wrap and has an extra layer of foil just to be safe."

"I wouldn't eat it. Why risk it? Even if it doesn't make you puke it's probably going to have that freezer burn taste."

"Wouldn't that be great if I could just eat her terrible cooking one more time? I'm going to try it. I'm going to fire up the oven."

"Well, if it's decent and you don't experience any gastrointestinal distress within the next few hours, bring me some when you come back. You're coming to the show, right?"

I was hoping she'd forget. I had been pondering bailing and now that I was slowly ingesting vodka it seemed nearly impossible that I would subject myself to another round of public transportation.

"Don't flake on me," she said. "Keith and I broke up and I want to go out."

"Keith? I don't even know who that is."

"We had three dates and it seemed like we were having fun, but it's okay. He's married anyway."

"Well, sounds like that situation is resolved. Okay, I'll come. It might take me a while, but I'll be there."

"Didn't your mom have a car? Just take her car."

The wagon. I'd walked right by it in the garage. '82 Oldsmobile, sky blue, wood paneling, eight-track player. I opened the cabinet where the spare keys were kept and there they were, dangling from a big brass ring.

"That's definitely an idea. It's a giant-ass station wagon. The battery might be dead and I don't have a valid license or any insurance, so."

"Perfect. Just go try it and call me back. We're on the list so we don't have to get there until at least ten."

I walked back out to the garage and looked at that beautiful beast. I pictured a map full of colorful lines showing all the places my mom had driven. A blue line to her job, a green line to the grocery store, a red line to the mall, a yellow line to church, an orange line to bridge club. The most boring rainbow ever. God, that car was enormous. It never made any sense that she drove it. She bought it at a time when a mom was supposed to drive a station wagon, but without a dad in the picture, it was only ever the three of us. What did we need a station wagon that seated seven for? The three times she got pressured into driving some kids from Scott's baseball team to pizza after the game?

The door was unlocked and I dropped into the blue vinyl seat, stunned by the intense memory jolt from the smell. Gas and tobacco and old chewing gum. Not unlike the inside of my mom's old purse. I laid across the seat and started to cry. Unlike many people I knew, I hated to cry and did so rarely. *Grief comes in waves* is what people told me. I decided I was crying because my mom's life suddenly seemed sad to me. The stupid part was that I don't know if my mom's life was that sad to my mom, so I was probably crying because my own life seemed sad and it was also going to end in certain death sometime in the next ten to thirty years. As a general rule, I was against therapy, so how was I supposed to know what was happening to me? It always felt like a guessing game. When I was done sobbing, and I did my best to keep it short and ugly, I put the key in the ignition and wasn't surprised at all to hear a very faint click. Nothing. What a relief to have an excuse to numb out there for the night. But Deirdre wasn't having it.

"I'm calling my friend Gilbert," she said. "I'm going to have him come over and jump you and fill up the tires or whatever it needs."

"It probably won't work. Or it'll just die again once I'm there."

"Yeah, but then you're here and not there."

"Who's Gilbert?"

"Just a super-fan from my shows. Really sweet. He lives some-where down there and he'll do it in a minute if I ask."

GILBERT TO THE RESCUE. He was cute; a chubby Latino dude with a pompadour and thick-ass sideburns. He showed up with a friend of his, a skinny white guy, Kip, who worked for AAA but was currently off-duty. It hadn't occurred to me that I should spruce myself up for the guys jumpstarting my car, but now I was ashamed of how I looked. My outfit was debilitating. I had put on a pair of my mom's old pants, jeans with a lengthy crotch and tiny pockets that made my butt look long and flat. Unlike having a huge forehead or being so pale you're blue, there was probably not ever a time in history where people aspired to the beauty ideal of having long, flat butts. I had also grabbed an extra-large white sweatshirt with lavender paint splotches that said Santa Clara Whiffers. No idea what that meant.

Gilbert wore his work shirt buttoned at the top, cholo style, and a brand new pair of black slip-on winos, the cheap canvas shoes with the gum sole favored by old drunks and scrubby white punks and skaters. Kip, the tow truck driver, looked like an illustration of a rockabilly guy as rendered by a competent teenage art student: white T-shirt with a pack of smokes rolled in the sleeve, hair in a greasy D.A., stiff Levi's with a four-inch cuff, and high tops.

"This is a pretty nice house," Kip said. "Run-down, but probably worth what, a million, million and a half?"

"Something like that," I said. It was supposed to be rude to talk about money, but I always appreciated when people did. Even if it made me uncomfortable like it did now.

"I mean, it's not mine. The house. I'm trying to get it together to sell. It was my mom's. I still live in the city, but we're close to being evicted. I'm trying to figure out where I'm going to go next, you know?"

"You could go anywhere," Gilbert said. "You could buy a place in Hawaii and retire."

"I don't know about that. I have to pay a bunch of bills off the top and then my brother gets some and our aunt gets some."

"Still," Gilbert said, "It's better than nothing. It's better than getting punched in the face or whatever the expression is."

"Oh, I know. It's pure luck on my part. Believe me, it doesn't feel good to have this responsibility, to be in charge of something expensive. I don't like it. I'm not used to it. I've worked at the same bar for twenty years and keep turning down the manager position because it feels like too much, you know?"

"Could you just stay here?"

"My family won't let me. I guess maybe I could for a while, but then I'd be living here. No offense or anything, but it's hard to imagine living here. In San Jose."

Kip was agitated. "There are so many rich young fucks around here that would give you so much money for this place. Tech fucks. If a tech fuck wanted to buy my place, I'd be all like, no way, motherfucker, you can't have everything you want just because you have money. Think they run the world."

"They kind of look like they do run the world. I mean, from what I can tell."

"Nah," Gilbert said. "They don't run my world. They don't even know how to order a taco. They get all nervous and have to check their phone to make sure they're getting the right one. The one that got a good review. If you can't order a taco, there's no way you can run the world."

"I don't even know anyone who works at those places. Apps or whatever," Kip said.

"Yeah, me neither. I think I'm too old," I said.

Kip was getting worked up now. He was getting loud and starting to sweat. "All my crew are like deejays and mechanics and electricians and cooks and shit. I like people who do real work."

"What about Lucinda, man?" Gilbert said. "Isn't she working for that CEO guy?"

"She's a nanny. She's the help. He and his wife are never home, so she's basically raising their kids. I told her she should raise them to be real assholes. Wouldn't that be rad? To go all stealth and raise them to be like Nazi Youth or something?"

"What the fuck are you talking about, holmes?" Gilbert said. "Yeah, that's just what we need, man. More Nazis and more hateful rich people."

I wanted to wrap up this transaction, but for Gilbert's sake, I didn't want it to end in a bag of downers. "Well, maybe she could just teach them random stuff that isn't quite right," I said. "Like tell the kids that when they first meet someone with red hair it's customary to sniff them behind their ears. Or that if someone holds a door open for you, you are supposed to take over holding the door until the next six people wearing boots have exited. Just little stuff that would add up to the parents looking like total idiots every once in a while."

"Disrupt, disrupt!" Gilbert laughed with his hand in front of his mouth, which I found adorable.

"But then they would just blame her and she's making bank at that job," Kip said. "She paid for our vacation to Greece. That was pretty tight."

Kip was making me cringe in self-recognition. Ready to froth up an opinion about The Man, but not a lot of follow-through.

"So you think you can start this thing?" I said.

Kip made a big show of positive-positive-negative-grounding the cables and I got in the driver's seat. It turned over right away and I left it running and got out of the car.

"You should probably drive it around for a bit to keep it charged," Gilbert said.

"I'm going to drive back to the city to meet Deirdre, so that should do it. Looks like it's got gas. How much do I owe you?"

Me and Gilbert looked over at Kip, who had started to walk down the driveway. He turned around quickly, like an invisible hand was grabbing his greasy duck's ass. "I don't know. How am I supposed to know? I'm doing this off the clock so whatever, man."

Shit. My wallet was still in the pocket of my jeans at the bottom of the pool. I sprinted to the backyard and tried to fish my pants out with the net. Futile. I gave up, ripped my clothes off, jumped in, and dove to the bottom of the deep end. Without drying off, I put my mom's clothes back on and ran out to the front. Gilbert took one look at me and put his hand over his mouth again.

I handed Kip two wet twenties. "This good?"

He looked them over and said, "Yeah, I guess so. Why are you all wet?"

"Wallet was in the pool."

He looked down at the money and shook his head. "It's kind of lame since you're going to make a million off this house, but it's cool."

I rung out my hair over my shoulder, making a small puddle at my feet. "Well, that's all I can do right now. It seems pretty fair to me."

Kip hopped back in the truck and revved the engine. "You coming, man?" he asked Gilbert.

"Maybe I'll take a ride with Edie, if that's cool with you. Can you drive me over to Moorpark on your way out?"

I locked up the house fast, conscientious about not making Gilbert wait. He was obviously the coolest person currently living in San Jose and I didn't want to come off as some high maintenance woman obsessed with my appearance. I rolled down the garage door and got in the wagon.

"That's it? You're not going to wear any shoes or bring a jacket or anything?"

"Oh, right! I forgot my boots. It's okay. Deirdre will have shoes for me to borrow."

"You sure? It's a little…."

I backed out of the driveway, bottoming out at the curb.

"How is Deirdre anyway?" he asked. "I can never get her to call me back."

"She hates the phone almost as much as I do. Where'd you meet her? A show?"

Gilbert smiled real big and I saw for the first time that he was missing a tooth on the top, about three back from the front. In the past few years, quite a few people I knew had lost teeth and not replaced them because it was too expensive. Hardly anyone I knew had health insurance, let alone dental insurance. I suspect middle class people probably used to go to the dentist more regularly.

"It was a long time ago. She was doing a show at a car rally in Hollister. I used to go to those all the time. Bring this old Charger I had. I took one look at her and, man, I was done. Done!"

"She's pretty hot shit, huh?"

"So we hung out a bit, you know. But she's up there in the city and really hard to get a hold of."

"Basically you had amazing sex with her once and you've been in love with her ever since."

"Damn!" He shook his head and looked out his window at a homeless guy sparechanging. The guy was holding a sign that had a drawing of a bluebird on it that said *Bitter*.

"So I should, uh, join the club or something?"

"About Deirdre? Yeah, join the club!"

We drove past the site where the headquarters of the biggest technology company in the world was being built. "Five billion dollars right there in that spaceship. Probably more, right?" Gilbert said. "Fifteen thousand more cars coming. Can you believe it? Already look at this traffic." We'd been sitting at the light through two greens. "Supposedly they're going to fill up the middle of the circle with orchards like there used to be."

I didn't want to talk about what everybody else was talking about and Gilbert picked up on this. Valiantly, he switched tacks. "Did you know that fruit cocktail was invented in San Jose? Supposedly. That's what my auntie told me anyway. My grandma worked for a canning company and they started doing it to use up all the bruised fruit."

"Huh."

"It's supposed to have booze in it. That's why it's called a cocktail. But I guess they started canning it during Prohibition so they had to leave the alcohol out."

"San Jose! Bragging rights to more than just that Dionne Warwick song! Do I have to refer to it as a Burt Bacharach song?"

"He wrote it for Dionne so I'd call it a Dionne song too."

"Have you lived here your whole life? Did you ever live anywhere else?"

"Nah. My family is here. I have a place to work on my cars. My dogs have a yard."

"I grew up in that house and by the time I was, like, ten, it used to make me crazy. Being here. It always seemed like everyone was doing something cool or exciting somewhere else. San Jose felt embarrassing. Even as a kid I was embarrassed to be from here. I had only been to the city a couple times, but I knew that there was a whole world out there and this place didn't matter very much. Did you ever feel that way? Like you were missing out on what was really happening?"

"No, not at all."

"Not even as a kid, as a teenager?"

"Not really. We'd cruise up to the city sometimes or go to shows at Gilman."

"I used to go there, too. I bet we were at shows together."

"Or we'd drive over to Santa Cruz and go to parties, go to the beach. But this is where I'm from."

Why had I completely missed the civic pride boat? Now it was too late. The tech world had claimed it.

"I feel like I'm from here too, but that's exactly why I wanted to get away. I couldn't get away fast enough. And even though I've lived in the city forever, I can't shake that I'm from here. The warmer weather, the parking lots, the freeways, the way the flowers smell, the '70s strip malls. I kind of like it, but it's hard to admit that when I've spent all these years staying away it."

"You just have to get into it. It's your birthright." He threw his thumb back over his shoulder at the construction we'd passed. "We don't want those people taking over. We got to stay here because they're here. We got to represent."

"Represent what, though?"

"White girls!" He slammed a palm on the dash and did one of those laughs like *HAW!*

I pounded my fists on my thighs and shrieked out the window.

"White girls who look like they just got hosed down at the car wash."

"That's better."

"No, I just mean you got to represent you as hard as you can. Whoever you are."

I did a quick assessment. Bare feet. Wet, stringy hair. Inflamed knuckles gripping the steering wheel too tight. Permanent sleeping wrinkles on one side of my face. Driving an old wagon with no drivers license. I turned to Gilbert, took my hands off the wheel, and pointed at myself. "But Gilbert, what is this? I don't even know how to describe what this is."

It was a relief to Gilbert that I broke into a laugh, so he knew he could laugh at me too. When I pulled up to his place, a little bungalow with a dead lawn and a squat palm tree in the front, he was still laughing. "All right now. Give Deirdre some sugar for me." He gave me a special handshake with four or five rapid-fire components and I tried my best to follow along. "I'll be here," he said.

FUCK THAT CLOWN BAND. We ended up walking out, lasting only four and a half songs. They were supposed to be so killer live, a lot of friends our age told us that, but all we could see were kids aping the styles of about a thousand other bands that came before them. Their look was so studied, it felt as prescribed as a platinum-selling boy band's. There was the moody white frontman with teased black hair and eyeliner, the black nerd bass player with thick glasses and a flattop, the Asian girl drummer with a tube top holding on for dear life to her big fake boobs, and the grizzled secret-weapon guitar player, probably fifteen years older than the rest, who played with his back to the crowd. He had great tone and was the only saving grace, but was also probably a drug addict who collected broken vintage gear and didn't pay his child support. Whoever told us to see this band was going to suffer later.

We walked back to the wagon, but of course it wouldn't turn over. The question was posed as to whether we should call for help or go out, have a good time, and not worry about it. The answer was obvious. Let it get the ticket for street cleaning at midnight. We walked back to the Mission and gorged ourselves on pork and cheese pupusas, had a few cans of beer, and then decided maybe we'd stop by the bar and see what was happening. It was a Wednesday, and getting late for all those money-making tech wads, so the sidewalks weren't too bad.

"This is so much better than the weekend," Deirdre said. "I don't even come down here on the weekend because it is *le shitshow. Le shitshow horrible.*"

"Nice French accent, though."

"Used to be a lot better."

"You learned it in college?"

"Yeah, and high school. And then I lived in Nice for a year."

"You lived in Nice? Why didn't I know that about you?"

"I was young. I thought about staying, or at least I thought I'd go back again soon. I remember getting on the plane home and thinking, 'I'll be back next Spring and rent a flat for a while.' That was in 1980."

"Why didn't I ever learn a language? Why didn't I go anywhere? One of my things now is trying to come to terms with my complete lack of ambition. It worked pretty well for years, but I don't know what happened."

"It's still working for you. When you question it, that's when it stops working. The confidence in not giving a shit can work for a long time. And you can always learn a language when you have nothing to do because you're living in San Jose."

We passed an old man pushing his ice cream cart through a throng of glass-petters blocking the sidewalk. They were waiting for a table at a restaurant with seven dollar lemonades served in mason jars. I felt triggered.

"God, can you move?" I snapped. "Stop looking at your phones and move out of his way!"

A few people looked up at me and I knew exactly who I was. Impatient aging townie mad at nicely dressed young people. Even the ice cream guy looked at me like I was obnoxious. What did I know anymore? Maybe he was stoked to be doing more business than ever. Maybe some of these newcomers were trying to have an authentic experience like the listicles suggested they do. Certainly the *helados y paletas* from this old dude were a top ten thing to do somewhere. *Be more than a gentrifying xenophobe! Buy ice cream from an old brown person!* I wondered if there was a young millionaires' guide to not acting like an asshole.

"Like, where does that guy live?" Deirdre said. "Where's his apartment, how many people does he live with, and how much is his rent?"

"I have an attitude problem," I said as we turned up an alley to avoid everyone. "It seems to be caused by my life."

"Well, yeah. A midlife crisis is real."

"But I don't want to be like this. I can't go on day after day hating everyone and everything."

"You don't hate me."

"That's true! I love you. I love you, but maybe you're the only one I can love because you expect nothing of me."

She laughed. "I'm fine with that. Plus, look at me. I've always hated everything and I don't worry about it."

"I think that's your new medication, though. You're a much happier curmudgeon now than you were in your thirties."

"Could be. I think I've just grown into it. I've settled into my true self, which is kind of a sybaritic misanthrope."

"What does that word mean?" I had no idea where Deirdre had picked up her extensive vocabulary.

"Sybaritic? It means I enjoy pleasure."

I whacked one of Deirdre's butt cheeks with my open palm. "Everyone enjoys pleasure."

"The stench!" Deirdre laughed. There were certain blocks of the neighborhood that were occasionally susceptible to an open-sewer bouquet. "I can't believe they can't get a handle on this, but I love that all the millionaires who live around here have to smell this too."

I pulled my shirt up over my nose so all I could smell was myself.

"Look there's more," Deirdre said. "It's an epidemic."

Someone had spray-painted on the front of an apartment building in fancy cursive writing *You're The One That I Want.* This self-affirming inspirational platitude was everywhere lately. It had been around since before the dot-com boom, but its origins were pure. The first time I saw it was one Saturday

morning long ago when I had woken up early to volunteer at the
Folsom Street Fair, the big annual leather and bondage street party.
A friend of mine who worked at a health clinic was recruiting
people to stand with donation boxes at the entrances. I had never
been, so I decided this was the way to go. Cooler than being an
ogler, less embarrassing than actually participating. On my walk
there, I kept seeing these stickers. Name tag stickers they use for
mixers or conventions that say My Name Is _____. All the
blanks on the stickers were filled in with the same kind of cursive,
written in colored Sharpie. My Name Is Bright Unconscious of the
Fern Bar. My Name is Reacharound Husband Constellation. My
Name is Be My Ambulance. And while I was working at the fair,
someone came by and put a sticker on my boob. My Name Is A
Jihad for the Crystal Egress. It was, like just about everything that
started underground and obscure, an art project that went off the
rails over time, and there was no sign, even with the tech influx,
that it was abating. The new iteration of it was warm and fuzzy,
lacking anything strange or absurdist. Same flowery script but stuff
like *Everything You're Doing Is Right On. We Belong. This Too Can
Be Yours. Protect Your Heart. All Is Not Lost. Be Gentle With Yourself.*

"Can there be a robust civilization when the graffiti is inspirational?!" Deirdre yelled.

"This shit has been going on for too long," I said. "Like
burlesque!"

The burlesque dancing "revival" had now officially been going
on for longer than in its original heyday.

"Watch," Deirdre said. "That graffiti is probably part of a viral
marketing campaign for some new app or something. Remember
all those stencils on the sidewalk advertising that music site? And
then they blew through all their money and disappeared, but their
dumb name was all over the streets for years afterwards."

"Rude."

"I would love to rent a sandblaster and sandblast that."

"Man, back in the day, we would have known like ten people

who owned their own personal sandblasters and they would have loved to roll them out here and blast away a huge chunk of the sidewalk and no one would have even called the police."

We spontaneously broke into a light jog to exit the piss alley and spill onto a bigger thoroughfare with more ventilation. Sweet escape into the exhaust from a passing bus. And standing right there was Trinket, Deirdre's nephew. Real name: Brandon. She hadn't seen him in months and I hadn't seen him in years. He was in his late-twenties and had moved out from Colorado to go to college, but never finished. After year two here, he was already coated in tattoos, mostly mystical shit involving the tantra and some paganistic-seeming detritus that I recognized from T-shirts on Haight Street. Last time we hung out, on Deirdre's bed at a party, he kept insisting he was a polyamorous pansexual though no one was arguing with him. *It's just what I am and if you have a problem with it, go talk to my wife.* He pointed at a woman with pigtails doing a whip-it. Deirdre was surprised to hear this news and he told her that the wedding had happened at Burning Man and she hadn't responded to any of his posts about it and she could fuck off. Then he left the party without his bong. She still had it on her mantle and was making good use of it.

Trinket shuffled from foot to foot in a pair of pink espadrilles while he told them about a party down by Duboce with bands and homemade absinthe. Trinket was big on raves and ecstasy, one of San Francisco's other scenes that wasn't exactly our territory, though we were curious about the party. It was always worth it to go to a place you hadn't partied before.

"We'll go with you," Deirdre said. "We'll follow you."

And just like that he was on fire, as if we'd lunged at him and ripped the carved walrus tusk out of his septum. "I AM NOT GOING! I CAN'T RUN INTO ANY CLIENTS TONIGHT!"

Trinket was also a hooker. He had told me before that most of his clientele were straight, married men, who just wanted a little treat at the end of the workday before they went home to their wives and kids. He had a cop who liked to do it in the back of the squad car, and told him that getting the cop's pants off killed five straight minutes, what with all the tools and weapons on his belt. Trinket was one of those three-minute-increment wonderpeople. Any longer than that and his shenanigans got tedious.

"You guys should go. There's a rad view from the roof," he said. "And I have extra spades you can buy off me for twenty bucks each."

Deirdre had mentioned he was now putting himself through massage school doing porn and selling drugs.

"What's a spade exactly?" I had tried not to learn that much about drugs. I remained willfully ignorant for years to keep myself out of trouble. This was based on a slight hunch that I might be one of those people who would eventually find my ideal drug and not want to let go of it. At least that's what I told people. Maybe I was just garden-variety scared of the unknown, too self-conscious.

"It's just a kind of X," he said. "It's a little speedy. You'll get all goo-goo and then probably get the shits."

"Bitchin," Deirdre said. "We'll take two."

I swallowed the pill outside the party and immediately regretted it. Now I was doomed to hold Deirdre's hand all night and keep my mouth shut for fear of saying something stupid. Most people took drugs so they could cut loose and not worry about looking dumb, but I wasn't like that. With drinking, I could get rowdy and dance and have screaming conversations with people. It felt more natural to who I was. Drugs got shady. I didn't trust them or myself. I would morph into a tiny country mouse who kept in the shadows and observed the city mice. I'd done this quite a few times. Taken some drug or other at the spur of the moment and then wished I hadn't. To me, all drugs were the same. I had tried a bit of all of them—speed, coke, mushrooms, pot, X—they all just made me feel like a moronic woodland creature. I kept trying them a few times a year to see if I would find something I liked, while at the same time hoping I never found one that resonated with me too deeply.

We walked through a beat-up door and down a long narrow walkway between two buildings to a rolled-up garage door. The place looked like maybe it was some kind of shipping office during the day. There were a couple metal desks, a fax machine, and a mountainous pile of foam packing peanuts that I promptly decided I had to take refuge in. I laid back in them and watched a short, sturdy guy with huge, meaty arms hang a piñata from the rafters. I had a soft spot for the kind of people who were described as being shaped like fireplugs. They looked like they were from another era and foreign geography. Broad chests and chunky hands that could easily knock you over with one punch. The kind of person you look at and think, "Now here is an animal who will protect my eggs." This guy's piñata was obviously homemade and he looked very proud of it. It was a giant blue unicorn with a hand grenade in its mouth and sporting a large pink penis. Masterful.

I felt a whoosh when the drugs started working. The tops of my ears tingled and my throat felt hot. I calmed myself by making a montage in my head of humans performing various tasks. I saw an EMT applying a defibrillator to someone's chest and shouting CLEAR!, a scrappy D.A. fighting to keep an inmate off death row in front of a packed courtroom, a frantic Wall Streeter bustling around the trading room floor, a baker removing a tray of perfect croissants from an oven, a pilot landing an airplane, and then this dude: crafting his unicorn-with-dick-and-hand-grenade for the big party that night. Everyone had their stations.

A young couple came and sat on the peanuts with me. I watched them make out for a bit, trying to imagine what their faces felt like all smashed together, until it occurred to me that they weren't as high as I was and I likely looked like a creeper. I flipped a switch and turned myself invisible. It was a trick I had recently learned. If I turned off my lights, people would look right through me. Luckily, aging made this trick much easier.

I scanned the room for Deirdre. The piñata scene was about to go off, people were crowding around, and I was sitting more or

less underneath its radius once it started swinging. I couldn't will
myself to move. An old-fashioned dyke with slices of hair pasted
onto her cheeks like sideburns started whacking the shit out of
it while the piñata architect was yanking the rope, pulling it up
and down, trying to get the crowd hyped. I lay there, slumped,
watching overhead as a series of arms took turns whacking it with
a Louisville Slugger. Finally, a lady in some sort of golden velvet
wizard robe broke the seal. Was I capable of diving for candy? Or
maybe I would luck out and candy would just fall on top of me?
I would enjoy a candy storm raining down on my prone body.
Where was Deirdre? And what was coming out of the piñata?
They were alive and how had I not heard the chirping before?

"Get up," a guy was grabbing my arm. "They're crickets.
There are crickets coming out of the piñata!"

People were screaming and running out the door, picking them
up and chasing each other with them, crunching them underfoot.

"I hate this town," I said to the guy as he helped me to my feet.

"Don't hate," he said, cupping my shoulders with both hands.
"We are in a scrimshaw of insanity as the earth's metronome goes
tick-tock-tick-tock and you need to make the conscious decision
to love it!"

"This is mean," I said. "Tell me what is wrong with a piñata
that is filled with candy!"

"I'm from East Texas so I want all the freak scene I can get!
I'm going to get my roommate's gecko and bring it back and let it
eat all the crickets."

I felt cross-eyed. I wished people would stop being so pleased
with themselves for feeling terminally unique. All I desired was a
piñata shaped like Snoopy with Smarties pouring out of it.

"Buena suerte," the guy said. "Buffet time, yo!"

I LEARNED LONG AGO there's a rule about following a hippie to a second location, but this was a biotech engineer wearing a rust sweater vest. The person, I was unsure of their gender, had arrived at the bar about an hour before closing and nursed a scotch while reading a waterlogged paperback by candlelight. Charming at first, but also inexplicably irritating. Perhaps it was the performative nature of it? How book-toters usually seem so poised and virtuous about the fact that they're reading in public. Them and their tote bags that said things like LIT HAPPENS. I almost asked what the book was, but stopped and admitted to myself that I probably had no idea who the author was and didn't want to get into a long back-and-forth anyway.

Opening up a conversation while working was always a boondoggle. Fragments, disjointed or repetitive, were swapped every time you traveled to their end of the bar, and you got the sense they had been thinking about what to say from the time you walked away until the next time you came back. Better to avoid it altogether. I brought change for their twenty, and they looked up, shut the book, and said, So what are you doing when you get off? I was floored. I hadn't been asked that question in at least three years, and never by a person who didn't appear remotely buzzed.

Getting with someone from the bar was bad news. They always knew where to find you and once they had, there was no escape. You were literally barricaded behind an enormous plank of wood. There'd been bartenders who quit because people they once (or twice) fucked kept dropping in to visit. You'd get paranoid that while your back was turned they were telling the other customers about the pile of dishes under your bed or your b.j. technique. Or maybe they were sending in their friends as spies to check you out. *Please refrain from fucking the patrons* was the best piece of advice my boss had given me that I had mostly heeded.

Back in the days when I had to field this question multiple times a night, I'd come up with a cache of stock answers. The rejoinders had to be definitive enough to halt the line of questioning without creating lingering animosity. Tricky. No matter how careful you think you're being, the use of certain words and phrases are likely to make a horny patron drinking alcohol think you're down to clown. Your excuse cannot mention anything involving smoking a doob, opening a bottle of wine, sitting on your couch, playing video games, watching a movie, or going to bed. Nothing that sounds like you're at loose ends or jonesing to relax. There was a classic dis that I learned from old movies, *I'm sorry, but I'm busy washing my hair tonight*, which was supposed to make you sound blasé, but that's a backfire straight-up. You're essentially asking the person to picture you taking a hot shower and running your hands through your hair. Who came up with that one? Hedy Lamarr? And even if you're trying to send the signal that you're exhausted, a woman has to realize that the sentence *I'm going to go home and pass out* comes off like an invitation to be raped. I had honed my list of uninviting but not offensively rude things to say to:

Sorry, but I've got to detonate a couple flea bombs.

I'll be hemorrhaging blood into a maxi pad.

Ringworm is no joke.

I'm exhausted from having sex with too many people.

And once I even tried, *I'm busy washing my hair... collection,* which had a witchy component I liked.

In heaviest rotation at this juncture was, "I'm going home to my sweatpants and my cat," neither of which I owned. It was astoundingly boring and only worked because of my age. A young woman saying that exact sentence would come off cute and cozy, as if her plans were actually an anomaly you might be able to talk her out of. Like, she might go home and do a facial mask and have a cup of tea OR she might stay put at the bar, drink a few shots of Goldschläger, and let you rip off her fishnets instead. Yes, when you're ripe enough to age into the sweatpants and cats excuse, you become the winning combo of sounding like a dud who's also self-satisfied. No one wants to chase that down.

It was a surprise to everyone who knew me that I poured the vest person a free shot and replied, "Nothing. Wanna party?" My wink-and-nod Spring Break answer didn't fully register, so I winked and nodded and made an awkward clucking sound to drive it home. They winked back. Still not sure they got it. Didn't matter. What did, in the moment, was that Lolly—it turned out that this butch brainiac's name was Lolly and she was good with being called she—possessed the quality that I had come to desire most in a person: she was new to town and probably didn't know anybody I knew. And as soon as Lolly started in about other bars in the neighborhood, hopping aboard the conversational funicular that kicks off with the phrase, "Do you happen to know…?" I told her to stop. *Shh, don't speak.* How I loathed the do-you-know-this-person game. It was yet another reason I refused to have a computer. From what it sounded like, the computer was actually an enormous lagoon where everywhere you looked, there they were bobbing around: people who knew people you knew.

The thrilling part for me is in being unknowable. The exciting part of Six Degrees of Separation is the *separation*. These days the steamroller of human connections is constantly rolling through your neighborhood with a full tank of gas and a live webcam.

I poured a beer for someone and checked myself. Was I really going to ask the other bartender to close up so I could skip out with Lolly? Perhaps I could resurrect a little of my old-fashioned slatternly behavior. I poured myself a shot of tequila, looked over at Lolly's serious "reading face" and decided sure. If only to get her to stop making that face.

We went out to the sidewalk, the rush of cool air so welcome on my sweat-covered brow, and Lolly asked if she should "summon a car on her phone." I insisted we either walk or take a cab.

"It's up in Twin Peaks," she said, gesturing up to the radio tower on the hill.

"You know this city is only seven miles across, right? Nowhere is too far to walk if you've got a couple hours."

She smiled. "That's cute, but let's take a car. It's already one."

I watched her changing in the nighttime lights, the streetlamps and passing headlights revealing different aspects of her face and body, second by second. Her head was a comforting square shape and she was supremely confident, as if her very bearing was a divine thank you to the universe for the gift of being a sturdy mannish woman blessed with a deep, calming alto.

"Okay, but let me hail a taxi." It was so irritating that people had forgotten about taxis.

After watching about fifteen black SUVs go by, I saw a cab. I had adopted a bold hailing style when I was a teen: one hand on my waist, the other arm stretched high, wrist firm, slow wave, staring straight into oncoming traffic, half in the street. I gave a sharp, earsplitting whistle. The Veterans Cab stopped and the driver asked how we were doing.

"We're good," I answered, a little drunk already. "This guy here wanted to call a car, but I insisted we take a cab. I've been in the city for a long time and have a lot of friends who drive cab." Drive cab. That's how cab drivers said it.

"Where you going?"

I was disappointed that the driver failed to congratulate me on my righteous stance to shun ride-sharing apps. Where was the praise for my old-school approach? I almost repeated myself, but

I knew they both had heard me loud and clear. Collaring yourself doing dumb shit, before you did even dumber shit, was turning out to be an important part of personal growth.

"So I don't know what this is going to be," Lolly said, checking her teeth in her phone. "It's a bunch of guys in my department at work, but since I'm new I figured I've got to take every opportunity to put myself out there."

"What do you do exactly? I heard you say biotech, but that's kind of like saying something in turtle language to me."

"What's turtle language?"

"I have no idea. You know what I mean."

"Do you really want to know? It's sort of tedious to explain."

"Okay, please don't then. Thank you."

We pulled up to one of those boring box buildings in Twin Peaks. I had been to parties in a few of these over the years. Looked like brutalist garbage from the street, but then you walk in and realize the place is all vertical and built into the hillside. From the front door it's about twenty paces to a giant wall of glass with panoramic views of the city. No matter how stunning the view, the damp weather inevitably turned the deck into oatmeal. I knew two people who died that way, from sketchy decks collapsing at two separate parties a few years apart.

I followed Lolly through the front door. It was incredibly dark inside, but still obvious, at least to me, that the three women visible on the premises were being paid to be there.

"Cool party," I said loudly. "Hookers and everything."

"I'm going to see if I can find Brock," Lolly said.

I wandered off down the hallway, repeating the name like I was burping. *Brawwwwwck.* A young woman in a cropped sweatshirt and metallic silver shorts was smoking out of her one-hitter.

"So what's the deal here?" I asked. "Who are these guys?"

"I don't know. I think it's some tech thing. My girlfriend and I just do it for the money and the alcohol and other stuff. There's two bottles of Don Julio. The big kind. We just get drunk and, you know."

My eyes adjusted to the light. I could have made a custom bingo card where each square contained an element of the decor and daubed a blackout, no problem. Large black leather couch. Matching black leather recliner. Wall-to-wall carpet. Multiple video game systems. Giant TV screen mounted on an arm on the wall. Four remotes. Embedded speakers. Microwave. One of those machines that makes coffee by squishing a pod. There was no art on the walls, no books, no CDs, or records.

I continued onto the deck where a very hairy man was in the hot tub, reclining backwards with his belly and feet breaking the water's surface, holding a drink in his hand. The wind was gusting billows of fog all around as if it were being triggered by machine.

"Come on in!" he said, extending his lowball toward my crotch. "The water's fine!"

The water's fine? What kind of Alan Alda movie was this?

I cocked my head like a spaniel and wordlessly held the pose as long as I could. Then I backed up toward the sliding glass door and went inside. Lolly was sitting on the couch with one of the paid companions in her lap, a bony pixie in a terrycloth tube top.

Lolly exhaled a long toke from her vape. "This is already the best party I've been to since moving here." She craned her neck at the girl like a ventriloquist checking in with her dummy.

The television screen played a decades-old music video that I remembered from the first days of MTV. That was what triggered a case of Party Crossroads. I could either get loaded and *force majeure* a dance party in the kitchen or quietly slip out the front door.

In an instant, I was walking down the hill. No reason to bust a nut for these turds. The pressure on the front of my knees was so painful that I turned around and started walking backwards. *I'm a woman walking backwards*, I thought. Or did I say it out loud? I had to watch that. I'd caught myself talking aloud lately, and not just muttering occasional phrases under my breath, but speaking full sentences at regular volume.

"God, that must hurt," I'd announced at the drugstore the other day, standing behind a guy with two Gold Bond Friction Defense roll-ons. "Extreme chafing of the balls." He turned around and I was caught off-guard, surprised at how he managed to hear my thoughts in the first place.

It had been a while since I'd been out on one of my night-time prowls. I'd gone through phases of doing this over the years, getting off my shift and roaming to places I never went in daylight, into the little alleys and coves, up the staircases and narrow streets in the hills. I continued my descent slowly, backwards, and when I heard an engine or saw the wash of headlights from an approaching car on the road, I turned around and faced it for a few steps until it passed, making a sporadic dance of full circles on my way down to the Castro. A few stray people lingered on the street. A buffed-out puker being propped up by his friends. A couple of teenagers doing a full body grind on the hood of a truck. A silver fox in a tuxedo walking a corgi.

I continued down 18th and saw the light was on in the kitchen window of an old boyfriend's house. I didn't even know if he lived there anymore. He was one of those people who disappeared from the scene, but supposedly still lived in town. I think I heard he was in a relationship with someone younger and professorial? Was that it? I couldn't recall. Maybe she worked at a museum? In textbook publishing? My memory was that his wife did something upstanding and normal. I'd never met her, but when she was described by others, I pictured him standing next to a tall marble column in a pair of expensive heels and a garland of laurel leaves. I paused out front, gazing at the window, its broken sash propped up by a familiar Italian cookie tin. I moved on before I got caught staring, continued past the frame shop and the old palm tree lot, down 15th to Mission. The street sleepers and drug jonesers were dotting my block as usual.

The warehouse was unlocked. Never a good sign. The entrance was a set of swinging glass doors, which made it look like a barely

functioning business; a shabby hardware store or shady credit
union. If it were left unlocked for even five minutes, someone
would come wandering in off the street because the artfart warehouse was known to the local street populace as a place where, if
you tried enough times, you were eventually bound to gain entry.
There were so many variables with its unpredictable residents,
including states of inebriation, relationship drama, or habitual spac-
iness, that it was a miracle the door ever got locked. You'd think
caution would be rampant in a communal living space, with all its
bed-hopping and disappearing peanut butter, but personal responsibility was a tough nut among warehouse dwellers. Because of
this, the place was being ripped off constantly, when plenty of
people were home. Bikes, records, stereo equipment, computers,
and musical instruments were easy to snatch and pawn. I, on more
than one occasion, had bought my own stuff back from Anthony
at Eagle Loan, but sometimes I was too late and everything had
already been sold. When my stereo got stolen in the middle of the
day while I was sleeping, my refrain was: *Well, at least I don't have
to worry about my stereo getting stolen anymore.* That's when I got a
padlock for my bedroom door.

I hesitated at the threshold for a second. Something was off.
It was raining. It was raining *inside*, but it wasn't raining outside.
The front workspace was dark, which was strange because there
was always a light burning somewhere, and there was water falling
from the ceiling. It smelled like rotting garbage sacks with occasional surges that were even more foul. Human. I rushed back into
the kitchen and there were my roommates Ed, Jen, Jake, Luke,
Luke's girlfriend Keisha, and the new British guy who had given
everyone tattoos with a gun he made from an old Walkman. They
sat in the red vinyl booth, a massive curved banquette that had
been rescued from a diner and was patched with duct tape, holding
umbrellas over their heads. A few tall votives burned on the table
and no one was talking. They barely looked up when I ran in.

"You guys! What's happening?"

They immediately sprang to life, like a switch had been flipped on grubby animatronic dolls. Answers came spilling out from everyone. *It's the fucking pipes!*

From up there! From the fucking hotel.

It's fucking toilet water from junkies!

It's shit water and shower water. It won't stop.

I was rarely surprised by anything anymore, but I did want to know one thing. "How can you guys just be sitting there while shit is raining down on you?" I took refuge under one of the ceiling's wider beams.

Out of the corner of my eye, I noticed a figure stretched out across the length of the dining room sofa inside a case for an upright bass.

"We've been bailing out garbage cans and buckets for six hours. We are so wasted right now."

"What did Ahmet say?" The asshole landlord who smoked skinny lady cigarettes.

"He won't answer. We've called him a million times."

"I think we have to call the city and have them turn off the water to the whole building," I said. "Tell them it's an emergency."

No one moved. Call the city? The warehouse, in general, was allergic to the idea of involving anyone in their lives who appeared "official." The fact that we were constantly under threat of an eviction made this more pronounced.

I motioned to the couch. "Who's that guy?"

"I don't know."

"I thought he was your friend."

"He's some old jazz dude who played here back when we used to run the music series."

"Okay, but we stopped doing that seven years ago. You didn't even live here then."

"Yeah, he was coming through town from like Bisbee or something. He just needed a place to crash for a few days. He's harmless. He's really old."

"Lawrence told us he used to play with Beefheart sometimes. Or was it Zappa? And he toured with Miles Davis in Europe in the '80s."

I peered into the bag at the old man. The few strands of his scraggly gray beard were in a skinny braid, held by a green twist tie, and he was snoring away. His face was vaguely familiar. I grabbed a candle off the table, and walked down the hall to my room like a ghoul. I noticed first the sludgy mess on the linoleum floor and then I was overcome by the smell. It was even worse in there. The dirty sewage water seemed to have activated all of the age and must and grime of my secondhand clothes and furniture, turning my darkened room swampy and putrid. Anything I had been convinced in a moment at Thrift Town was treasure, was now obviously trash. I glanced over at the freestanding closet I had built. Maybe the things inside were safe?

Calmly, I did a 180 and exited the front door, without locking it, and walked two blocks down to the storage locker place. This was not the type of corporate storage enterprise with a signature color palate and cheery billboards meant to ease your mind about the decision to pay a fee every month because you were incapable of letting go of your garbage. This was a janky one-off, a cavernous space where plywood units had been hammered together decades ago.

I found a woman behind a desk, looking like a hairless cat in a gray Caesar wig.

"I need to rent a small space from you like right now." I said. "What's the smallest you got?"

She pincered her fingers into the drawer in front of her and handed over a key. "Go take a look at number nineteen."

I walked down the labyrinth of dingy hallways, littered with trash and cigarette butts. I passed a unit with an open door and inside was a couple squatting on the floor rifling through their boxes and bags. They had a bucket of chicken and a few tall cans of beer. Possibly their home for the time being.

The lock on nineteen had been cut. I yanked opened the wooden door and peered in. The space was about as big as two refrigerators and already had someone else's caved-in boxes and bursting grocery sacks in it. A few items were scattered on the ground, VHS tapes and manila file folders, as if the space had already been looted. Grim, but since I wasn't picky about much of anything, a perfect fit.

Back at the desk the woman had fallen asleep with her skinny arms corpse-like across her chest. I watched her for a moment. Her nose veered off toward her shoulder, her mouth slack. She looked younger than she had before, but also mostly dead.

"I'll take it," I said loud enough to startle her. "It looks like there's some other stuff in there, though."

Her eyeballs popped. "Guy died." She hoisted herself out of her seat and began ambling slowly away. "I'll clear it out."

I eyed a couple old dollies in the hall. "Can I use one of those?" I yelled after her. "I'm just a few blocks away."

"No bringing the dollies outside," she said without turning around. I was halfway out the door when the woman yelled after me. "You're free to use a shopping cart. They're around the corner. People ditch 'em here all the time."

It wasn't often I was conscious of my own breath, but I took a deep inhale and tried as best I could to let it out slowly and evenly. And then I approached a shopping cart and pushed it out of the mouth of the building onto the sidewalk. I found exactly one cartload of salvageable things in my closet. There was an antique dinnerware set I had never eaten off of, a set of leather-bound encyclopedias embossed with gold leaf, and some vintage dresses that needed repair. After all the years of interacting with homeless people in my neighborhood, some with whom I was pretty well-acquainted, I had never experienced the sensation of rolling a grocery cart filled with all of one's earthly possessions down the sidewalk. I ran into a guy I knew named Clarence. He was rolling his cart toward me.

"How's it going, youngster?"

"Not that great."

"You out here now?"

"No, not really. The pipes in our place exploded so it's been raining inside for a few hours. I'm trying to rescue some of my stuff."

"That's terrible," he said. Terry-BULL. "You need any help?"

"No, I'm good. Thanks, though."

"You need that cart when you're finished? I got a friend who's looking. They stole his."

Clarence and I shambled side by side back to the lockers and I handed off the cart.

"So you off the block now?" He said this with his palm flat on top of my head.

I reached up with both my arms and pressed his hand more firmly, creating a deeper pressure, as if I were afraid my head would blow off, geyser-like.

"Think so," I said. "I think I'm off the block."

We hugged and he headed out, pushing the empty cart forward and dragging his own hefty one behind. I found the woman asleep at the desk again and woke her up with a vaudeville-worthy throat-clearing.

"You get a discount if you pay for three months up front," she said.

"That's okay. I just need it for a month."

She let her chin drop to her chest and looked up at me slyly under her droopy lids. "That's what they all say."

I should have let it go, but it bothered me to spot someone's catchphrase. I kicked my hip out and said, "You like that line, huh? It's kind of your 'thing' you love saying to people." I imitated her right to her face using a drunk Joan Crawford voice. "*That's what they all say!*" Didn't faze her.

With my belongings safely inside the storage locker, I walked straight past my warehouse without even looking at the cracked front door. The wagon was parked on Shotwell, so I figured I could take a nap in the backseat. Until I discovered someone was already taking a nap inside my car. Two people, actually, had folded down the seats with a sleeping bag unzipped and splayed open to cover them both. One looked like a little kid. I walked up to Deirdre's place and felt underneath the gate for the extra keys. No dice. She must have had a visitor come during the night. I didn't buzz. I could sleep in a booth at the bar with a towel over my face for a few hours, maybe bring some lunch over to her later.

Oh shit, the casserole! I had left it out on the kitchen counter with the oven preheating two nights ago. My first thought was that I had ruined my only chance to ever eat my mom's cooking again and it was my second thought that the house might be currently burning down. Last came the thought that if there were a fire, at least I wouldn't have to worry about dealing with the house anymore. Scott and I could split an insurance check and be done with it.

Should I call the San Jose Fire Department and tell them? Race down there and make sure everything was okay? What was the actual likelihood of a horrible fire from a preheating oven? Scott was flying in that night. I could wait in the limbo of not knowing until then. I'd recently heard about the idea of a liminal zone and I liked it, probably too much. It made me think that my whole adult life had been a liminal zone and I hadn't realized it. I had spent the last twenty-five years thinking that I was *there*, that I had arrived at my destination and was staying put, but maybe that wasn't the case. Maybe I had merely been on my way from one place to the next this whole time and I only became aware that the trip was starting to feel a tad too lengthy. I let myself into the bar and plunged into a stress nap.

When the cleaning crew arrived a few hours later, around 7 a.m., chatting loudly with cups of coffee in hand, they hushed and treaded lightly, like perhaps I was a dying sea serpent washed ashore. I did my best to play it off—*just sleeping in the bar again!* Something about the looks on their faces, the embarrassment and pity, sent me scrambling for a Sharpie. I left a note for the owner and taped it to the register.

Harry, I won't be in for a while. I've got to deal. —E

It was Sunday and I stalked the early morning streets like a jilted cat. So many new businesses had popped up in the last year, replacing the old bookstores, cafes, and copy shops. It was mostly fancy meats and sweets and liquor. Plus a shop called The Wolfpack that appeared to sell typewriter supplies, bamboo bicycle frames, Mexican blankets, iPad cases made out of yarn, and salt. In a flash of self-preservation, I bought a gallon jug of water from a corner store and started guzzling it as I made my way to the park to nap. These civic institutions can really come through for you when you're feeling put out, as evidenced by all the sleeping bodies dotting the grass that morning. I plopped down on the hill, soaking my pants immediately, and watched the dog people do their thing. I added "dog ownership" to my growing list of stuff that automatically makes people seem like they have their shit together. When I woke up hours later, I was uncomfortably damp, my back wet from the grass, my front sweaty from the sun. Not exactly refreshed, but at least rested enough to move through the crowds of brunchers, strollers, and weekend line-standers, on my way to my old favorite bar on 17th Street.

It should never be considered too early in the day to have your first drink. It's when and whether you have your second and third that the problems start. As I walked passed the wagon, I saw the sleepers had vacated, but noticed the driver's side window was halfway down, off its track. My antenna had been busted off to make a crack pipe.

The bar had just opened an hour before and I was craving the quiet and the dark, only a threshold away to a different world. I was expecting to open the door to the sweet sight of an empty room and cranky old Karen working, but what happened was more like a high school reunion. The bar was packed and loud, unheard of for 11 a.m. on a Sunday. I recognized almost everyone in the place.

"Edie, oh my God!" It was an old bartender's girlfriend. She squeezed me tight into her chest. "Isn't this the best? It's so freaking cute."

"What is it? What's going on in here?"

"You didn't see the post? That's hilarious. You're just here on a Sunday morning? Why are you so sunburned? No, Lynn and Jen's twins are in a band and they're playing. Look at them!"

I looked over at the stage and saw four mini-adults going about their business like they were in a real band. Plugging in amps, tuning guitars, checking drums.

This was some kind of bizarro world. I took a seat at the end of the bar and ordered a drink from the specials board. Three bucks until noon, pretty good. The glass arrived, tall and frosty, with a swamp of fresh mint on the bottom. I took a big swallow and slammed it down on the bar. It tasted like carbonated toothpaste.

"Hey, Karen! I don't want to piss you off, but what the fuck is this? You forgot to put the booze in my drink."

"It's a fauxjito," she said and turned her back.

I looked at the board again. Mocktails. Right. For the kids.

This pissed me off and I didn't care who knew. I launched into a line of inquiry, very loudly, directed at no one. "Why the fuck do kids have to have their own scene in a bar when they're still in middle school? What happened to feeling special because your mom let you get a Shirley Temple at a steakhouse once a year? On your birthday!"

"Calm down, woman," Karen said. "These kid shows do pretty well. The parents get drinking and, you know."

"What, they're not cool enough yet? How about leaving something for them to discover on their own when they're grown up? Let them turn twenty-one and then they can go into a bar and order a drink like a grown person does. But no! They've already played in a band to an adoring audience and had cocktails in a bar before they've even entered high school. Great preparation for the real world! Fuck off!"

Everyone was staring at me now. Karen dumped a glug of rum into my glass and I calmed down. What did I know? Maybe this rapid acceleration of experiencing the world was part of evolution?

Maybe you could gobble up every new experience whenever it presented itself and that was how your life progressed and advanced. Maybe these kids lives would be better than mine because they were trusting that something new and exciting was always around the corner. Like, if they cleared this experience out of the way when they were eleven, what might life have in store for them between now and twenty-one. Imagine! I couldn't imagine, at all, but maybe someone less jaded could.

Something came into sharper focus as I sat there, tucked into the Naugahyde captain's chair with my back to the wall. I convinced myself early on that I'd found everything worth looking for in my snug little art scene, so at some point, I completely stopped looking around. I worked at a cool place and knew cool people who were doing cool things. Then I got old. The end. I was no different than those Goth lifers I saw on the street. Now in their fifties, they schlepped to their office jobs or waited in line at the ATM, the fishnet sleeves and black leather of Siouxsie Sioux long abandoned for comfy cotton separates in shades of black that didn't quite match and chunky orthopedic shoes. Looking like stagehands, their powdered-milk complexions dusty, lips in a deep carmine. I was white-knuckling my past and losing my grip.

Sock Monkey Chicken Party fired up another three-chord punk rock classic. The girls sang and looked sexy without quite knowing they were looking that way. It reflected poorly on me that I thought the girls were sexy, I knew that, but I also knew what I was looking at. The signifiers were there. Karen walked back over.

"It's confusing how mesmerizing it is to look at girls like that," I said. She was still mad at me, so I had nothing to lose.

"Wunderlich, you're disgusting. What are you saying? What's wrong with you?"

"Nothing. Just probably what a lot of people are thinking."

"I don't think a lot of people are thinking that."

The belligerence swelled in my belly like a dirigible. "Okay! It just seems fairly obvious to me that those eleven-year-olds are kind of sexy even though that is the exact wrong thing to say. They're hot preteens acting like how they see people act on TV. Or on their phones or whatever!"

"Enough!"

"Everything happens, Karen. Everything you can imagine actually happens and it doesn't make it any less true if we refuse to talk about it. Our city is gone. People have sex with infants."

"I hate you."

"I'm just saying that it happens."

I saw a woman I recognized as the former girlfriend of one of my old roommates at the warehouse. Shelton? Shelby? She was wearing a pink boxy shift dress and white go-go boots. She jerked her head back, like she thought I was going to keep saying terrible things.

"Did you hear about what happened at 1943 last night? The shitstorm?" I said.

"Oh, it's insane," she said.

"Where is everyone going to go? At five this morning, I was actually wheeling my stuff to a storage unit in a shopping cart!" I laughed.

Her face froze. "You know, it's not okay to laugh at other people's misfortunes."

I was confused. "But it's my misfortune too. I've lived there for seventeen years."

"I mean the shopping cart comment. Some people live like that full time. That's some people's *reality*."

I stopped. I didn't scream.

"You're the only one who left, by the way," she said. "They're, like, going to mop it out with a really strong bleach solution."

I kept it even. The too-even that shows you're barely in control. "So they're going to keep living in a place where shit water, water with feces and bits of toilet paper in it, was raining down on them and their things?"

"Well, they're going on a rent strike. That place is like four thousand square feet! Where else is Luke going to find a place to do his work? He's using all these huge concrete slabs now. No one has space like that anymore. Not everyone gets left a house by their rich mom."

So that was the story? I leaned back in my chair, watching the parents in the crowd. I had known some of these people since they were in their twenties and I had never seen most of them looking this happy. Without them being on drugs, I mean. They looked so proud of their sexy kids, who weren't really sexy, but just feeling uninhibited and carefree and wearing tight shirts and shaking their asses in a way that would be legally considered sexy seven years from now. "I Wanna Be Sedated" as performed by sixth graders with fun purple streaks in their honey blond hair. I finished my drink, grabbed my bag, and went to the next bar over. It was a new place that had spent a lot of money on a wall of tropical fish and a lighted dance floor. I ordered a beer and a shot.

In the corner, there was a couple sequestered, making out. This type of behavior had become more and more grating to me the less frequently I experienced it in my own life. I started to wonder if I would ever have a real lover again. There had been so many, but not anyone in years. From what I heard, it might even be as easy as it ever was to find someone to fuck, using a phone, but I doubted I could find a person who could see the real me and then love me anyway. I tried to pinpoint what was different about me now than back when I was having all that sex. I mean, besides my sagging boobs and aging face and crepey arm skin. There was a distinct gelled bitterness now. It was in how I responded and reacted to everything. It was on my face and in my body. I sipped on my beer and tried to scroll through the sex snapshots I had in my mind, trying to get lost in some hot reverie, but I couldn't do it. The irony. Out of all the sex I'd had, I'd never committed any of it to memory because it never occurred to me that someday I would want to look back on it. When you're used to having something, you can never imagine there's going to be a time when you won't.

I tried harder. There was a memory trick I learned where you could dip into your past by focusing on what was under your feet at the time. Did the bedroom have carpet or hardwood floors? Try to remember a pair of favorite socks or favorite shoes. I went back to my early twenties and saw a scratched parquet floor and a pile of dirty clothes in the corner and started to remember a guy who would always braid my hair when he came over. We would climb on the bed and he would take off all my clothes. Then he would grab a comb and a couple rubberbands and give me two tight braids down the back of my head. There was another person from that room, someone who was crazy about my bones, who would touch every part of me, pressing down hard through my skin to get at my ribs, my scapula, my femurs, reaching under my collarbone, hooking their fingers and thumb around it like they were pulling apart a small animal. I was stretched out on my stomach, feet hanging off the bed, legs together, waiting. I would get pulled onto my knees, hands grabbing my hips. A person so joyous about putting their tongue in my ass. Or maybe they were just drunk and acting out? I would let a cock get hard in my mouth. Pull the hips tightly into my face. Sometimes I would try to keep as still as possible so the orgasm would overcome me with no movement at all.

That was me?

I guess I would have to wait and hope again for the sweet, weird, exciting sex of a real creature feature. When I was ready. When I was feeling less amorphous, less like I was in transit. Right now I was stuck in the middle. It was like the '70s song except the clown to the left of me and the joker to the right were also both me. What a bummer threeway.

I WAS HARPOONED BY Marco from the get-go. We had been at a party at some guy's apartment on Market and Sanchez the night a wildfire broke out in Point Reyes. Everyone was on the roof looking for smoke, even though it was freezing up there. I was huddling in a group, my beanie pulled down low to warm my ears, the collar of my peacoat turned up. I'd seen him in the neighborhood a bunch and now here he was, sort of a narrow-shouldered, small guy with dirty hair and a scruffy mustache. The kind of look that used to break my bones. Everyone's hair was dirty back then, but this was quite a few years before guys were growing joke mustaches, ironic mustaches, fundraising mustaches. Mustaches were still for dads, gay men, and sportscasters. A straight young white man with a mustache in San Francisco was unusual. Grunge may have been on the brink of a land grab, but dirtbag culture was still mainly in the jurisdiction of the city's badass dykes.

I overheard a girl asking him about his photo studio. He said it was over on Florida, near an old mayonnaise factory, not far from the abandoned Hamm's Brewery that punks had taken over. The Vats. I'd been to a few parties there over the years, at different dwellings that had sprung up inside the beer vats, yeasty and abandoned. You'd crawl through holes that had been bored into the metal to get inside people's "apartments."

I half-expected Marco to float the idea of the girl coming by to do a photo session with him, like most male photographers talking to women in their twenties at parties did, but he didn't. He had no interest in taking pictures of women. Or of people in general.

"I like ugly industrial things and just garbage really," he said and I was intrigued. He said he felt like his camera limited him, that it was like being suffocated, having to express himself with even a massive Hasselblad. There was something slightly troubling that he equated the size of the camera with the depth of experience, but I was still way too young to start putting up boundaries on people who seemed like a lot of work.

"It's not a lollipop," I said.

"What? What's not a lollipop?"

"Your photos. Like, you know those oversized lollipops, the swirly kinds with all the colors? Their main job is to be impressive when you're traipsing around the boardwalk and other kids are looking at you, right?"

"Traipsing around the boardwalk! In a striped bathing costume? With a parasol?"

I ignored it. "But those things don't taste very good and you never want to finish them."

"I have no idea what you're talking about," he said.

I was fully aware I was trying too hard. Attempting to be interesting is the least interesting thing there is, so I tried to recover by saying, "I know what I mean in my mind."

Marco stopped for a second and then peered inside my ear like he was looking at my mind. I whipped my head around so we were face to face.

"Can I kiss you?" I asked.

"Hold up." He disappeared down the ladder on the side of the building.

I debated whether I should just leave and go to the bar, when he came back to the roof with a bottle of whiskey in his jacket pocket. We shared a cigarette and passed the bottle back and forth.

"Sorry I asked you that," I said. "I start drinking and then it follows that I usually want to make out. It's embarrassing. I'm trying to get a handle on it."

"It's all right. My friend downstairs just warned me about it."

"Great."

"I mean, sort of. So a lot of people know you? That's what Lawrence said."

"Well, I work at a bar that everyone goes to and I lived at the House of Pi for a while. I'm sure you've been there for a party or to see a show, right?"

"And he said you used to play with Corey's band? Or sing or something?"

It was widely acknowledged that my stint in Beaver Damage had been a failure.

"I subbed for a bit when Gina went to rehab. I was pretty not-good. I wrote some lyrics. You know Gina?"

He glanced around the rooftop. "I don't think so."

"You want to get out of here?"

By the time we climbed down from my bed the next afternoon, the loft was littered with condoms.

I could get very nostalgic for Marco, but I didn't miss having sex after finding out about AIDS. Everywhere you looked there was a bowlful of condoms, posters about condoms, flyers about condoms, people giving you handfuls of condoms on your way out of a movie, a party, a club, or a show. Every one of my jackets had condoms in the pockets. Every tote bag or backpack I owned was full of condoms. I drew the line at dental dams. But man, I never again wanted to re-live those years of unfurling rubber after rubber. Rubbers going on dicks that immediately got soft. Ditching a rubber midway through when it started to chafe. Rolling out another rubber and lubing it up. Holding a rubber up to the light to see if it had a hole. Getting mad at rubbers that didn't hold their jizz. Fishing out rogue rubbers from inside my body. Tying rubbers in knots that had done their job. Wrapping rubbers in toilet paper. Throwing rubbers in the trash. Tossing rubbers out the window. Flushing rubbers down the toilet. Digging through a coat or drawer or a bag for yet another rubber. I hoped to never have to look at another one for as long as I lived.

I heard a lot of senior citizens were now catching sex bugs now because they were hooking up online and not using condoms. No wonder. By the time you're that old, you've completely had it with putting a sheath on a dick. You figure you haven't gotten HIV by now, you may as well risk it. Maybe it was like the 10,000-hour rule. How you're supposed to become an expert in something after you've done it for 10,000 hours. How about after 10,000 rubbers, you've somehow mastered the craft of warding off infections. You've done your penance and it makes you immune to whatever's coming to get you.

I eventually got tested for HIV, though I put it off for months in a panic, convinced that I must have contracted the virus from being such a slut. My sluttiness was something I was neither proud nor ashamed of. I simply recognized that I had led a life in which I crossed paths with a lot of people and it just happened that a lot of those people were people that seemed interesting to have sex with. It wasn't always the best idea, but it was an idea in which I was able to exhibit remarkable follow-through. It made me feel accomplished. The night I met Marco, I was getting out of some thing with another guy and Marco was sort of seeing this person, but they had just moved to LA, so we were both in the clear as far as how "clear" was being defined in those days.

I procured a sub for work that night by promising the girl I'd bring dinner to the bar later, and Marco and I went off down the street to the Thai place, holding hands like a couple of goofs. The whole neighborhood looked different. Lopsided and golden.

"I think the best part about this place is that when you walk in, it smells like a barnyard, like the hippo enclosure at the zoo, but the food is so good."

"I know!" Marco said. "How does she do that?"

"She" was the woman behind the counter who was the only employee anyone had ever seen working there. She was one of those old/young people. Probably not more than forty, but looked at least sixty. She took your order, she prepped, she cooked, she rang you up, and she did the dishes. She scowled, but it was completely understandable why and therefore gratifying to witness.

I usually had no problem polishing off one of her enormous bowls of soup, but neither of us could make a dent that day. We were dazed, giddy, drugged. Starving, but with no appetite. I felt like my body was emitting a low hum, like a crank at the base of my skull had been turned and was ever so slowly unspooling itself.

"We can stay over at my place tonight if you still want to hang out," Marco said. "But if you have to pee in the middle of the night, you're screwed. The bathroom is down the hallway and you have to bring a flashlight because the lights are always burned out and someone stole the ladder tall that's enough to reach them."

I didn't care that he didn't have a real apartment, that he slept in a single bed in his studio and didn't have access to a shower. Who was I supposed to be? Princess Di? He liked that. He liked that I lived in a warehouse, had built my own bedroom, and worked at the bar. He was glad I had no interest in talking about whether we were dating exclusively or just seeing each other or wanted to call each other boyfriend/girlfriend or if we had ever thought about getting married and having kids. Not one heart-to-heart about the status of our relationship ever took place. We thought we were evolved, too smart to resort to such clichés.

Marco began building his own cameras, giant ones, so big that they needed to be hauled around by a trailer he hitched to his pickup truck. I helped him get his traveling rig together and he dragged those cameras all over California and the Southwest, doing 35 mph on backroads, but not to get to the Pacific Ocean or Bryce Canyon or Joshua Tree. His landscapes were mostly abandoned office parks from the '60s and '70s, public sculptures that had rusted out and been graffitied, and rundown shopping centers on the outskirts of small towns. He would buy the film in huge rolls and spindle it himself around plastic drainage pipes. The whole process from rolling the film onto the pipes and developing it in huge tanks was cumbersome and messy and time-consuming and expensive. Like a private performance he did for himself, or for me if I happened to be around. Part of the whole deal was that the photos were often damaged by light or scratches, imperfections of the rigorous process he went through each time. You know how it's a compliment to say that someone makes something look "effortless." Marco's art looked very effortful.

It was so warm the night of his first big show. It was October and during that era, it was the closest San Francisco would get to summer. After '89, when the "Indian summer" would come, everyone would start whispering ominously, *earthquake weather.* But warm days were few and far between back then, not at all like now where there are outdoor cafes and restaurants, where people dine at tables on sidewalks as if they were living in a normal city. The weather used to be so different that it's hard to imagine the only outdoor places to eat were the backyard at Zeitgeist, the biker bar on Valencia, and The Mission Rock and The Ramp, two water-front spots that were like taking a trip to another era. Sometimes a cafe would put out a bench or a couple of chairs, but you would never walk through the Mission and encounter an *al fresco* dining scene. It was a weather issue, of course, but it also felt too showy. Gauche. Go ahead and hunch over your taco in a doorway, inhale your burrito at the bus stop, or brown-bag your beer at the park, but the minute you're using a fork and knife on the sidewalk or drinking out of a chilled cocktail coupe in a made-up word called a *parklet* while broke and homeless and working poor people trudged past you on the street? There was a time when that kind of activity was considered far too let-them-eat-cake-y for San Francisco.

Marco's gallery was on Treat Street, a dark little alley that continued to hold the warmth of the afternoon even after the sun set. He had been working on the show for nearly a year, the last three months obsessively. He blew through so much money buying chemicals, the kind to develop photos and also the ones to fuel his creative process, that he began to borrow from me. Just a fiver here and there a couple times a week. I wasn't worried. I knew that to feel a bit on edge, to plummet and spin out a little, to experiment and turn yourself inside out every once in a while was okay. The best view is always from the edge, right? I trusted I would always come back to what was more or less level. I trusted he would too.

My b.o. that night was out-there bad, like burning tires and damp Chex mix. I had gotten called in to work an afternoon shift and hopped right out of bed. The plan was to go home before the opening, to rinse the bar off me, and change into a better T-shirt, but I was too jacked-up, too excited. As soon as someone arrived to cover for me, I borrowed a bike and pedaled the twenty blocks to the gallery. It was a mob scene. There was no longer room inside. Everyone was drinking cans of beer and smoking out in the street. When I finally located Marco, he was completely wasted, sitting on an upside-down milk crate surrounded by people. His beard had grown long and scraggly, his fingers and nails were filthy, and his hair hung in two oily sheaves on his shoulders. It's a look often described as Mansonesque, the opposite of the showered version, Jesus, but he didn't look like either. His eyes were so large and kind, he mostly resembled a bearded toddler during a time of famine. Marco stretched out his arms to me and smiled. I recognized his euphoric state of exhaustion, another of his preferred drugs. I leaned the bike against a fire hydrant and pushed through the crowd toward him. We pressed our foreheads together and spoke with our lips touching.

"You did it, little one. Look at your crazy art party."

He put his hand on my cheek and whispered, barely audible. "I am so high right now. I need to just sit here and stay mashed into your face for a while."

I knelt down in front of him and kept close, attached to his breath and his sweat. A mass swirled around us, laughing and shouting, while our friends' band started playing in the street. A trio who banged on washtubs and scrap metal—staunch opponents of anything that required an electrical outlet. People screamed along to their cover of John the Revelator. Dirty white artists in a Latino neighborhood really going apeshit on a blues song because they were feeling it. That moment was the essence of how being with Marco felt: on the inside of something that was outside, in the middle of everything, but slightly wasted and removed.

"I think I sold a few things," Marco finally said, his eyes closing in an extended blink. "There was that old guy here. The one Tina told us about who produced those movies with the guy."

He looked like he was going to drift off.

"Baby, that's great. You gotta just rest after this. Promise. Let's go up to the hot springs or something. We could go camping." Camping was something I had never done, but we had been talking about it ever since we first met. Our camping "plans" had crossed over into a rather depressing zone. We were far too young to keep talking about, but not doing, a thing that seemed so simple. A theme had emerged.

His head floated on his neck, a day-old helium balloon. "Okay. I'm going to stand up now. I'm going to get another beer."

We walked connected, hipbone to hipbone, back to the bathtub of beer and popped open a couple cans. I had seen most of the show in progress around his studio in the past months, but it was impossible to take any of it in that night with the crowd. I would come back alone. We headed to his place and the streets faded quiet behind us. Whenever that happened, calmness in the night streets, I asked myself what the date was. Quiet streets at the beginning of the month usually meant the junkies were in their rooms using after social services checks came out. Crazy streets meant everyone was out of money and looking, using whatever they could get their hands on. Tonight was quiet. Everyone was on a mission.

I locked up the bike and threw Marco over my shoulder and carried him up the stairs. He was so light, like a tall sunflower stalk.

I brought him into the dark of his studio and collapsed onto the bed. By the time I wiggled my pants off, he was deeply asleep. It took me a while to wind down, to slow my hummingbird heart, to move my breath from my throat to my stomach. As he snored loudly next to me, I lay there and listened, trying to match his rhythm in and out, in and out. Still I couldn't sleep.

I flipped on a small light and grabbed the sketchbook he kept by the bed. I turned past his drawings and notes until I came to a blank page. With a grease pencil, I began to draw the scene outside the gallery that night. I never had any talent for drawing, but I wanted to capture it. The street, the band, the dogs, all of it. My street scene was flat, with no dimensionality. How to draw something as simple as a pair of shoes? Where did the sky start? I made a brief stab at rendering a set of bongo drums and the result flustered me so deeply, I yanked out the page, folding it neatly over and over and placing it underneath the mattress. Perhaps my talent was for the more abstract? I would instead try to capture the electricity I felt. I hovered the pencil over a new page, moving my hand quickly above it without touching down. I tried sparking lines and shadowy figures, but it didn't make me feel like I was "on to" anything. Eventually I tucked the book behind the bed and clicked off the light.

I was still lying there awake when the birds started to sing. I tried to block everything out except the numbers one through 100, which I counted down and back up three times, before I started seeing the familiar signs. I was getting to the drop-off point. There were lights and spirals, mouse holes and mossy caves, a lemon slice, a tangle of vines, a seashell. The dizzying lightheadedness of traveling to sleep. When this happened, I would delve into a spiral or head toward the light, taking myself deeper and deeper, until I got lost in it, until I let myself be whooshed away.

I saw my mother. She was at the Japanese tea garden in the hills of Saratoga, sitting on a rock, wearing a yellow rain slicker. She was relaxed and smiling, unfamiliar, leaning back on her elbows with her knees bent. I walked to her and she reached into the koi pond, grabbed one of the bright orange fish, and tossed it up into the sky. I waited to catch it, but it never came down. Eaten by a hungry cloud with a purple tongue. What the hell. Dreams, man. I guess there are reasons we should keep them to ourselves.

At two the next afternoon, Marco finally stirred. I reached over and rubbed his hip, trying to gently wake him while pretending that wasn't my intention. (I would sometimes lightly touch his dick until he would start to get hard and stir a little and then I'd pretend I was asleep. A game.) His eyes opened to half mast and he whispered, *Can I just?* before falling off again. I gave up. I hadn't been out of the city for a year, out of my neighborhood in months, and I was itching to go somewhere. The city had a way of sucking me in, like I was on the clock, working, guarding, noting the changes. Paying attention in case no one else was.

Marco stayed in bed all day, waking briefly to have a few bites of the scrambled eggs I made, leaving the rest to get cold on the bedside table. I sat down in the kitchen and tried to write about the night before. I smoked cigarettes. I began a letter to my childhood friend Josie.

Dear Josie, Last night was so wild.

I began a letter to myself as a child.

Dear Young Me, Your boyfriend is an amazing artist and a good kisser.

I began a letter to an outside observer. *Everyone was drinking cans of beer and smoking out in the street.*

It felt idiotic to write; pointless. I made tea. Agitated and antsy, I rooted through his pockets for the garage door opener we'd been handed last night. I would go fetch the car we were borrowing, just in case he got up. If he didn't, I'd go somewhere on my own.

Late afternoon and it was arctic. I should have worn a jacket. I had finally gotten used to the fact that it was never going to be possible to predict the weather in this city just by looking outside. There was a surrender involved. My hands jammed into fists and retracted inside my sweater sleeves, I climbed the hill into the fog until I passed the last of the shops and the rushes of wind had chapped my nose raw. A couple zigzags until I saw Sunny's shitty building with its rusty fire escapes and chocolate-milk paint job. I hit the button on the thingy and up went the door for the big reveal. 1968 Impala, royal blue, totally cherried out. It had been left to Sunny's uncle, a San Jose hot rodder who died of AIDS a few years before. He kept the gift going to anyone who could afford to put gas in it. Friends would take it for the weekend and there were a couple mechanics in the neighborhood who volunteered their services, promising to keep on the road. I fired up the engine, getting chills at the echo of the roar. I'd never driven a car like that, so powerful you'd leave your heart in your throat every time you accelerated from a full stop. When I got back to Marco's, he was just getting in from somewhere.

"He walks!" I said.

"Oh yeah," he turned around part-way, "I just had to step out for some fresh air."

And that's when I knew. There were probably real people who used that expression *step out for some fresh air*, but I had never met one. He could have easily said he was having a cigarette or getting a coffee at the corner, but he chose the autopilot expression of someone who was lying. I held his shoulders and tried to look into his eyes, but he grabbed me in a tight hug and pulled me down on the bed. We lay there entwined until he was asleep again.

I left him there and got drunk that night. I pinballed between the three bars we all hung out at until last call, when I walked with a few people over to someone's apartment to make grilled cheese sandwiches with a clothes iron. Everyone was talking about Marco's show, how he had sold over half the pieces, how they heard a gallery in New York was interested. His hollowed-out hippie look, his sweet and spacey personality, his dedication to his art, his oversized landscape photography of neglected par course structures at suburban parks; it was all working for him. He was preternaturally magnetic, as those able to simultaneously exude internal strength and vulnerability often are. I had noticed it the very first time I saw him on the street. I could see it in the reverent way people talked about him, in their expressions when he interacted with them. He was a fixture in the neighborhood, but in no way was he one of the gang. He was present and available, but didn't fit. Which is why he became a hero to everyone.

Usually when I stayed out late I spent the night at my own place, no need to bring my sloshy drunkenness to Marco, but something told me to go back to him. It had a little to do with him *stepping out for some fresh air* and something to do with the leftover energy pulsing from the night before. And possibly from my inability to capture it on paper through writing or drawing earlier. The occasional twinges I got, small signals in light or sound that came to me without warning, were confusing. They told me to create but I didn't know how. It was like having a sharp pinch in my gut accompanied by soft white halos of light or streaming colored orbs. I jokingly told Deirdre the feelings were my "white light spirit guides." Some New Age shit I tried hard to squash.

When I walked in, Marco looked like he hadn't moved at all. He was naked and face down, feet hanging off the end of the bed. I stood very still until I heard him breathing, and then I pulled the blanket up over his torso and crashed.

The next morning, I woke to the sounds of him packing the car. Clean T-shirt, clean hair, putting blankets in the backseat, two hot coffees in peanut butter jars.

We crossed the Golden Gate, underneath the rainbow banner of the tunnel, and within minutes were in another reality; hills and grass and sky. Hippie country, rich yuppie fuck country. Inside the suburban towns, I knew there were people like the ones I'd grown up with. The kind who put their personal comfort above anything else. People who wouldn't live without three-car garages and kitchens with two ovens and chandeliered entry ways. People who raked in money from corporations and didn't give anything back. I sneered at them from the car as best I could. I flipped them off in my mind. The suburbs made me sick to my stomach and I could never articulate why. I thought that most people who took refuge in the city had grown up poor or queer, people of color, immigrants, abused or neglected. People for whom the city was a way to escape, to experience freedom, to be who they truly were. But the suburban world was designed for people like me, wasn't it? I'd always regarded my upbringing as if it had been some vast assault on my very being. Which it wasn't. Rationally, I knew this, but how did I come to reject it so thoroughly? If I was confident in who I was, if I was such a solid person, why did this overplayed rejection of my past have such a tight grip on me? The word suburbs, which in the beginning was purely geographical, had come to connote so much more. Wealth, comfort, safety, whiteness. And the word urban—urban schools, urban population, urban music—basically just meant black. The impulse to always pare things down to black and white was strong and I wanted everything to be grey. Like San Francisco used to be.

We drove in silence for miles and when we hit Petaluma and stopped for gas—god how that thing guzzled it—I decided to ask him. I wanted to look into his eyes while I did it.

"You're not addicted or anything, are you?"

The way he said no was enough, with his eyes downcast and a kiss on my cheek, and I acted like I believed him. He knew I didn't.

We cut over to the coast and stopped to get oysters and a six pack of beer near Point Reyes. On the beach we pried the oysters open using a combination of three tools; a bottle opener, a flathead screwdriver, and Marco's rusty Leatherman. I could have eaten a hundred. It was like being dragged through the tide by my hair with my mouth open. We lay under a scratchy army blanket in the sand and for a few hours I tried to forget I was in a love with a drug addict.

I took the wheel for the rest of the way up the coast, listening to the oldies station, singing.

"It kills me how you know the words to every one of these songs," he said. "How?"

"I can't remember learning them. When I was a kid, I had this little clock radio that I loved. It had a dial on it that you could set for an hour so you could listen to music while you fell asleep. I'd set it to a station called KLOK that had this really sweet jingle. *K-L-O-K!* I think that a lot of the songs must have seeped in while I was sleeping."

"Osmosis."

"I guess so. What do you think that'll do to a person? Having all those songs about magic and sailing and finding love on the dance floor drifting into your head every night?"

He petted my head. "It's probably why you're so sweet."

"Am I sweet?" That didn't sound right. "Maybe that's what made me so complacent. Is that the word? A little fine just doing whatever."

"That's the best way to be. It doesn't get enough credit. It takes a special talent."

I wasn't convinced.

"People pay other people to teach them how to be like that," he said.

We arrived at the hot springs, pitching our borrowed tent in the woods at the perimeter of the property. I wore a long T-shirt until I got to the edge of the pools, but Marco had no qualms stripping down in front of anyone. (I could be an exhibitionist, but only if it felt like a dare.) He made strolling around naked among strangers seem entirely natural. It might have had to do with a term Deirdre coined: The Quiet Pride. The Quiet Pride was the way a semi-reserved or seemingly shy guy was actually extremely confident because he walked around all the time knowing he had a big dick. I teased him about it, and showing perfect form, he acted like he had no idea what I was talking about.

After a dip in the pools, we went back to our tent for a snack and a nap. We ate some figs and cashews with rosemary and Marco pulled up leaves of wild sorrel that grew nearby. "This would be a great life," he said. "To live like a fancy squirrel."

Marco started to get sick. First the sniffles, then the watery eyes, and eventually the chills and nausea. I left him to sleep and spent the day by myself in and out of the pools, trying to do things I never do: meditate and read. I was incapable of quieting my mind. I found a book in the free bin at the front desk, about U.S. history from the point of view of workers and people of color, but I couldn't focus. I kept falling into a stress-induced sleep, wondering how long he had been doing it, keeping it from me.

We drove back to the city the next day with me behind the wheel and Marco in and out of sleep. I looked down at him, head in my lap, and I knew. I had to leave his soft corners and open heart behind. He reminded me of an aerialist resting on his back on a taut wire a hundred feet in the air. He looked so relaxed up there, like he could stay suspended forever. I heard through the grapevine that he left the city for the desert, and a few months after that, he lost his balance and fell.

MY BROTHER LANDED IN San Jose later that night looking pretty flawless for having gotten up at 5 a.m. Boston time and putting in a full day of work before getting on a cross country flight. His orange and white checkered shirt was neatly pressed, as if maybe he carried an additional, backup, *fresh shirt* to put on after he landed or had somehow managed to iron it in the airplane lavatory. If he was engaged in that level of personal grooming, I didn't want to know. He also had no discernible stubble. Had he shaved twice in a day? Once in the morning and once in the airport? On the airplane? I thought I understood people, but I realized I did not. He threw his bag on the back seat and slid in next to me.

"Bay-bro!" I squealed, grabbing the parking ticket that was on the dash and stashing it under my thigh, hoping he wouldn't notice that my window wouldn't roll up. The first three seconds of reuniting with my brother was my forte. After that, I struggled between borderline hyperactivity and crippling silence.

He pecked my cheek. "Nice ride!"

"Can you believe Mom drove this car for half of her lifetime? I feel like I'm getting a new perspective on her. It's ridiculous. This is like in that board game, the Game of Life, when you start and you're just a stick in the driver's seat and there are all those empty holes for other sticks."

"What?"

"You know how that game has the cars you drive around the board? After we left, Mom was like a solo pink stick sitting in this thing for twenty years and all the other holes were empty. No more sticks."

Were we even blood-related. There was the telltale nose, the slight hook and deviated septum, but he looked more like a catalogue model, one from a midrange apparel company located on the eastern seaboard. Or someone profiled in a food magazine for hosting a stylish dinner party where a flayed goat was roasted on a spit. In contrast, I ate all the lipstick off my face within ten minutes of putting it on and was usually rubbing my nose or marathon-scratching one of my itchy tear ducts in an OCD-like snit. Some people were more comfortable inside their skin. It didn't mean they *should* be more comfortable in their own skin, they just were. How did that work?

Deirdre divided humans on a spectrum of which the polar ends were "scaly" and "all one piece." All-one-piecers were like self-cleaning ovens, people who were put-together and looked lightly photoshopped. Scaly meant you were sloppy, like a reptile sloughing off bits of itself as it crawled. Scott was all one piece. Deirdre was all one piece. I was scaly.

"You're looking all right," he said. "Still skinny at least." He patted his nonexistent paunch and flashed his bleached teeth. "This guy has to work to stay at fighting weight!"

My metabolism had been my saving grace my whole life. Calories? Fat grams? Spending more than twenty seconds on a toilet? I burned up whatever I ate and drank so quickly that I was embarrassed. I knew to keep quiet about it. There wasn't much that was less relatable than a middle-aged woman who didn't think about her weight.

The oven came back to me. Ever since this morning, I had gone in and out of staccato panics about leaving it on, but I didn't dare mention it. I'd feign surprise when we arrived at the house.

Or maybe try blaming it on someone else? Turn it off quickly and try to keep him away from it while it cooled down?

We drove down the boulevard past carpet wholesalers and car dealerships, ancient strip malls, and supermarkets. Scott wanted to go to the taco place we always went to in high school. Taco Bravo. The food was pretty terrible—greasy meat, orange cheese, runny beans—but of course it also tasted perfect. Scott loved to nostalgia-eat. Even in elementary school, he would beg our mom to buy the teething biscuits she used to carry in her purse when he was a baby. He would eat at a Chinese place that gave him food poisoning one out of every five times he ate there, simply to remember what it was like when he went there on his first date.

"It's supposed to be ugly here," I said as we passed an old der Wienerschnitzel A-frame that had been turned into a Korean BBQ joint, "but I kind of love it."

"Makes sense. That's kind of your deal with everything, isn't it?"

"I never really thought of it that way, but I guess so."

We ordered tacos and sat at the smooth concrete tables outside, watching the cars cruise by.

"So, how's everybody? What are the kids like?"

I had only met Henry, his oldest, right after he was born ten years ago. They came out to visit and we spent all afternoon looking at the baby, though my mom didn't want to hold him. Scott placed him in her lap and she lifted her arms like she was being held at gunpoint. "I've done my time!" she joked and didn't get any laughs.

"Kids are great. Vanessa is taking piano and Henry is doing soccer again. Maya is a complete brain and is into science, tech, math and stuff. STEM kid."

"I don't know what that means. Stem kid. I can't believe you have three of them."

"Why? What's that supposed to mean? Like it's too many?"

"What does stem kid mean? No, I don't know. It's just odd. Like you're a grown-up."

"Science, technology, engineering, math. It's an acronym that everyone uses now. You know what? I'm going to say something and it's going to sound like I'm being a dick, but it's getting kind of old. Simply because someone has a family or a job, you, a forty-six-year-old woman, are calling them a 'grown-up' and it's somehow surprising to you that people do that? It's what most people do, isn't it? I don't know what happened that you think it's some foreign concept to buy a house or own a car or pay your bills."

"I pay my bills."

"Come on. What bills do you even have? Rent for one-seventh of your warehouse space, or however many people you live with."

I'd been on the fence about whether to tell him about the shit-storm. I didn't need him thinking I was even more disgusting than I was. Or knowing that I was now homeless.

"Do you even have health insurance?"

"No, but health insurance is ridiculous. How is someone like me supposed to have health insurance?"

"I don't know. You worked at that bar long enough. You'd think maybe they'd give you something."

"Do we have to go through this again?" I paused for two seconds to reset. "I'm doing fine. I'm sorry I said the thing about you being a grown-up. You're right. I'm getting pretty tired of myself, too. I'm going to make a concerted effort to stop exoticizing your normal life."

"Thank you. It's like people believe the trend pieces about extended adolescence. Are people really surprised that they're adults? I'm 'adulting.' That kind of shit." He reached in his leather manpurse and pulled out a small black box. "I bought you something."

Sometimes a gift is given and you know the person bestowing it saw that item and immediately thought of you, knew you would love it, and had to buy it. Other times, you receive a gift because the giver decided they were doing you a favor. This was one of those.

"You bought me a fancy phone?"

"It's going to change your life. Really."

"There's a reason I don't have one, Scott. I don't want one."

"Look, I'm paying for the first year. If you don't want it after that, you can get rid of it."

"I can't take this. It's too much."

"It's not. It's really not. It's nothing."

I knew that a new phone and its monthly bills were nothing to him.

"And believe me, you're not going to get rid of it. After you have it, you're going to want to have it forever."

I smiled one of my laziest smiles, tucked it back into its little box, and put it in my bag. Scott looked disappointed that I didn't want to start playing with it immediately, but kept his mouth shut. Owning a cell phone was going to alter who I was.

All that remained of our burritos were the greasy pieces of yellow paper they'd been wrapped in. Scott folded his neatly over and over again until he couldn't fold it anymore. He held up the rectangle. "Seven times, remember?"

We had read when we were kids that a piece of paper, no matter the size, could only be folded seven times, and we refused to believe it until we had folded so many pieces of paper seven times that we finally asked our mom to run over one of the squares with the car so we could try to get an eighth out of it. When she refused to get off the couch, we took the keys and tried to do it ourselves. The car rolled back into the street, eventually getting clipped by a passing truck, and we had to drag her outside to drive it up the driveway. We didn't even get in trouble.

"Do you want to go to The Nest?" I asked.

The Nest was the old-man bar that had been downtown forever. We used to go there when we were younger, when you could still use the kind of fake IDs that looked absolutely, one hundred percent, fake.

"That's still there, huh?" He looked out at the street and I watched his face shift. He was too tired. "Let's go tomorrow, okay?"

"Of course. We don't even have to go at all. I don't think I'm ready to run into people we went to high school with anyway."

Scott got up from the table, leaving his trash paper square and cup. I waited until we were at the car, to test him, and then called him on it. "Why wouldn't you even throw your trash away? Like it didn't even occur to you."

"Dude, shut the fuck up. The trash will get thrown away, don't worry."

"Yeah, by someone making minimum wage who's probably more tired than you."

"Okay, Dolores Huerta."

"Who?"

"How about Erin Brockovich? Does that ring any bells? What about Julia Roberts? How much of a cave have you been living in anyway? Sometimes I feel like you're getting dumber."

I ignored him and hit the gas, bracing to arrive at the charred remains of the house.

"What's wrong with you?"

"Nothing." I rolled through a stop sign. "I was just thinking about how I was at the house earlier to preheat the oven because I found one of mom's old casseroles in the freezer and thought it would be cool if we ate it."

That didn't come out very smoothly.

"What a stupid sentence, Pajamas. You left the oven on?"

All he ever did was assert his superiority. It was pathological.

"Peej, I don't know if you're up for any of this. You have to step up. This isn't just about you."

I kicked myself for mentioning the stupid oven. Of course the house was still standing. I jumped out and ran ahead of him, bursting into the (extremely warm) kitchen. It reeked like burnt sugar and grease. Scott walked over to the casserole, lifted the foil, and we both stared at the gloppy pool of noodles speckled with green-gray peas. He pulled the trash can out from under the sink and dumped the whole thing, Pyrex and all.

"This is what you have to do with everything," he said.

THE NEXT MORNING, HE woke me up by putting a donut next to my mouth. He was holding a whole pink box of them.

"I can't believe you bought a dozen," I said.

"Go big or go home, right?" Scott had an arsenal of phrases like this, things that he said in a bro-voice as a joke, but if you looked at him and didn't know him, you'd think he was saying them seriously. It was a strange subterfuge. "I've already had four, but I saved the strawberry one for you."

I loved strawberry donuts so much that I had stopped eating them at some point. It seemed too treacherous to love something that was so cheap and easy to get.

"Coffeeeeeee," I said. Haunted-house voice.

"It's out in the garage. It's all out there. There's bubbly waters and I got us beers for later. I decided that neither of us are allowed to leave the garage until everything is gone. We can piss in those old Alhambra jugs if we have to, but we can't come back inside."

I followed him and was surprised to see all three garage doors open and a sign in the driveway. "Wait. We're having a garage sale?"

"Yeah. As long as we're getting rid of it, we should make a little money. It's more fun. You can keep it. I've already made you forty-three dollars while you were sleeping."

I had never, in my whole life, seen all the garage doors rolled up and I felt very exposed. Our mom was a fairly neat person, especially when we lived in the house, but for some reason, the garage was consistently a war zone. It didn't seem to fit with her personality at all. A completely tidy home and yard, but with the garage of a Level Two hoarder. It was an indication of something, but what? I started to analyze it using the rudimentary psychology skills I learned from friends who read self-help books, but couldn't put my finger on it. Secrets? Putting up a front? Controlling chaos?

"Why do you think Mom has a hoarder's garage?"

He brushed it off. "I don't know. She never felt like cleaning it. Is it time for beer yet?"

"Let me enjoy the mania of the coffee and donuts and then I'll use the beer to come down later."

"Poor man's speedball," we said at more or less the same time.

I was looking forward to seeing who would stop at our garage sale. When I was in high school, my friends and I would drive all over the Valley picking up records and ugly art and old cameras. Our demographic that day was distinctly not the young tech workers I was always hearing about, but mostly older Asians and whites who could barely see over their steering wheels. We got rid of a lamp made out of a piano leg, an enormous red shag rug, a vacuum cleaner, and three bikes. An old Chinese guy haggled for ten minutes over four TV trays, those little metal folding tables that you set up so you can eat your dinner on in front of the screen. He refused to give us five bucks for the set and I wouldn't budge. He kept walking toward his car and then turning around and coming back up the driveway.

"It's a good deal," I was saying. "You're getting a good deal already. Jesus!"

Scott was enjoying the hell out of it, laughing at both of us.

"Three fifty!" the man barked.

"No! They're five dollars! I could get a lot more on eBay." As if I knew how to do that.

"Then put them on eBay!" he yelled back and walked down to his Chevy Citation. I watched him tear off, tailpipe farting.

I turned to Scott. "I'm probably going to be cheap when I'm an old person too."

"Probably?" he laughed in my face. "You've always been cheap."

"But why do I also think of it as a Chinese thing?" All I could come up with was a bunch of hack Hollywood shit. I was disappointed in myself for not at least having more interesting source material for my long-held racist belief.

"I think of it more as a Jew thing," Scott was unsurprisingly matter-of-fact.

"Well, aren't we a couple of privileged whites!" I said, distinctly pronouncing the "wh" like a country club matron to get a laugh.

"We're actually part Jewish," he said. "On Dad's side. The Poles."

"Really?" Here I'd gone my whole life assuming we were just Basic White Person. "You'd think someone would have mentioned it."

"Maybe Dad didn't know. Or he never told Mom because they barely knew each other. Anyway, I did one of those genetic test kits."

"I can't believe you fell for that. Sending part of your body to a corporation."

"Let me know when you find something that doesn't offend you." Scott and I were tiring of each other already.

Three little kids, maybe about seven or eight, came walking up with their colorful plastic wallets.

"Check out this crew," Scott said. "Big spenders."

I loved the way the kids were holding their play wallets. Out in front of their bodies with both hands at chest height like they were divining rods leading them to what they needed. There weren't many kids in the neighborhood, not that I'd noticed anyway, and definitely not like when we were little and ran around the streets all day long. Or maybe there were kids around, but they just went from their cars into their garages into their homes.

"You guys have any toys or kid stuff?" the boy said.

"No. Not really," Scott said. "We have some used medical equipment and an old microwave. Or maybe you're interested in a variety of scratched teflon pans?"

The shortest one made a frowny face and walked straight into the garage.

"Most of the stuff is out here," I called after him.

"Did the lady with the dog who lived here die?"

"Yeah. That was our mom."

"I heard her dog died first and then she was so sad that she died. When I was little, in pre-K at Explorers, she gave me so much candy on Halloween. Then last year, she didn't answer her door."

"She was getting old," I said. "I think she wasn't here on Halloween."

"No, she was here," the kid said in his annoying short-vocal-cord voice. "She was just pretending not to hear us. We kept ringing and ringing the doorbell and then Darla started yelling to her that we could see her in there watching TV."

Scott ignored this, a broken weed whacker in each hand, holding them up in the air. "Two of these," he said. "Neither of them work."

"Why would somebody yell at a nice old lady?" I asked the kid.

"Because she wasn't answering the door."

"Maybe she couldn't hear it."

"She could hear it. She just didn't want to give us any candy."

"Yeah," his sister added. "She was pretending."

Now they were pissing me off. "Well, maybe she forgot to buy candy so she didn't have any to hand out."

"She had candy all the other years."

"Maybe she was tired," I said. "Or maybe she was having trouble getting up. You don't know. You don't know what it's like to be seventy-five years old and have little kids begging at your door for candy, for like the millionth year in a row. Maybe you just get sick of it. Maybe you're tired of handing out candy to kids who automatically expect it. How would you like it if you just wanted someone to go away, but they kept harassing you? That probably happens to you. You want to go in your bedroom and shut your door, but your parents or brothers or sisters keep bugging you. It feels pretty shitty—sorry—crappy. It feels pretty crappy when someone does that to you. Doesn't it?"

Scott turned around and held out the box of donuts. They pounced on it.

"Okay, go home, you guys," he said. "Take the donuts. We don't have anything else you want here."

"I want that," the younger girl said pointing to a polyester scarf with orange and blue polka dots. "I want to buy that."

I picked it up. Mom's. My whole life I had never seen her wear a scarf. I never wore scarves either. It looked like the type of present a man who doesn't know a woman too well buys for her. But the six-year-old was right, it was kind of cool. Maybe I would start wearing scarves. Maybe scarves would be part of my new thing after I quit the bar and moved somewhere else and had a new life. I would have a cell phone, a TV, a fun scarf, and a sex life.

"How much is it?" the kid asked. "I have three quarters, two dimes, and twelve pennies. And four dollar bills at home, but I didn't bring them. My mom said nothing at a garage sale would be more than a dollar for a kid."

"You know what?" I said. "I'm not going to sell it. I want to keep it."

"That's not fair!" She lunged and tried to grab it.

"I'm sorry." I held the scarf over my head. "It's just that it was my mom's and she died and I think I want to keep it to remember her by."

"You have her whole ugly house to remember her by," the older brother said, walking down the driveway with another donut.

"You live right there, right?" I said, pointing to a house in the cul-de-sac that was exactly the same as ours, just with the floor plan flip-flopped. I tied the scarf tight around my skull like a pirate or a fortune-teller. "You and me? We have the same ugly house."

"Ours is better and we have grass. You have rocks."

"You're scary," the littlest girl said. "You don't like kids."

I could feel the skin on my neck and face burn as they wandered off down the drive.

"You look like Rhoda," Scott said when he turned around. "You look like Valerie Harper if she had a meth habit. Not a terrible one, but just like six dark months in the speed hole followed by a spiritual awakening with some cult leader who took all her money."

"Why don't you get rid of all this shit by yourself?" I grabbed a donut from the box and walked across the cool cement floor of the garage and into the house.

"This is why you're alone!" he yelled after me.

Good one. I fought the temptation to say something like, "And this is why you're married with three children living in a colonial house in the suburbs and working at a job that is contributing to the downfall of the American middle class!" But I didn't. He would just make fun of me for that too.

BAY-BRO WAS BACK TO Boston in a puff of vetiver aftershave. We'd been grilling hotdogs on a portable Smokey Joe we found in the garage when he dropped the bomb on me. The house had to be on the market in the next month.

"It's go-time, Peej." He made a V with his fingers, pointing them at his own eyes and then at mine. "If you start flaking, I'm going to roll right over you."

I assured him I would get it done in a manner that was entirely sincere in that three-beers moment. It wasn't until he left that I grew nervous. Sure, I could manage to schedule the painters and plumber and landscaper; he had made a spreadsheet with all the phone numbers and deadlines for me, but what was I going to do when this was over? What was the next rectangle on my *spreadsheet of life*, man? How could I pull the trigger on leaving San Francisco after twenty-seven years in order to float without a plan in San Jose? I could already hear the gossip. *Guess who's unemployed and living in The Hose?* There was no way Edie Wunderlich would ever do that, but I was starting to think that maybe Paula Jane could. Like, what if I got a job-job in Silicon Valley? Scott would see that I was trying to improve my circumstances and he'd cut me some slack and maybe let me stay in the house for a little longer. What if I were able to remake myself in the image of a normal person?

I could try living one of those regular lives I saw all around me. How hard could it be? Literally millions of Americans were able to appear as if they had their shit together and if I put my mind to it, I probably could too. Whiten my teeth and buy a belted cardigan from Ann Taylor Loft. Get coffee every morning in a cup with my name Sharpied on it. Open a bank account. I was pretty certain, however, this meant getting over at least one major hurdle: I would have to learn to use the internet.

Hating the internet was a semi-popular claim made among people who used it regularly, but few Americans, besides the elderly, impoverished, and incarcerated, had as little experience with it as I. Hating the internet was part of my whole thing, like being anti-cellphone. It helped define me, not only to others, but to myself. It was a morale booster to say, "The internet? Oh, I don't do that." People at the bar would gawk at me like I was a sideshow freak. *The Phoneless Woman. The Lady with Zero Google Results.* Once I started turning into a relic, rejecting the dominant tech culture made me feel like I was doing something interesting. Kind of like when kids moved abroad after college, it absolved them of having to "do" anything. *They were living in Tokyo, for God's sake, that's what they were doing.* Women who carry expensive designer handbags operate under a similar dynamic. They sashay around like, *This is a three-thousand dollar purse, what else do you want from me?* Men with ridiculous cars. A thing like that could become your whole personality. The bold gesture that is powerful enough to shut down petty trifling.

There was a regular at the bar who went to a meditation retreat where he couldn't talk or read or write or look another person in the eye for two whole weeks. It was like the Second Coming when he returned. *What did you think about? Did you ever freak out and just lose it? What did you learn about yourself?* Do you think I should do it? In a way, I felt like the rejection of technology was my perpetual meditation retreat. It automatically made me seem formidable at a time when I was losing my power.

That morning, I woke up and picked out a fresh outfit from my mother's closet to wear for my big trip to the public library. Loose khaki pedal pushers and a light blue scoop neck T-shirt. We wore the same size shoe, though her feet were long and slender, while I was more of a Fred Flintstone. I put on my old boots, which looked ridiculous but I couldn't pull the trigger on a pair of her comfy beige sandals or slim lady loafers. A shopping trip loomed, now that all my clothes had been shitstormed on, but the thought of going to the mall to buy shoes made my stomach feel like it was prolapsing into my rectum.

The sun was coming up strong over the mountains when I passed by the Sklamberg's house, the neighbors who had been there since I was a little girl. Mrs. Sklamberg was doing some weeding, squatting on her drought-resistant berm in a pink sweat-suit and matching visor. Poor Mrs. Sklamberg. She had gotten divorced sometime in the mid-'70s after her husband took off for Grass Valley with the lady who sold vitamins at The Nut Hut, the sad old health food store in the nearby strip mall. Everything in it was brown or brownish. (Interesting that when natural food got what was essentially its sex appeal makeover in the '90s, everything purportedly au natural went from brown to green.) When Mr. Sklamberg, a pilot for Pan Am, moved out with Nut Hut Donna, Mrs. Sklamberg raised five kids by herself, getting heavier and more outwardly Fundamentalist every year until finally, the last kid, the checker at Albertsons, left the house and she kind of fell apart. She even stopped going to her megachurch, the one that had the wooden Jesus, whittled real skinny, on the corner of Moorpark and Mitty. Scott and I once threw frozen peas at Him from the way back machine of the station wagon, shouting, "Crucify Him! Crucify Him!" and laughing our brains out.

I averted Mrs. Sklamberg's gaze. The last thing I wanted was face time with anyone in the neighborhood, especially someone who had known me as a kid. The route I picked would bring me past my old elementary school, so I could get a wee buzz off the melancholia. Huffing a bit of nostalgia would hopefully alter my internal chemicals enough to prime me for the momentous leap I was about to take.

It wasn't until I was almost right up on the school that I remembered it wasn't there anymore. It had been torn down years before by a local developer to build houses. When I looked up at the street signs, I laughed out loud. Via Escuela now butted up against Merlot Way, Chablis Place, and Janice Court. The first two, a blunt nod to the fact that the developer was also a winemaker, and the latter, for his wife. Ex-wife now, I'd heard. I watched a woman back a Lexus out of a garage and I hoped she knew that she was living in a cul-de-sac named after a racquetball champion who got caught screwing the installer from California Closets.

After a purposefully circuitous route that took me past homes where I'd been to sleepovers and birthday parties, streets where I'd played Kick the Can until dark and kissed boys in bushes, I arrived at the library. Surrounded by a heritage orchard of old fruit trees, it was built out of redwood in an architectural style reminiscent of '70s ski cabins in Lake Tahoe. They'd done some remodeling and ruined the vibe with an addition, but it was still beautiful. This would be the first library I'd been in since the one at my high school (not counting a few emergency trips to the bathroom at the Civic Center branch in San Francisco.) It was definitely the first time I'd gone into a library with the intention of learning something. I was going to learn the internet.

I never really "got" the library. Adults were always telling kids how wonderful it was. *The library is so wonderful!* Was there some secret I didn't know that made teachers and parents get all twinkly whenever they mentioned it? As far as I could tell, the only reason the library could possibly be so wonderful was for the obvious reason that it was full of free books. Is that what they meant? I never read much. Nancy Drew I got into as a third- or fourth-grader, until it dawned on me that the sick feeling in my gut was because Nancy and her friends were so perfect and polite, talking about "luncheon" all the time. I felt like they were judging me. A few books I read as a teenager stuck with me, *Lord of the Flies*, *To Kill a Mockingbird*, and the one where the black guy lays out how supremely jacked it is to be black and living in South Africa. But everyone liked those books. It was normal to like those books. Classics. For the most part, I just skimmed what I was supposed to read for the tests and papers, knowing that if I ever wanted to read those books, I could rest assured they would be around forever. And so would millions and millions of other books, readily available and free at the library. Clearly, reading could wait. In my twenties, I'd sometimes go out to live readings, to hear writers read their own work. There were tons of events every night for a while, people reciting poetry or performing angry rants or rhymes. I got onstage a few times and read what I called my "live public transpo reports" where I gave short breakdowns of what happened on the bus or at the bus stop in front of the warehouse. It was fun but I didn't expect anyone would ever want to sit down and read it.

I was already agitated about my decision to use the computer, which, coupled with my disjointed feelings from the walk over, had me about ready to hang myself from a heritage apricot tree. I had only been inside the building twice, and both times I'd gotten in trouble for talking too loud to my friends. But a different feeling whirred around me as I entered. I felt mildly awkward, but not prohibitively so. Not like the sinking pit of my stomach when I accidentally stepped into a clothing store that only sold brushed alpaca sweaters or a cafe where bearded men were ministering medium roast coffee from hammered copper urns. It was immediately clear that I was in a place meant for everyone. It was nearly empty with a few scattered people quietly doing their own thing. I once heard someone say that a proper city functions on the social lubrication of mutual indifference and that's what the library felt like. I walked up to the woman behind the desk. She looked to be around sixty with an icy white pageboy and beautiful thick-rimmed specs, reading a newspaper in an unapologetically poised fashion. Like she was behind museum glass. A benevolent queen in plum lipstick.

"Hey, can I just, like, use a computer? To go on the internet?"

"Go right ahead," she said, crossing a black leather boot over her knee. She pointed to the computers by the far wall in the next room.

"I want to go to the Craigslist website and look for jobs," I volunteered. The Craigslist website. I knew that sounded wrong.

I admired the serious people skills the librarian had for not making fun of me. The ability to simply pretend it was the '90s and escort me to a monitor so she could commence instructing an adult on how to use the internet.

"Just click this here and then type it in," she said. "See, it's already in the cache. This is one of the most popular sites people go to here."

"Craig," I said, eyes on the screen, begging myself to remember how to do this for next time. "I met him a couple times. In San Francisco. That's where I live. I don't live here." I cut myself short before I performed my boring one-woman show entitled *I Left the Suburbs for San Francisco A Long Time Ago.*

"Anyway," I said, "Super nice guy."

"I've met him too," she said, sitting down on the chair next to me. Those boots. Up over the knee and a buttery calfskin. "My sister-in-law works for a nonprofit and he spoke at their annual fundraiser."

"He came into my bar once and I told him that I thought it was stupid to advertise for a roommate on the computer when you could just hang up a flyer at the laundromat."

The librarian laughed, tucking a stray piece of hair behind her ear and smoothing it down. "Which is completely valid if you want to limit your potential roommates to people who use laundromats."

Good point, I thought. Never would have occurred to me. I looked down at my outfit, suddenly sheepish. She was all one piece. "Yeah. Well, thanks. I appreciate it. It's sort of embarrassing being this lame with computers still."

"You'll get the hang of it. It's easy. And there are a lot of other websites now where you can upload your resume. Just let me know if you need any help."

"Okay, I'll stick with Craigslist because of my personal connection to Craig." What a cool answer! So committed to Keeping It Real.

The woman returned to her desk and I wanted to cry, relieved to have made it over this hurdle. As I started clicking around, it came sharply into focus how few jobs I was qualified for without a college degree, valid driver's license, or willingness to go back into restaurant or bar work. There was a natural gas company that was expanding and a casino looking to take their customer service to the next level of excellence. Both these listings said they were accepting applications for all levels, but they were looking for full-time employees. I had never in my life worked a full-time job.

Some jobs that I wasn't qualified for included:

Egg Donor: Way too shriveled
Door Repair Technician: Experienced only
Vehicle Purchaser, Carshare Driver: Valid driver's license
Faerie/Pirate/Mermaid: Friendly, likes kids

The jobs that looked possible, no college degree, part-time, on an easy bus line, were:

Security guard
Sunglasses sales
Flyer dropper
Sign waver
Arthritis medical study
Dry cleaning presser
Average hourly: $9.00
Average commute time by bus: 40 minutes

I was looking at a listing for an employment agency that

wanted people to come in for interviews when I realized I was going to need an email address. At one point, I had one. Some friends had set up a server at their house in the '90s and threw a party where everyone was wasted and got their first email addresses. What was the website called? Monkeybars, Monkeybrains, Monkeytime? Chocodile@monkeybrains.net? Was my email handle my favorite childhood snack food? Or was chocodile my password? I couldn't remember. I had tried to use it a few years ago so Scott and Carolyn could send me pictures of the kids, but I forgot my password and couldn't figure out how to change it. So then Carolyn went back to putting the kids' school pictures in an envelope and mailing them, which I liked better. Though come to think of it, I hadn't gotten any new ones in a while. Had I ever written her back to thank her or confirm delivery? Certainly not.

There was a brief period where either you had email or you didn't and it was fine. Personal preference. The tipping point came around 1997 when I noticed that not having email made people look at me curiously and I enjoyed that. Rudy and Alex from Monkeywhatever were probably still in SF, even though they never came to the bar anymore. They would have helped me out. I could call someone who had their number, but I no longer spoke to Fletcher, Maggie, Chris, Jeff, and Moe for various reasons involving sex, alcohol, and money. I resigned myself to making a new email address using the website that everyone used. After the first seven names I tried were already taken, I gave up. Maybe there was a workaround? Maybe a prospective employer would see it as an indication that I was some kind of rebel genius with an elevated mind if I had no email.

Ah, I don't see your email address here.

I don't use email.

What? Wow, well, can we have a phone number?

I don't have a cell phone.

Very cool. How are we supposed to contact you if we want to hire you?

(Grab my crotch and flip him off)
You're hired!

Okay, so that wasn't going to work. I let the screen go dark and thought about it. I could walk out and go back home without any plan whatsoever or I could admit that I didn't have a mind that was any different from everyone else. This was the Generation X paradox, wasn't it? You balk at anyone who thinks they're special, but then you think you're special for realizing that no one is special.

And so I created an email with a bunch of random numbers in it that I felt no connection to. In just over an hour, I figured out how to make a resume, though there wasn't much on it. It was incredible what I knew how to do just by listening in on people's conversations at the bar. I waited at the librarian's desk to pick up the printout.

"You figured it all out, huh?" The woman handed it over without glancing down at it.

"There are a lot of little pictures that help. The tiny printer totally looks like a printer! What do you think," I asked, "about me dropping this off in person? As opposed to emailing it? Do you think it'll make a difference?"

"Well, it's not what most people would do, so maybe you could try it. That's what I did when I got this job. I found the listing online, but I came in so that they'd remember me. Face with the name. It was so competitive and I think it helped."

"Being a librarian is competitive?" I didn't mean to sound condescending, but it was surprising.

"Believe it or not. I worked in marketing for years and got tired of it so I went back to school. I really lucked out with this location. Some people have to work in middle schools."

I responded with an exaggerated poopface. The only time I had gone to the library in junior high was to carve my name into a table with a pitting knife. Larissa Gruber ratted me out and I was promptly suspended.

"Or some people go the academic route. Or corporate. There

are a lot of different types of job for librarians."

"Huh. And you just help people find books and shit? And stuff, I mean. That's cool."

"More or less. I sit here and read and help people get where they need to go."

"Like a life coach."

"Or just a librarian."

Making jokes about life coaches was as played out as making jokes about mimes and yet, I said it anyway. Before I could retreat in embarrassment, she waved a manila folder at me.

"Want to put your resume in this? So it stays crisp?"

An angel. I walked back home, taking the shortest way this time.

DEIRDRE WAS NOT A delicate flower by any stretch of the imagination, but she had an air of dignity that didn't reconcile with being left waiting alone in a commuter train parking lot. I got to the station early, mid-afternoon, and the sun was really starting to cook. It was more punishing than the one from my childhood. Less golden and patient, more *Cancer Time!* I riffled through the glove compartment and fished out a pair of my mom's supermarket sunglasses and a flattened pack of cigarettes and then reclined onto the windshield with my legs outstretched, buns toasting on the hood, leaving the car running so the battery wouldn't die. I fired up a stale Benson & Hedges. It tasted so terrible that I decided to give it a few more puffs out of sheer incredulity that I used to do this all the time.

"There's no smoking in this lot."

It was the woman parked next to me. All the windows of her minivan were down and she was reading a newspaper, folded into quadrants, with one pencil in her hand and one tucked behind her ear. She was wearing a terrycloth visor that had yellowed from its original white and had dirty brown smudges on the bill.

"You look like a bookie," I said, jabbing the cigarette out on the sole of my shoe. I tossed the butt on the ground. The woman set her paper down and peeked out the window a little. Real hair or wig? I couldn't be sure.

"I'm not a bookie," she said. "I have an associates degree in Business Administration from De Anza Junior College. And you just littered. Also against the law."

Normally, a stranger's reprimand would piss me off, but I had an idea what might be going on here. "Sorry," I said, hopping off the car and picking up the butt. "You look like maybe you're going to the horse races or something."

"I've been to the horse races once in my life," the woman said. "Golden Gate Fields. 1991. June sixteenth. My dad won forty dollars on a two-dollar bet. Winning horse that day was Sisterwife."

I walked the butt over to the trash can. One thing I really enjoyed doing was talking to people who seemed to be on the autism spectrum. It loosened me up.

"Wait," I said, "there was a horse named Sisterwife back in 1991?"

"Sure. Polygamy is as old as Methuselah, even though as a practicing Catholic, I don't condone it."

"I understand. It just hasn't been a popular term to throw around until recently. So who was the jockey that day? The one riding Sisterwife?"

The woman paused, staring out at the train tracks. "Well, I'm glad you asked because the name escaped me for a minute, but then it just came back." She turned quickly to look in my general direction, but not quite at me. A little off my shoulder. "Javier was his name. Javier Carbajal. From Spain by way of Florida. Tampa, Florida. Population 346,203 last time I checked."

"When was the last time you checked the population of Tampa?"

"June 16, 2011. The twentieth anniversary of Sisterwife's victory. When I was wondering what old Javier Carbajal was up to."

"You know what time the train from San Francisco is coming in?"

"Yep."

"Cool!" I laughed. "And what time is that?"

"Two-sixteen. It's late about eleven percent of the time. We have at least six more minutes."

"You're here regularly?"

"Sure. I come here on Wednesdays after I get done volunteering at the senior center."

"That's great. That you volunteer."

"Miss Brenda is always looking for more people if you're interested."

"Thanks for the info."

"I didn't give you the info."

"Right. What's the info?"

I actually wrote down the name and address she gave me. I knew she'd call me out if I didn't, but maybe I was also interested.

"My name is Joanna and if I recommend you and you work out, I get a free pizza."

"That's cool."

"You chose a good word. Miss Brenda is very cool. I plan on splitting my pizza with her if you join our team of helpmeets."

I took off the sunglasses to see if I could tell if it was a wig or not. Maybe not a wig, but more of a tightly coiffed and sprayed salon 'do. "You wouldn't split it with me?"

Joanna was nonplussed. "No, I wouldn't. I've known Brenda for nearly five years."

Definitely a wig. The light had changed, accenting a plasticine luster to the curls. "Hey, I'm sorry about the cigarette, Joanna

"It's the law: plain and simple. It's not a personal issue." She pulled off her visor and started up her car. Not a wig, I decided.

"You going? I thought you were waiting for the train."

She pointed at the tracks, where the train was slowly pulling in to the station. In a very literal sense, she had been waiting, not for a passenger on the train to arrive, but for the train itself. And she was for sure wearing a wig, though now I was ashamed for being so obsessed about it. Maybe I'd go visit her sometime at the senior center. I used to love talking to strangers, or listening to them rather, but it had gotten to the point in San Francisco that I was suspect of everyone's reasons for living there so I never wanted to talk to anyone new.

The train doors opened and Deirdre stepped out wearing a carnation pink linen capelet and matching pair of cigarette pants, as if she were arriving to Paris with a steamer trunk in the '50s. She even paused once she was on the platform, looking out on the horizon for a second, before pulling out her compact to reapply her lipstick. What a piece of work. I knew her well enough to know that she wasn't performing this. It was in her bones. What I would give to see Deirdre in a pair of ratty sweatpants and a hair scrunchie.

"Gorgeous!" she said, getting in and kissing my cheek. "I've thought about it and what I really want to do right now is get some burgers and milkshakes at an old-school place. Is there a drive-in where we can get curb service?"

"Because you just time-traveled?"

"Feels like it. And then maybe later we can cruise on El Camino Real."

I remembered a great burger place I used to go to as a kid, but it was a bit of a drive.

"Don't take the freeway," she said, angling the A/C vents toward her face. "We have all day."

We rolled past car dealerships, carpet stores, office parks, and one of my favorite restaurants from childhood, By Th' Bucket. I couldn't believe it was still there. You ordered your food at a window and it all came out in buckets. Fried chicken in a bucket, spaghetti in a bucket, a stack of hamburgers in a bucket, clams in a bucket, fried catfish in a bucket. The whole gimmick was this bucket. We'd eat at one of the picnic tables or sometimes in our car. The place had a new sign, which wasn't even a giant bucket anymore. Blasphemous. The vagaries of nostalgia and vintage idolatry were confusing. When does something old get elevated, and what's the tipping point when it becomes dated and sad? Attempting to modernize old things could fall as flat as attempts to retro-ize the new. What was anyone supposed to do? Let everything deteriorate or knock it down? Allow the figurative kudzu to take over and strangle everything to death? That felt like what was happening to me. I was letting the creeping vines of my formerly cool life squeeze the life out of me.

Deirdre kicked her heels up on the dash, her ruby-painted toenails like perfect jewels on her parched, knobby dancer's feet. Everything else about her was so refined that I found enduring pleasure in the state of her feet. She once made me laugh for an hour straight by telling me she had spent an entire day with two popcorn kernels and the small metal flange from a bolt lodged in her heel without even noticing. *They're like hooves*, she said.

"The show last night was basically the Regal Beagle with Jack, Chrissy, and Janet." Deirdre was talking about the show she'd been to the night before, yet another event I'd bailed on at the last minute, unable to motivate myself to make the drive. "It was all the regulars. Julie, Creighton, Walter, Kelly, Little Blue Bill." We called him Little Blue Bill because he was very slight and his skin had a Dr. Seussian blue hue to it. "And Olivia is such a mess now." She was a painter who had lived with me at the House of Pi for a while. "She goes from shy and reserved to laughing to cackling to silent and legless in like an hour now. And she doesn't make any sense when she talks anymore. I think she's totally wetbrained." Deirdre looked over and then out the window. I could tell there was something else coming. She put the bottle of iced tea she was drinking up to her forehead and exhaled. "I'm almost...fifty."

"Shut up! No, you're not. You can't say you're almost fifty when you're forty-five. It doesn't work like that."

"No. I'm almost fifty. I'll be fifty in September."

"You're fucking kidding me! You've been lying to me about your age all this time?"

"Well, not exactly. I mean, I don't think you ever asked me."

"That's probably true, but we had that big party for your fortieth five years ago. And then ten years before that, we celebrated your thirtieth. And all the years in between were celebrated sequentially." Deirdre was one of those adults who made a big deal every year about celebrating her birthday.

"That's true. But what does it matter, really? You know what I mean?"

We were at a stoplight. I was still deciding whether to be offended that she had lied to me. "I guess I could imagine you lying to everybody else about it, but me too?"

"Anyway, as I was saying, I'm turning fifty."

"Red Hat Society!"

"Hush your mouth. I'm finally starting to think about what I'm going to do when I retire. Can a person technically retire if they don't have any money?"

"You can come and live here with me."

"Imagine if we lived the rest of our lives in this wasteland."

"We could rent it out on one of those websites for a bunch of money and then do whatever we wanted." That was never going to happen and we both knew it.

"I mean, I guess at some point I can start making money by being the oldest lady on the burlesque circuit. Sort of like a novelty act."

"See? You should just tell people you're sixty now."

This wasn't the first conversation we'd had about what the hell we were going to do when we got older. The first ten years of our friendship it never came up, not even once. Then we had a few friends die, of cancer or AIDS or heart attacks or overdoses, and we started looking around the Rave Up on a Sunday night taking guesses at what was going to eventually become of everybody. Not us, at first. Just how were all those *other people* in our scene going to deal with paying their rent or affording medical treatment. We joked about how the bar was going to have to lower the bar stools and install a buffet with a sneeze guard to adapt to the aging clientele. Our friend had recently started something called the Coalition of Aging Rockers that put on shows with a firm 6 p.m. start that wrapped up in time to be in bed by nine. The logo was a ripoff of The Clash's *London Calling* cover, but instead of smashing a bass, it was a guy wielding a cane. People brought walkers as props out on the dance floor and you got in free if you presented junk mail you'd received from AARP or rode up on a Rascal.

"After you sell the house and make a million dollars, you won't have to worry about retirement anyway," Deirdre said.

"I told you it's not like that. There's a lot of bills to pay before I split it with my brother and aunt and then the taxes are bananas."

"You'll be at least a hundred-thousandaire."

I was hoping the chunk of money would motivate me. "I should find somebody to help me invest it or something, but do we know any people like that? A money guy? What are they even called? Investment person?"

"It's stupid that we don't know this stuff. Like a financial planner, maybe? That's a job, right?"

"Have you heard of bondassage?"

This is probably how we got so old without knowing basic things about finances. There was forever something more interesting to talk about. "What's that, a bondage massage?

"Do you remember Kayla, that waitress who was really nice from the diner? She started doing it a few months ago and is making so much money. She basically shows up in full bondage gear, like with the whip and everything, and then ties the guy up, puts a ball gag in him, blindfolds him, plugs up his ears, and leaves him there for a few minutes, wondering what's going to happen. While he's lying there, getting a hard-on about whether or not she is going to destroy him or smother him with her man-eating pussy, she goes and changes into shorts and a T-shirt and gives him a massage. When the time's up, she changes back into her costume before she lets him go."

"Huh. That sounds pretty easy, but aren't you leaving out the part about the hand job?"

"Yeah, there's that. You'd probably have to give a few handies, but not everyone wants one."

I told her about the spectrum-y lady I met at the train station. How I liked talking to her and maybe I could parlay my affinity for that into some kind of job.

"I even made a resume for the first time ever in my life this morning. At the library. On a computer."

"You'd probably have to go to school if you didn't just want to be a volunteer," she said. "I forget if you ever graduated from high school."

I looked around. I hadn't been paying attention and now we were way out east by the dusty brown hills. I had no clue where to take Deirdre. Downtown San Jose? What was even down there now? Over the years, I'd heard that some locals were making something happen, opening nightclubs and coffee shops. A guy from my high school may have started an art gallery. There used to be an old movie theater where I spent a lot of time during my last year of high school. I'd bug out early and go there. That theater changed my life. One day in the early spring, when the countdown to graduation was really on, I'd blindly walked into a film called *My Beautiful Laundrette*. I'd never been affected by a movie that way; I didn't understand why a story of two working class gay men in Thatcher's London made me feel so lonely, and especially didn't get why the compulsion to experience that feeling was so strong that I returned and saw it three more times in a week. For most of the '80s and '90s, the city hammered on with its beleaguered campaign of *San Jose is Growing Up!*, but the truth was that I didn't remember anyone wanting to hang out down there. It was depressing, thanks in large part to that beast Ronald Reagan, cutting the funding for veterans and the mentally ill, until downtown became flooded with homeless people. The Mexicans had lived downtown forever, but the white families retreated to their Sunnyvales and Saratogas, their Campbells and their Willow Glens, making the drive to San Francisco when they wanted to get their culture fix. Black people, who made up a perplexing *two percent* of the city's population, mostly lived in Alameda County. So that left the rest of the sprawl to the hundreds of thousands of immigrants from Vietnam and Cambodia, Iran and India, China and El Salvador, Korea and the Philippines. It might sound like a recipe for a thrilling place to live now, but in fact, it was the opposite, at least back then. Everyone was too preoccupied with how to survive in a new country to do shit I would have been interested in.

We rolled down East San Carlos Street, past Original Joe's. Its retro vibe was right up Deirdre's alley, but it was one of my mom's favorite restaurant and I wasn't in the mood to feel the feelings I was going to feel if I went in. Instead, I pulled over in front of a park and we got out and walked.

"I know you'll object to me getting on my phone and looking up a restaurant nearby," Deirdre said, "but maybe I can hop on for a second and find us some sexy singles for us to hang out with tonight."

"That is my exact nightmare."

Deirdre laughed and scrolled through her phone. Was there a startup house near my mom's place, she wondered. A place where a bunch of app-making guys lived? She assumed they were everywhere. I thought about the people in my mom's neighborhood, mostly low-key rich families who didn't want anyone to know how much money they had. "Dudes like that are going to be way too young for us anyway," I said.

"I go out with plenty of guys in their twenties and thirties," Deirdre said.

I made air quotes. "Go out."

We kept walking through the quiet streets until we reached the small stretch of blocks that made up Japantown. It was cute. An old tofu factory and a Buddhist temple, depressingly offset by an Edible Arrangements in the middle of it all. If I ever wanted to drag someone, I would send them an Edible Arrangement.

"I'm getting cranky," Deirdre said. "I'm getting hangry."

I bristled at the word. We never claimed to have coined it (*Noun. The state of being so hungry you start to get angry.*), but we'd been using it for nearly fifteen years.

"You know that word finally made it onto TV commercials, right?" Deirdre said. "Like, why didn't we think to buy Hangry. com? We could be like Jonesy." Lyle Jones was a guy we knew who had bought a bunch of domain names in 1996, including Large.com and Small.com and made a fortune. (He regretted that he hadn't bought Medium.com.) "Or FOMO.com? I heard some entrepreneur lady on the radio saying she had been the first to blog the phrase and then talked for ten minutes about how social media created the Fear of Missing Out."

"What bullshit!" I was happy to have something new to rant about. "FOMO was passing out and missing the secret Prince show at the Hotel Utah in 1991. FOMO was getting to The Farm after Nomeansno played and all anyone could talk about was how rad it was. FOMO was arriving at the party after all the drugs were gone!"

"Guess we should have had a blog, girl. The minute the internet started we should have uploaded every piece of information we knew and attributed it to ourselves. It really is endlessly confounding that so many people have so much to share all the time."

"You know what you did that never caught on?"

I know there had to be approximately a hundred legit answers, but I shrugged.

"Using a plastic VHS case as a wallet." I used to throw loose dollars and change inside one of those cases and carry it around.

We were standing in front of a Mexican restaurant. Japantown had come and gone that quickly. Deirdre lifted her sunglasses onto her head and sighed directly at the disappointing brown vase full of dusty cattails in the window. "If we must."

"Just think of it as the suburban restaurant version of showing up at a crusty warehouse where Flipper was playing a show when we were twenty," I said. "I've been trying to think of a lot of things that way while I'm here. Like I'm not returning home to the suburbs I hated, I'm discovering a whole new place." I didn't tell her what I really believed: there was a finite amount of joy to be experienced in San Francisco and I had reached my limit. I walked around the city like I had blinders on, like I had seen so much that I'd scorched my senses.

Under the wholly unflattering lights, families and couples filled nearly every table and they were almost all Latino. Way more than there would be at any restaurant in San Francisco these days. It reminded me of a neighborhood place we had eaten at least twice a week for years and years. Its closing was the usual gentrification story, but particularly tragic because it affected me. There was a woman named Lupe who made the greatest chicken soup in the entire Bay Area, with corn and yucca and huge chunks of bone-in chicken, slices of avocado and a lemon to squeeze on top, and she would no longer be serving it to anyone anymore because she couldn't afford the rent in the city where she had lived for thirty years. It was like everyone was expected to adapt by doing a food truck. There was a time when the concept of a food truck was exciting, back before it made every chef I knew who tried to do it go insane. Who was responsible for glamorizing this gigs-n-hustle way of living?

"Maybe I could live here," I said.

Deirdre laughed in my face. "So to clarify, you would be happy for the rest of your life being a white lady living someplace with a lot of authentic and cheap ethnic restaurants. Is that all it takes?"

"What else is there to get excited about anymore?" I said. "It's nice not running into anyone I know. It feels good to be ghosty."

"Ghosts are sad. Or angry. Even Casper was in the dumps a lot because he was a dead kid who couldn't get anyone to play with him."

We ordered margaritas and enchiladas, and I decided to go out on a limb. "Can I ask you some really dumb questions that I've always wanted to ask you?"

Deirdre's interest was piqued. She would have been happy

to be a guest on a talk show every night of her life. "I would say 'there are no dumb questions' but of course there are. So many dumb, dumb questions. Anyway, go ahead."

"Your whole vintage thing. Does that feel like who you really are? Or is that something you wanted to be and so you became it? Like, is the real you underneath that or is that just the real you now?"

Deirdre lifted a brow, but launched right in. "I don't know if it makes sense, but I was always into movie stars and old Hollywood glamour and I loved the way my mom used to dress. I've been dressing this way for longer than I haven't so it would be really sad if it wasn't me. If it were an act. I'm naturally classy, I guess."

"Because everything about you seems so perfectly pulled together that I think how could anyone be doing that unless they were so self-conscious, you know? It looks exhausting. You wear a watch that you have to wind and take to the repair shop."

"It's not a lot of effort if you like it."

"Most of your clothes have to be dry-cleaned! Your makeup is always perfect. Your plates are worth twenty-five dollars apiece."

"I think I keep my life fairly chaos-free by mostly living as if it were fifty years ago. I love the internet, and my Botox, but my quality of life is better if I don't buy gross clothes at Target or force myself to eat paleo."

"Can we talk about your Botox?" Deirdre's beautiful, unlined face sometimes made me crazy with envy. And other times it made me think Deirdre was vain, irrational, and insecure. "Besides the expense of it, the fact that you've sometimes had to sell books or records in order to finance it, plus the hamster wheel feeling that must go along with keeping up. Don't you think there's something strange about erasing time from your face?"

None of this fazed her. "The fact that women have always been obsessed with trying to look younger makes me think that it's not strange, but perfectly natural. It's a normal thing to want to do and since it's possible to do it, why not?"

I always assumed it was impossible to offend her, but I wanted to be careful with this next one. "To me, it seems like the same impulse that anorexics have. To control and to disappear and to not be visible in a way that can attract any type of criticism. Disappearing your wrinkles seems to me like you're disappearing yourself."

"Strongly disagree. And you're the one who likes being a ghost. Middle-aged women are so invisible in society, so making yourself look younger is actually making yourself more visible."

I hid my frustration poorly. "But that's accepting this patriarchal bullshit double standard for women."

"But that's the world I'm living in." She licked some salt off the edge of her glass and dabbed at the corner of her mouth with a napkin. "And that's the world you live in."

We carefully laid out our cash on the table, going halfsies as we'd always done. Walking back to the car in the light smog of dusk made me feel deflated. I wanted to snap my fingers and decide not to feel alone, unsure of my future, and ugly anymore. Instead, I snapped my fingers when I remembered that we needed to bum a jump for the car.

"I think you're doing this on purpose," Deirdre said, as I walked up a driveway toward a woman sitting on a folding chair in her garage. "You're trying to introduce yourself to everyone in San Jose, one jumpstart at a time."

"What's up?" the woman said.

"I hate to bother you," I began.

"At least you're learning to ask people for help," Deirdre said.

I had a headache and fell asleep on the couch, while Deirdre stayed up watching TV and going through her phone.

The next morning I watched her walk up to the Caltrain platform and buy her ticket back to SF. I turned away for a second and then turned back trying to see her with new eyes, to see the person the other people on the platform were seeing. Deirdre looked like a fashionable, glamorous woman straight out of a magazine from 1964. A glamorous older woman.

ANOTHER MORNING AND BAFFLING that it was only 9 a.m. and I felt so spectacularly rested. Not staying up late drinking, in addition to giving my gut a break from a constant diet of burritos and pizza, had made a real difference. I was eating a lot of oranges from the branches of the neighbor's tree that were hanging over the fence. I'd been in the pool every morning for the last week.

The swimming pool brought memories, crystalline shards of them, reflective prisms that rained from above, breaking the surface of the water. As they slowly started to sink, I swam through them, grabbing glimpses from different angles as they spiraled. It was impossible to catch them all before they hit bottom, before they broke apart. *Like sands through the hourglass so are the days of our lives!*

Doing slow laps that morning, I remembered a party inside an old fire station in Pacific Heights. It had been converted into a house and belonged to some society fag dandy. All the walls had been covered in gilded mirrors and there was thick white shag carpeting that had its own special Lucite rake, that rose up an inch and a half off the floor. The furniture was Lucite too, all these see-through tables and chairs and swiveling stools, and in the middle of the room, the inevitability of the gleaming metal pole. If your interior decorator was a bindle of coke, this is what your house would look like.

An older man with a bright golden hoop in his ear and a
Navy-issue peacoat pulled me by the hand into a bathroom that
had a sunken onyx soaking tub and a white bearskin rug. We
both got down on the floor and looked into the bear's dented
face for a long time. We tried giving it different names—Orville,
Soloman, Tate—but none of them were good enough for this
giant regal polar bear. I dipped down underneath the animal, let it
weigh me down for a minute before rearing up on my haunches.
I crawled around the party, becoming the bear, as people took
turns riding me until that got old and it was time to climb up
the fire pole. A laughing girl with white feathers and sage leaves
in her hair, spit into her hands and quickly disappeared into the
ceiling. I jumped as high as I could, wrapped my body around
the pole and shinnied up after her. The boudoir, the entire floor,
was an enormous wardrobe closet with a California King smack
in the middle. The loft was overflowing with clothes. Short silk
bathrobes and satin pajamas, wide wale cords and pink polo shirts,
cashmere sweaters and soft leather belts, paisley ties and argyle
socks in cool lavenders and grey-blues. Golf pants. Linen sportcoats. Icelandic sweaters and leather chaps. We tried them all on.
Records were fished out of alabaster cabinets and played on the
turntable. Sly and the Family Stone. Wagner. Herb Alpert. Ohio
Players. Donna Summer. Bowie. Soon everyone wanted up.
They shambled up the pole one after another, coming out of the
hole in the floor like sardines slithering out of a giant can, shiny
and silver. A couple swung from a rafter beam using a knotted
bedsheet. Someone said, is that a noose? Let's make a noose. A
bald girl pretended to hang herself and came close. When we slid
back downstairs, people were playing a modern parlor game. A
ropy yoga guy was naked in a headstand with his legs in a V and
someone had slid a hot dog in his asshole. A woman handed out
slices of bologna. *Now grab your slice, fold it in half and take a bite out
of it. Open it up. Use it like a meat frisbee! Try to throw your ring of
bologna around the hot dog!*

I came out of that world and up for air.

"Hello! Anybody home?"

Someone was yelling over the fence. I climbed out of the pool and wrapped a towel around myself. Peeking over the gate, I spotted a landscaping truck idling in the drive. The yard. Scott had left a message on the machine with a number for me to call to get it cleaned up, but I hadn't gotten around to it yet.

"Just a minute!" I yelled. "I'll meet you at the front door!"

I ran inside and threw on one of my mom's old robes. It zipped up the front, had a yellow floral pattern, and hit me mid-shin. I wrapped the towel around my head and went to the door. Two men were standing in the atrium, backing off from me while I talked.

"We take the rocks," one of them said. "And we put in the plants."

"Go for it," I said. "Do I pay you?"

They didn't know. One handed me a business card. I shut the door, just as the answering machine was picking up a call from Scott. *Dude, you there? Someone's coming to do the yard. They said they're ringing the bell.* I probably should have picked up, but didn't bother because, look, it was already being handled. Scott didn't trust me with anything and it was starting to get on my nerves. Things with him were much easier when we only spoke twice a year.

I sat on the edge of the bed, momentarily paralyzed by the thought of what to wear to drop my resume off at the employment agency. Dressing to go into an office felt challenging, but dressing to go most places was confusing these days. I wouldn't have owned anything appropriate, regardless of the shitstorm, but now I was relying on solely what was in my mother's closet. I put on a skirt I remembered her wearing to an Easter party, an A-line denim one that looked like it was ripped straight from the wardrobe department at the Children's Television Workshop. There were still some pantyhose in her drawer, even one brand new L'eggs egg that I could give Deirdre to sell online. But I wasn't sure if professional women wore pantyhose anymore. I suspected they didn't, but there was no way I could go out with bare legs.

One of the regrets I had about my body is that I realized too late that I would be dragging it around forever. My shins were full of dents and scars that I probably could have avoided if I realized that one day it might be important to have legs that looked decent in a skirt. All those years of climbing over fences to get into closed parks, slamming into kegs in the basement in the middle of a shift, falling down while dancing, moshing around in a pit. The soles of my feet were hard and callused, my toes were smashed and deformed, my elbows dry and rough. I had the disorienting thought that my meat probably wouldn't taste very good. That if I were ever to be eaten, be it by mountain lion or cannibal, my flesh would be chewy and gamy, requiring extensive marination or a lot of pounding to tenderize.

I pulled on a pair of ancient black tights, so old they emitted a blast of dust when they snapped onto my leg. I was absolutely certain they looked wrong with this summery skirt, but I wore them anyway. I yanked a white oxford shirt, impeccably pressed and smelling faintly of cheese, off a hanger. When I tucked it in, it created a lumpy roll around the waistband that I couldn't get rid of. Then I folded up the sleeves to my elbows. There had to be a ten-year-old bottle of Jergen's around here somewhere. Would I pass now? Perhaps a necklace of some sort? I opened my mother's jewelry case, a wooden box with burnt umber mushrooms painted on the top, and pulled out a thin gold chain with a four-leaf clover pendant.

My hair was fighting its own battle with depression, too long and frayed at the ends, an uneven mousy brown woven with wiry gray strands that stuck out. I pulled it back in a too-tight ponytail and juiced it with a can of hairspray. I felt like a woman who had recently been freed from prison and was trying her best to fit back into with society. Like the serial killer Aileen Wuornos. Years ago, I had seen a documentary about her. I felt bad for Wuornos and didn't give a shit how that made people feel when I said it. Hollywood eventually did their version of the story and a scene haunted me. Wournos gets out of jail and tries to re-enter society. Sweaty and determined, wearing a terrible outfit not unlike the one I was wearing this very minute, she rides her bike all over town going on job interviews and getting rejected. I related to Aileen. A misfit attempting to work her way back into the good graces of a society that didn't care about her. I rooted for her the whole film because I forgot the ending. Dead by lethal injection at age forty-six. My age.

One drunken night at a rock club, I met the actress who played her in the movie. This was before that film came out, so instead of serial killers we talked about the subject of her current role, non-Hodgkins lymphoma. She had done *a lot* of research on non-Hodgkins lymphoma. And she was so gorgeous, it was distracting. Like how sometimes it doesn't seem possible that two people are from the same species. She was infinitely all one piece, trying earnestly to talk to scaly old me. She happened to be dating a guy from a San Francisco band, a band loathed by everyone I knew, a band that made millions with a bunch of radio hits. I couldn't keep up my end of the conversation, so many details about stem cell research and kinase inhibitors, so I wandered off, creating a vacuum for someone else to get sucked into. Eventually, she broke up with the rock star and as far as I knew, he was still living rent-free in the basement of a multimillionaire's mansion in Pacific Heights, occasionally touring casinos, playing corporate parties and considering a run in local politics. It seemed like a thousand years ago, to be drunk at a club talking to movie stars and rock stars. I remembered how annoyed I was that *they* had come to *our club*, trying their best to be regular person cool instead of fake celebrity cool. What a relief not to worry about something so stupid anymore.

I had been sweating a lot lately, intermittently, yet like a demon when it happened. Yet another affront to my sensibilities. There didn't seem to be a way to control it, but driving to the employment agency as opposed to taking the bus and walking seemed like a good way to avoid it. Should I call Deirdre to get Tony's number for a jump again? It was too embarrassing that I hadn't yet replaced the battery. I took a deep breath. Mrs. Sklamberg was probably home. She had been a living, breathing symbol of everything I did not want to become and now she's the one who had the spark that I needed.

A middle-aged woman walking barefoot in public was surely a sign of instability, but my boots were airing out in the back and I didn't want to subject myself to a pair of my mom's shoes until the last possible minute. She answered the door in the same instant I was ringing the bell. She looked directly down at my feet.

"I'm sorry to bother you, but I was wondering if I could get a jump for my car—my mom's car. I have the cables and can do all of it myself. I'm really sorry." I hated over-apologizing, but I noticed it was a popular way women expressed themselves when they needed something.

"It's not a bother," she said. "Just let me turn my beans down so I don't scorch them and start a fire."

I suddenly felt affectionate toward Shirley, who was now retired and living in the house alone. She had worked full-time as a receptionist or a secretary, but like many moms of my mother's generation in the Valley, who were nurses or teachers or cashiers, she was also responsible for the shopping, cooking, laundry, and cleaning. Divorced or not. It was the dads who got to be the scientists and engineers, at Xerox or Hewlett-Packard or Lockheed, or the doctors, who were generally regarded as snobs. There was an occasional realtor dad in the mix, driving a nice car and the butt of everyone's jokes. But the moms, with their low-paying jobs and Toni home perms, were tasked with trying to hold everything together.

Shirley came down the street in her Corolla at a glacial pace, as if someone had put a dozen eggs on her bumper. I instructed her to turn off the engine, pop the hood, and I'd take care of the rest. I appreciated the favor and wanted to make it easy on her, but I also imagined I was giving the woman a gift of sorts by presenting her with an opportunity to be useful. It wasn't until the wagon was running and Shirley backed out of the driveway that she showed her true colors. She braked in the middle of the street, rolled down her window, and yelled, *I know how to jumpstart a car! I was born in 1939!* I left the engine running while I went inside and grabbed the box containing my new phone, still yet to be turned on. I threw it on the front seat, checked the map in my mom's Thomas Guide, and blasted the adult contemporary station to calm my nerves. For the first time since I was a child, I scream-sang to the band Bread.

Hey, have you ever tried
Really reaching out for the other side?
I may be climbing on rainbows
But baby, here goes

The office park, located on a tree-lined street in Santa Clara, looked like an architectural model set up behind Plexiglas. I smoothed out my skirt, grabbed my phone box and my resume, and walked onto a shrub-lined path and into the display. I tried to walk extra tall, extra poised. This plan could work if I wanted it badly enough. There could be a lifetime of calmly walking through office parks with prominent water features if I wanted it. The girl at the reception desk, a chubby white twenty-something with dyed gray hair and red cheeks, looked up from her bedazzled phone case. A princessy accessory like that could really set me off, but I caught myself in time. I successfully thwarted a scowl and put my resume on the desk while my ass worked buttonholes.

"I'd like to get some sort of a job."

The young woman swept her phone into her giant leather bag. "I'm sorry. Do you have an appointment? I don't see anything on the schedule."

"No. No appointment. I just wanted to drop this off and see about working somewhere."

She mumbled and gestured for me to take a seat. This was a real curveball in her morning routine. I sat with the phone box in my lap, paging through a copy of Time magazine without registering anything inside of it, only noticing how different it felt in my hands from than the last time I had touched an issue decades ago. The feel of the pages dampened my spirits. So flimsy, so thin. I looked at the other two people waiting, looking at their phones. Maybe this was the time to break it out? Did times feel desperate enough? Instead I fixated on the office workers. Like fireflies, they seemed invisible until they lit up here and there, performing tasks. I watched, imagining myself in their place. Carrying a water bottle to refill at the cooler. Cradling a phone receiver in the crook of my neck while scribbling something on a Post-it note. Giving a computer monitor concerned looks in between tapping away at a keyboard. It had been so long that I'd been anywhere that felt so clean and professional and efficient.

"Paula?"

It took me an extra beat to realize that was my own name and I had put it on the resume. The woman gave me a quick up-and-down, though I was unable to discern any negative judgment. Just Basic Eyeballing 101 as she passed me off to a willowy blonde in a chambray shirt dress.

"So, do you have a phone number? I didn't see it on here. And it looks like you've been working in…" She looked down at her desk. "The beverage industry?"

"Yeah. I managed a bar and worked with bands and artists and things."

"Uh huh. In San Francisco. That's exciting. You live here now? At this address?"

I nodded. There was an official document saying I lived in San Jose now.

"And I don't see any computer programs listed here? Word. Excel. Photoshop?"

"Well, you know, I'm a little late to all that stuff." I could feel myself starting to get thorny and defensive. "I mean, I worked at a really cool bar and I was helping artists set up shows and bands do different gigs. It was very *real life*. I didn't need computers for anything. But I've been going to the library."

The woman cut me off. "So at the bar, you were a manager?"

"Not officially by title. That was my choice. To have a mellower position."

"You handled the money?"

"Yep. I did the drawer every night I worked for fifteen years. I trained people."

"Okay, that's great experience. You should put that on here. And did you use any accounting software? Quicken?"

"Nope. Just a calculator. Should I have put that on there? That I have experience using a calculator?"

"Um, no. Not worded like that, no."

I fidgeted with the phone box in my hands. "I know it probably seems really weird, but I was just too busy out there living, I guess." My own sad chuckling made me cringe. "I'm not very experienced with things humans do using screens."

Why was I talking like this? *Things humans do using screens.* I tried to right myself. I pictured a small human figure in the architectural model.

"But I'm ready to be. I mean, I've had a great life and a lot of cool experiences, but now it's time to make a change and figure out a new path. Career path."

The woman smiled. "And is there any industry in particular that's interesting to you?"

I wracked my brain. Why didn't I think of this before? She tried to help. "Or think about what you're good at? What skills you have?" I remembered the woman at the train station the other day.

"Something with people? People who have problems talking to other people? And old people."

The woman set down her pen and looked at me. "Like social work? That's not an area we serve here, so I imagine you haven't checked out any of our online webinars?"

Webinar. Webinar. Webinar. The twenty-first-century word clanged inside my head.

"No, not yet. Also, you know, I'm interested in tech. Technology. Apps etcetera."

"And are you up for taking some classes? I'd recommend a few classes, so you can get up to speed with what's happening now. You went to college?"

"Some. Yes," I lied. "Yes. I'm definitely interested in learning."

"We just put up a new video last week. Why don't you watch it and then check out some of our links and come back and see us a little later in the process?"

The woman sat me down in front of a computer and cued up a video. In stark black and white with an instrumental post-rock score, the minute-long piece showed me the Colosseum in Rome, a man climbing a winding staircase, time-elapsed footage of a sunrise, an old man posing with a surfboard, a woman smiling in front of a copy machine, the wisps blowing off a dandelion. *We help people wake up to the new world of work. This is who we are. This is what we do. What do you do?*

The woman watched with me, over my shoulder, looking as proud as if she had shot and edited the video herself.

I smiled at her. "But the problem is that I do need to get some sort of a job. Do you have anything I could do while I'm figuring out the computer thing?"

She looked me up and down. "Are you willing to do light industrial?"

I suddenly felt my temperature soar. I think I was having a hot flash. "Sure," I stumbled, dabbing at my forehead with the heel of my hand. "What does that mean?"

"It's like packing boxes or shredding files or moving things. Nothing too difficult."

"More of a physical situation?" I clarified. Rivulets of sweat came down from my temples.

"We could get you working immediately."

I sat in the car in the parking lot for a few minutes and let my nerves off-gas. The suspense was killing me. Would or would not the engine fire so I could roll down the windows? I decided that if the engine went on right away, it was a sign I was doing the right thing. Click. Boom! The engine turned over and I privately rejoiced. Then I caught myself. What was I so happy about? That I didn't have to go scavenging for a jump for the car that I should have bought a new battery for a week ago? Happy that I had received a sign from the universe that getting a light industrial job from a temp agency meant I was on the right path? I pulled off the freeway a few miles away to get a bag of potato chips and a grape soda to cheer myself up, removing the phone from its box for the first time and putting it in my pocket. In the same parking lot, near a vape store called Up In Smoke, was a sign that read Nickel City. A young black guy with a kinky fade mohawk was smoking a cigarette out front. I resisted the urge to bum one.

I pointed to the logo on his shirt. "What is it?"

"It's an arcade. It costs two bucks to get in, but then most of the games just cost a nickel." I liked his laid-back vibe. Classic affable stoner. "Some of them are even free. Like Pac-Man and Frogger and Donkey Kong. I don't know if you're into those old-school games, but they're hella fun."

I took off my sunglasses, allowing him to fully drink in my advanced age. It felt so satisfying to see it register on his face.

"Oh yeah, so you know already. Go on in."

"So do I give you the two dollars?"

"Just go in," the guy said. "No one's here yet. Jump over the turnstile. It doesn't get going til two or so. After school's out."

I stuck a five in the change machine and put my nickels in a plastic cup. When I was a kid, going to the arcade was mostly about talking to boys. I never played the games much. I'd stand behind my friends watching them play, but it was too much pressure to be the one on display. I was always worried about embarrassing myself. I walked across the floor, across the zany carpet with a multicolored zigzag pattern, to a Frogger machine. The knob was sticky and loose and the frog was getting crushed way more than it should have, but I couldn't believe how relieved it made me feel. I didn't need to be good at it. I could die as many times as I wanted and keep getting up. I could make risky decisions that were of no consequence whatsoever. For zero money. Maybe this should be a small goal to set for myself. I could get really proficient at Frogger. Maybe I would even discover I had a latent love of video games and get a job at one of the big video game companies around here. As my frog got smooshed by a car over and over again, I realized this probably wasn't going to happen. Truthfully, it wasn't that fun anyway. It had probably been the buzz from the soda because it all happened in about fifteen minutes. I moved on to an arcade game where the goal was to catch bumblebees in a little plastic net and dump them into a honeypot. I excelled at that one, probably because I was physically holding the handle to a yellow plastic net and catching actual plastic bees that were being blown around by a forced air machine.

I took a few laps around trying to figure out what to do next. I dumped coin after coin into a machine called Tip Top, just to get rid of them. It was loaded down with nickels on different levels and a little sweeping arm that pushed them toward a ledge. If the coin landed in just the right spot, it could upset the whole balance and push coins down even farther so that they spilled out into the tray. I started breathing faster and my heartbeat got fluttery. I must have dumped about two dollars' worth into the slot when I finally got a payout. As the pile of coins dropped, I screamed. Less than I had put in, but it made an impressive sound. The machine spit out a long tongue of red tickets that folded up on each other. I brought them to the guy up front.

"I won!"

He was talking on the phone.

"Oops, sorry!" I said. "Not important!"

"Dude, call you back in a sec." He put his phone on the counter. "No, this is really important. Just go back there and stick them in the machine and it'll count them for you. Then bring me the receipt." I came back up and handed him the piece of paper.

"Well, it looks like you only have forty-two tickets. But I'll round it up to fifty. You can either get a keychain or the bottle of bubbles in the shape of a cell phone."

"I'll take the cell phone because I don't actually have a cell phone." I waited for him to be impressed.

"What's that in your back pocket then? Looks like a phone."

"First of all, I think that means that you noticed my ass."

"Bubbles it is," he said, ignoring the comment. "Pink or green?"

I went back to Nickel City the next two days in a row, trying to budget ahead of time so I wouldn't slide out of control. I was supposed to be clearing the rest of the garbage out of the rafters this week because Scott had scheduled a big trash pickup from the city, but I hadn't managed to find a ladder yet.

I walked in, shooting for spending a total of 200 nickels, and then switching to the free games. The same guy was working, and he let me jump the turnstile again. His name tag said Jonah.

"So what else do you do besides play very moderate amounts of arcade games?" he asked.

My cheeks flushed. Please spare me from another hot flash right now. "How dare you!" I yelled like I was in a theater production. "I'm just kidding. I don't know. I'm just around for a while getting my shit together. Trying to get a job."

"What kind of job?"

"All I know is I can't be a bartender again. I'm totally burnt."

"That seems like such a chill job though. I would totally do that."

"That's because you're like sixteen."

"I'm actually twenty."

"Same thing."

He came out from behind the counter and sat on it. "So my dad has this company…"

"Like he owns it?"

"Yeah, founder and CEO. And I want to be the bartender for their company party, but he said I couldn't because it's illegal for me to serve alcohol. Which is lame because he lets me drink beer at home and the party is in our backyard. I'll literally be twenty-one in less than three months."

I turned on a deep man voice, slamming my palm down for emphasis on each word. *It's! The! Law!* He laughed and I felt relieved.

"I'm trying to get a real job there, but he won't hire me until I finish my requirements at community college, so that's why I'm doing this. But when I start working there, I'll be making real money. Then I can upgrade my vehicle."

"What's his company?"

"HydroCrunch. You heard of them? Hydroelectric power. It's pretty cool."

"Like at a sawmill with, like, a waterwheel? Some steampunk shit? Why is that cool?"

"Just like the sustainable energy thing. I don't know. What, you're into nukes?"

"No, I believe you. I really don't get the regular world, the straight world, whatever you want to call it. I'm kind of an old punk, but without the tattoos."

He scrutinized me with a lot of doubt.

"But all of the damage," I added. "I'm trying to figure out why people want to do the jobs they do."

"I want your old job. Bartender."

I made a farting sound.

"Here's something. Why don't you be the bartender at my dad's party and I can help you out? Be your barback. We can both probably make bank. They'll pay us a lot because, you know, Silicon Valley and everything. Everyone is bending everyone over here. Plus tips."

I looked into his eyes and squinted as if I'd find my answer on one of his irises. I thought about the other bartenders I knew, the strippers and hookers. How hard it is to stop doing a job when the money is so easy. Always getting sucked back in.

"When is it?" I stopped myself. "You know what, it doesn't matter. I don't have anything going on. I'll give you my number and you can call me. I'll do it if the money is good. Just this once."

HERE COME THE CLONES, I thought, as the young professionals wandered into the backyard of the hillside home, headed straight for me. I had been told on the phone by the event coordinator that everyone at the company was invited, from "top brass" to "Russian IT geniuses." The woman also made a point to say that I could wear whatever, which was nice, because if I was required to wear black pants with a white button-down shirt, like a caterer, I would be triggered and end up acting out. If you put me in a uniform, eventually I will do something unbecoming of an officer.

I whispered to Jonah, "I'm scared."

"Don't be scared," he said. "They appear to be very well-moisturized."

Jonah was all right. He was funny, and by the time I got there, he had already done all the prep work. The whole bar had been loaded in and set up by the pool and he had even put a few blue hydrangeas in a pitcher. On the tip jar, he taped his caricature of a young Kris Kristofferson that said *Tip Tipstofferson*. Jonah may have been a rich kid, but he was a weirdo one who had a job and drove a shitty car. Early '90s Toyota Tercel with a front panel that looked entirely made of Bondo.

I scanned the crowd to see if I could guess which one was his dad. I hadn't seen a single black person yet and Jonah was dark-skinned.

"I don't know where he is," Jonah said. "Probably showing off his motorcycle to someone in the garage. He never rides it anymore, but he pretends he does. He has a maverick complex."

I popped open a few more beers and poured a bottle and a half of pinot gris in rapid succession into the stemless glasses gripped by women's tiny hands. It was easy work, though every so often a renegade guy whose shirt had nontraditional detailing—colorful stitching or a small silkscreened picture of a skyline on the breast pocket—would ask if I could make a martini. Or I'd get quizzed about the whiskey selection in order to allow the guy to act disappointed. I tried to pinpoint exactly what it was that I was feeling. Something had been happening in my face ever since I got here. It felt like I had been smiling for an extended period of time, something I never did anymore. I was relieved to be busy. To stop thinking about my future and just do something.

A handsome man in a slim-fitting seersucker suit with a tan that looked airbrushed approached, his hand extended. He was the only person on the premises not dressed for Casual Friday.

"Thanks for being here. Jonah tells me you're pretty miserable at Frogger."

I gave Jonah a decent punch on the arm.

"So this is my dad," he said. "He's kind of a joke machine."

Jonah had a white dad. A gay-ish-seeming white dad. Who was younger than me.

"Don't be embarrassed!" the dad laughed. "Someone's got to give some love to those old games. It can't be all Xbox all the time! You like pinball? My game is pinball. Talk about old school! You think you're old school, I'm old school!" He sobered briefly to make eye contact with me. "Very glad you're here, Edie," he said before walking off into the crowd.

I finished pouring yet another glass of white wine for another slim white woman. "He's a Cool Dad, huh? He must think I am such a loser."

"He's not like that," Jonah said. "He was just worried that you might be a child molester. Hanging around the arcade in the afternoon. You know."

"God."

"I'm just kidding. He didn't say anything about it. Look at him. He doesn't care. He's a single gay man who adopted a crack baby. You could be standing here naked with your bush on fire and he really wouldn't care."

"You weren't a crack baby," I said. "I've met crack babies."

"You probably gave birth to a crack baby!"

I slapped his shoulder and then looked down at my outfit. "But maybe not having any clothes on would be better than this." I was wearing a pair of pleated white pants and a lavender blouse. All of it was mostly polyester and I was starting to sweat.

"Yeah, what is this you're doing? Every time I've seen you, you look like you're an '80s movie version of a working mom."

"Jonah, you've met me at a high point of my life. All my clothes were rained on by shit water and so I've been putting together various ensembles from my dead mother's closet."

"Whoa, that's heavy. Shit water. Well, if you need to go shopping, I can come with you. I've got a decent aesthetic and I might be able help you out of this mess."

A guy leaned an elbow onto the bar in an attempt to be casual. The space was jammed with bottles and glasses, and the surface was only a little higher than his waist, so it didn't quite come off smoothly. He was bending over awkwardly with his butt sticking out. He nodded his head in the direction of Jonah. "So are you both related to Ted or just this guy? Is this a family affair or what?"

"No, I'm just freelance," I said.

"Very cool. Freelance mixologist. You do a lot of corporate stuff?"

"Oh, I do it all. Right, Jonah? Soft openings, soft launches, IPO picnics, coke blowouts, *gizmo romps*."

Jonah laughed. "Oh yeah! Frogger strategy meetings, Pong pings, bing bongs, strategy rips, aptitude levelers, leveraged paninis, hand-crafted takeovers, cloud buyouts. She does everything, Andrew."

Andrew held out his hand for me to shake. I briefly considered doubling down on making fun of him, but nixed it. I was managing not to be annoyed today and I was rather impressed with myself. This guy was too confident, automatically semi-annoying, but I let it wick right off me like moisture on an athleisure tee.

"I used to be a bartender up in the city and now I'm just doing extra work here and there."

"Cool, cool. Where in the city?"

I started to look past him to the next person in line. "The Locust. In the Mission."

"Oh, I know that place. I've had some crazy nights there."

I almost started to tell him how much crazier it used to be back in the day, but stopped. Progress.

"You do look kind of familiar." He finally pulled his arm off the bar. It was a relief to not look at him in that ridiculous pose anymore, but then he clasped both hands behind his back and started swaying side to side. "I mean, I was always super-wasted when I was in there with my brother. Man, my brother used to go there all the time. That was his regular spot. He loved the jukebox."

"It was legendary. They use an internet-based algorithm machine now. I'd probably recognize him. I practically lived there."

"His name is Isaiah. Tall dude with brown curly hair and one of the first bros to get gauges in his earlobes. Big black plugs."

"Ew. I'm sorry," I said. "That's the worst body mod there is. I guess horn implants are worse, but punk really went off the rails when that started happening. It seemed like they got their wires crossed with the Burning Man urban primitive thing. They were like a new breed I didn't understand."

"He was around a lot in like '96, '97, but we had to get him out of there. He was totally ruining his life."

"I saw a lot of people do that. Jury's still out on whether I ruined mine."

"Ruined sounds a bit harsh, don't you think? You're here, aren't you?"

I shrugged. "I survived."

"So you're down here in the Valley now. Weather's a lot better, huh?"

Weather remark. I almost commented on it, but went instead with an enthusiastic, *Yep!* At least no one had been a dick to me yet, which was unusual. Dicks had been flying across the bar at me nonstop for years.

When things started to quiet down after the first wave of drinkers, Jonah told me to take a break. I slunk over to a corner with a pile of barbecue and Andrew walked across the yard to join me.

"Sorry, should I leave you alone? You need a minute?"

"No, it's okay. It's been really easy. Everyone is nice, which makes a huge difference."

"I bet. Yeah, this is one of the best offices I've ever worked at."

"What do you for them? What's your job?"

"I manage sales. Pretty standard, but I believe in the company and the product, so that's good. I've had to sell some pretty stupid things in my life."

I've always had a lot of patience for hearing tedious shit about people's regular jobs. It's oddly exotic. "Like what?"

So he told me about his first job in college, selling home alarm systems door-to-door before he worked for a small newspaper doing the classifieds. Then he worked at an electronics company for a long time before he got headhunted for this job. He said he felt lucky, to work at a place that could make a difference in the world, a place about where the people cared what they were doing.

"And what is it that you sell though?"

"Energy. Water power."

"How do you even convince people that they want that? Aren't we in a drought?"

"Environmental reasons mostly. It doesn't take a lot of water to do it."

"What would you have done if this job hadn't come along? I mean, could you have just lived your whole life selling shit that you didn't really care about?"

He started to answer and then took a long pause instead. "Don't take this the wrong way, but I mean, you're a bartender. Do you ever feel like maybe you should be doing something more meaningful? And I swear, it's not an insult." Normally, this kind of thing would set me off, but I took it in. He was curious and potentially attractive. "Are you like, an artist or something? On the side? You kind of have an arty vibe."

"Yeah, I'm trying to do some temp stuff to figure out what's going to come next."

"But you're an artist? Were you in a band or something?"

I should have lied and said yes. Why didn't I ever have a band? The indignity of it stung. It would have been so much more satisfying to sit here in this suburban backyard as a woman who had stories to tell about being in a band in the '90s.

"Nope. Just a bartender. And I'm not just saying that to make you feel uncomfortable and like you just said a dumb thing, though that's something I tend to do."

He laughed. "Well, it might not be your thing, but we should talk to Miranda over there." He pointed to a group of Mirandas on the patio. "We're growing super-fast and I'm sure you could apply for something. It's a great opportunity to get in now. Before it blows up."

"That's super-sweet, but I don't think you really get it. I have absolutely no skills whatsoever."

"From what I can tell, you have decent people skills. Bartenders can talk to anyone."

"I used to feel that way. Now I just feel really out of it. Like I've been kind of stuck in a time warp."

"Well, let's tell them to call you if anything comes up. Ted doesn't do things the way a lot of people do. He'd love to have an old rock-and-roll bartender on the team. That's totally Ted."

"If he really wants to be a renegade, maybe he should hire some black people. He has a black son. It seems a little strange that his whole company is white."

"There are Asians! Look around! But what are you doing? Advocating that a black person get a job over you?"

"Well, kind of. Only in that I'm sure there are a lot of black people who are out there actively seeking this kind of employment." I stood, shook his hand in an uncharacteristic display of professionalism, and reconsidered. "Sure, if you would please tell them to pass over a black person and let me know if there's something easy I could do, that would be great."

At the end of the night, Jonah handed me a check for $300 in addition to the nearly $400 in tips we'd split. Ah, the disorienting sensation of easy money. It must be an okay place to work if everyone was tipping so freely. I said my goodbyes, but then remembered that I'd probably need a jump to get out of there.

"Just get a new battery already!" Jonah laughed.

When the engine fired up, I gunned it a few times. "See?" I yelled out the window. "Why get a new one when this old girl is still working?"

"You're an old girl who's still working!"

On the way home, I stopped at the all-night grocery store, leaving the car idling in the parking lot. I walked up and down the aisles, thinking about how much time my mom spent at the grocery store. She stopped in almost everyday on her way home from work. On weekends, she'd wake up late and head out for groceries in the afternoon.

What are you getting, Mom?

I don't know. I'll see what I feel like when I get there.

My mom was either a complete mystery or the most boring person on Earth. She'd come home with a grocery sack and throw some dinner together, macaroni and cheese from a box or Sloppy

Joe's on soft white hamburger buns. We'd eat on trays in front of the TV, rarely talking. She drank a lot of white wine, usually from a box, though she later moved on to large format bottles. What else did she like besides grocery shopping and white wine? Game shows. The oldies station in the car. An occasional bubble bath with Palmolive dish soap. Reading Dear Abby and romance novels. There must have been something else. The happiest I remembered her being was when she threw her peanut shells on the floor at a restaurant. She got a real kick out of that. "Isn't this crazy?" she'd said, throwing another shell on the ground and grinding it to dust with her white Tretorn sneaker, a pair of shoes she called her "tennies" that slowly yellowed over their twenty-year lifespan. "They want you to do this here. You're *supposed* to!"

When I first came back to the house after she died, I thought I would find something that revealed who she had really been. There would be a stack of letters, a journal, even an unexpected piece of clothing or book. But everything inside was just as it appeared. Linens and towels. Old bottles of Bactine and Kahlua. Cork coasters with the Chicago skyline. Decks of playing cards. Birthday candles. Too many baskets. Could it be true that sometimes there are no secrets, no mysteries, to a life? That to scrape away at the surface gives way to one surface after another? As a child, I was convinced that my Dad must have been the interesting one. This mythology worked for a while because he wasn't around to refute it. I wasn't even a year old when my parents separated, so all I had to go on were a couple photos and a few flash memories of him holding me above his head, holding my hand, holding my bottle outstretched. He had been in the Army and seemed to have lived a whole lifetime before he met my mom at a Lutheran church in Sacramento. It must have been him who held the secrets, the ones that accounted for my restlessness, my discomfort living in a house with people who were supposed to be my family, my ambition to flee.

I looked down at my cart. Besides the box of cheap popsicles, I had grabbed stuff with interesting names: fennel, pomegranate, mango, arugula, pecorino, boquerones, soppresata, winesap. I paid for everything with my fresh wad of cash and walked out to find the car still running in the lot, exactly like I was 85% sure it would be.

I was attempting to throw out all the expired food in the pantry while moths fluttered in and out of bags of flour and boxes of potato flakes. I'd just chucked a few cans of supermarket-brand turkey chili when Miranda from HydroCrunch called. Her enthusiasm was sweet, unexpected even, but it needed tempering.

"You know I have absolutely no experience in an office, right?" I told her. "You know I'm old."

"We know. No one cares. We didn't become an industry leader by thinking inside the box."

The silence was interpreted exactly as I meant it.

"Sorry to use corporate office speak," Miranda said, "but come on! Come in tomorrow and shadow the other Miranda. You have good energy. You're smart!"

I looked at myself in the hallway mirror and tried to remember the last time someone told me I had good energy. All I could see were two eyes framed by a proscenium of dull, unhealthy hair. Three years since I'd had a haircut. I marched to the closet and grabbed the scissors, pulled my hair back in a ponytail, and then cut the entire thing off, breaking into goosebumps immediately. When I shook my hair out, the blunt choppiness of it made my entire face look like an ancient cliff dwelling. Harsh, notched, and weather-beaten. It made me briefly question whether I was mentally ill. I yanked it right back into a stubby ponytail and walked to the shopping center to get it fixed.

Blonde. Blue. Mouse. Pink. Greenish yellow. Yellowish green. White. Silver. Jet black. Orange. The first time I dyed it I was twelve, after hitching to Berkeley to walk among punks and homeless people and college students. I rested on curbs with a fifty-cent cup of coffee in my hands and took it all in. Scrawny rat kids in glorious tatters, inflated balloon men tucked inside their grimy layers, misanthropic geniuses in big black overcoats, clunky boots, and disheveled hair. All these people, clearly brilliant and misunderstood I thought, until they set themselves free on the streets.

There was a boy I went out with in high school, a computer genius who sculpted his hair with Ivory soap and never studied, but got a perfect score on his SATs. We would make out in the park after school and drive around in his parents' old Volvo squareback to get tacos and ice cream. He played me music with sad lyrics by femmy men with big hair and became a vegetarian and taught me how to watch TV the right way. I hadn't realized that you could watch a dating game show in the middle of the afternoon solely for the purpose of laughing in disbelief at the whole wide world. It was a salve. It eased the invisible wire in my jaw. To laugh at the studio audience on the TV while they were laughing, rather than to laugh with the studio audience as they laughed. That was a revelation to me, especially when you could never figure out what the audience was laughing at anyway. I began to doubt most of them even knew.

The boy bought pants from thrift stores that looked like the ones earnest dads wore on '50s TV shows. I would visit him in Berkeley long after he had new girlfriends, other girlfriends who weren't still high-schoolers, just so I could disappear into the grayness and fog and spend a weekend in a messy old Victorian flat with giant textbooks and packs of ramen; and nobody had a real bed, only futons. To not own a bed, but amass piles of vinyl. To start your own band. What more could you want than a degree in theology and a hit song on college radio. That was perfect living, I thought. The way not to be in the studio audience of life. But I never did become one of them. I never completed my metamorphosis.

I think I had tricked myself without even knowing it was a trick. I had learned that if I could say the right words, if I got the obscure reference, if I could pronounce the correct names, I was already there. Arrival. A quick study without the study. I paid attention to the way people said these words and who said them (very important) and then I could figure out if I was supposed to file it away in my head for later. Like in comic strips when they show how a dog hears something. I was like a cartoon dog, only hearing bits. Blah blah blah Bergman blah blah blah Brecht blah blah blah Basquiat blah blah blah Big Black. And those were just a few of the Bs. There was a scrap pile in my head that commingled slicing up eyeballs with The Eye. Cockroaches and existentialism brushed up against Lux Interior and Rashomon. Anarchy in the U.K. elided into Borges, Rumi, Didion, Fellini, and City Lights laid down with 4AD, the Weimar Republic and Valerie Solanas. Inexplicably, they rung the same bell in my brain like a strong man swinging a hammer at a carnival. The high strikers. Raymond Carver. Ding! Matthew Barney. Ding! Stockhausen. Ding! Cindy Sherman. Ding! Karen Finley. Ding! I could tell you a sentence or two about each of them, but never saw any picture in its whole. And then at some point in the last decade I simply stopped hearing the bell. What was the apple that toppled over the cart? Which straw was *the* straw? Was it Lars von Trier's career or the final Sonic Youth record I didn't bother to listen to. All those apples had piled up so high and I never thought to actually eat one.

Twenty–five dollars for a haircut, huh? It seemed like a lot to pay, but I was used to not having to pay at all. There used to always be someone around, offering to do my hair for free, or for trade in drinks at the bar or an offer to be my plus-one on a guest list. Some of them were friends, or friends of friends, and others were young people who came up to me on the street asking if I wanted to be a "hair model." Kids from the styling schools. Had I ever paid out of pocket to have my hair cut? I went with my mom when I was little and after that, I either cut it myself or had a friend do it. In the kitchen. In the backyard. On a roof. Haircut parties. Put some records on the turntable, crack open a beer, and break out the scissors or electric clippers.

When I got invited to get my hair done at the fancy salons, because someone wanted to try a new cut or learn more about color, I would make sure to dress extra sloppy. I'd slouch in the front door with my sunglasses on wearing the T-shirt I slept in. All those upscale places had such pretentious names. Architects and Heroes, Cowboys and Angels, Festoon, Frolic, Oxenrose. People like to make fun of the Hairports and Curl Up and Dyes of the world, but those are no worse than sitting in a chair at a place that was for real called The Owl and The Pussycat. I'd walk in and the rich bitches getting blonder and blown-out would clock me, questioning. Did it make the salon better or worse that someone like me was there? I'd hug and kiss the stylists who invited me, as if I'd known them my whole life, and then roll out a few hours later, leaving too big a tip.

I'd probably had haircuts that were just as ugly as this one, but when you're young, a bad haircut can be a fierce and pivotal statement. I resented the uptick in personal grooming that was supposed to happen in middle-age, but this went beyond that. I looked disturbed. An older Vietnamese lady took me to a chair and I pulled out the ponytail holder.

"Ohhhhhhhh," she said. "What happened?"

"I just need a trim," I said, staring at myself in the mirror and seeing only the cracks and divots. "Just even it up or something."

"And you come back for color maybe?" the woman said. "We can make all over brown to cover the gray? Or highlights? Foils?"

I wanted to get out of the chair as soon as possible, to stop facing myself. The blunt bob I walked out with was not exactly flattering, but much less egregious. More like the haircuts that surrounded me.

I crossed the intersection to a bigger mall, trying to figure out which kind of clothing store wouldn't make me angry. Would it be more upsetting to buy inexpensive clothes that were going to fall apart, or would it make me feel worse to spend money on better quality clothes that were conservative and boring? Both options sounded hideous. I tried the cheap store first.

The last time I stepped foot in a mall was about four years

before, to pick up something for Deirdre after she'd had knee surgery, but besides that, it was sometime in the '80s. There was once a time when I loved the mall. Not as a teen, I was too far gone by then, but as a kid, a fifth or sixth grader. Shopping for new school clothes at J.C. Penney, trying to work out a fashion strategy for the small budget my mom gave me, getting a frothy Orange Julius as a treat. The mall was always filled with other people from other neighborhoods who went to other schools and had other lives that I couldn't see anywhere else except for there. The mall as a portal to the world. But then one day, I walked in and noticed that the magic was gone. I darted from store to store, but all of it was tired and sad. The kids didn't seem cool or interesting anymore. The clothing stores didn't sell anything I wanted to wear. The little record store didn't carry the records I'd heard on the radio. I started thrift shopping and hanging out at the Tower Records on Bascom Avenue in Campbell. I began to drink black coffee and smoke cigarettes at the cafe across the street. I caught rides with older kids up to San Francisco or Berkeley to go to shows.

I tried hard to ignore that I felt the exact same way about the mall as I had felt that day. Thirty-five years earlier sapped by the fake air, tamped down by the lighting and echoey sounds, all these boring sheeple with their open mouths and giant shopping bags full of crap. The food smells still sickened me, their oil and sugar stench, the overlay of melted plastic. I could smell the chemicals in food like this, as if there was one ingredient—I imagined them as crystals, layered on top and set under a heat lamp to sink in. Eating a fat, doughy pretzel seemed like a good idea until I bought one and it balled into a lump in my mouth. How do you roll back your taste buds and savor a fast food chicken nugget? Was it possible to recapture the kid feeling? What a wild gift it had been to experience such anticipation and pleasure while wandering through a hellscape.

I walked inside a store with the name Casuals in it and everything looked like it belonged in a commercial for paper towels.

Slacks. Separates. Sets. I couldn't bear to try anything on. The clothes were going to fall apart or pill up after three or four washings, but I bought a couple things anyway, without trying them on. Khaki pants, a blue button-up blouse, a black cardigan sweater. I thought I had successfully given up on caring whether I looked like everyone else, even though the existential dread I was experiencing was rooted in my desire not to look like everyone else. I guess I hadn't achieved enlightenment yet.

I called Jonah to tell him I'd be making an appearance at HydroCrunch the next day. "Looks like I'm getting in before you. My stock options are going to be worth more!"

He'd already heard. "I'm coming over with a new car battery and leftover food from the party. You can freak yourself out by putting the food in the refrigerator in the break room next to everyone else's lunches."

When he got off work, he stopped by and installed the battery. "Look at your hair," he said. "Very normcore."

I tried to give him money, but he laughed. "Please use it to buy yourself some clothes that won't make me sad."

I was touched. It had been years since I'd made a new friend, so I decided not to tell him about the outfit I bought at the mall.

He grabbed my shoulders in a quick hug. "Good luck tomorrow. Don't pee in the punchbowl."

The next morning I poured fresh milk over cereal in a Corning-ware bowl and ate while I read the itty-bitty, flimsy little local newspaper. I hadn't subscribed, but once I moved in, the *San Jose Mercury News* started showing up in the driveway. As a little kid, my favorite section was called *Living*. It had the comics and advice columns and celebrity profiles. The paper didn't have that section anymore. I remembered my mom poring over the classifieds, fantasizing about other jobs she could get but never applying to them, encouraging her cousin to move to San Jose when he left the military. *There are fifty pages of jobs! Everyone and his brother are building these things called semiconductors. Have you heard of them? We saw a company in the parade carrying a flag with an apple on it, all rainbow-striped. They're going to put computers in everyone's homes!*

I made coffee in the old auto-drip and poured it into a prehistoric commuter mug. Before America's second-wave obsession with coffee, when a cappuccino was still something you could only order at a specialty Euro cafe and cars were not manufactured with drink holders, there was a short time where all manner of mug shapes and accessories were developed to aid the commuter with the coffee problem. I would give them to my mom as presents. One model was a regular mug that fit into an accompanying cup holder that had been mounted on top of a beanbag. One was a vinyl beanbag attached to the bottom of the mug, which prevented it from ever going in the dishwasher. The cup I was using now was one Scott and I had given our mom on Mother's Day. It was gray ceramic with a dripping sky blue glaze, and was a conical shape that flared out into a wide, flat cork bottom, a built-in coaster that was approximately the circumference of a coffee can. It even came with a pamphlet that explained how the "technology" worked. You were supposed to set it on your dashboard and let the magic of physics take over. Your coffee still spilled, just less often than it had before. I was sure that young people didn't understand how dicey commuting was before temperature-regulated vacuum-lidded thermocups. Did they care? No. Why should they? Why did I?

It was cold enough outside that the windshield of the wagon was still fogged up. I grabbed a beat-up paperback from the backseat and tore out a few pages to wipe it off. I looked at the cover: *Coming Home To The Cattleman*, one of Mom's cheesy romance novels. With my economy haircut and brand new clothes, still with the creases from being recently unfolded, I fit right in with what I imagined the book's target market to be. Single working lady. Lonely. I placed the oldfangled commuter mug on the dash, pointed the car toward Cupertino, so grateful to my new friend

Jonah for bringing me that battery. As I navigated morning traffic, I mentally prepared myself to "shadow" someone fifteen years younger than me. *Be humble but not a donkey, be fun but not a spaz, be curious but not a dummy. Be yourself but not too much.*

The parking lot was full of Priuses and Hondas and MINI Coopers. There wasn't a single car more than five years old. Walking toward the building, I watched my reflection in the smoked glass. A scampering rat, a skittering cockroach, a spook in cotton blends. I pinned my shoulders back, as if I could vertically mobilize myself into a higher confidence level while my every screw-up, bad decision, and minor transgression flashed in my mind like some sort of deathbed fanfare. It was like my past had been vacuum-wrapped over my skin like an energy drink ad on a Smart car. How I wished to walk through those doors and start a new chapter, but the receptionist took one look at me and raised her arms in the air. "Woo-hoo!" she howled. "Tequila shots!"

I reacted by extending my hand in a regal manner, like a queen or pope. *Kiss the ring,* I thought. She grabbed it with both hands and said, "It's so awesome you're here! Was I totally wasted the other night or what?"

I clicked back into what was more or less my real personality. Be normal. "Am I shadowing you?" I said. "Are you the one leaving?"

Her hand flew up in front of her mouth, flat like a fan, showing off her Tiffany-blue manicure. "No way! You're going to admin in the sales department, not for the whole company. Girl, I ain't giving up this position. I'm the first thing you see when you come in. I'm the face of the company!"

I took a seat on a low, chunky sofa. Of course they wouldn't want me to be the face of the company. I wouldn't want that humiliating job anyway. How could anyone here take work seriously when there was an ironic mural of a Pegasus arcing over a rainbow painted on the wall? When twin dachshunds wearing hoodies waggled in? When a man in a fun-fur hat just rollerbladed in to bring me a juice? Miranda came to fetch me, and I put a pin in my mood. Most of the employees remembered me from the party and made jokey references to alcohol or vomit or hangovers. A bartender's cross to bear. I was instructed to simply "get a feel for the HydroCrunch vibe" but it was hard not to have a task. I was encouraged to wander around, but all I felt comfortable with was visiting the coffee machine. By 10:30 a.m., I was three coffees deep and becoming jittery and agitated. I ate a complimentary banana out of the fruit basket, noting the presence of several Red Delicious apples in the mix. That boosted my mood. Red Delicious apples are commonly described by everyone as the worst apple known to humankind so how fancy could this place really be? I thought of taking a bite of one just so I could spit it out and slam-dunk it in the trash. How did people assimilate in such a sterile environment? How did they accept that they worked in something called a cube or a pod? I washed my hands and looked at the activity calendar on the refrigerator. Why did co-workers want to meditate together? What was W00tRoulette? I was hoping to get the satisfaction of being a small but necessary cog in something important, but not if this was where I had to be day after day. I stepped outside and faced the sun for a second until I became self-conscious. When I went back to the kitchen, a big pink pastry box full of donuts had materialized. People were standing around it, oohing and ahhing at the display. I grabbed a large square one that had been glazed and dipped in toasted coconut.

"This is ridiculous!" I said immediately, still chewing the first bite. It was of course impolite to talk with your mouth full, but I thought there were exceptions. With something so decadent and presentational, wasn't part of the communal experience to make it a performative act? To relish in the extravagance as a group? Not everyone thought so.

"Um, hey," the guy in the rollerblades said, holding a serrated knife aloft. "We usually cut them up so everyone can try a little."

I looked around and noticed I was the only one with a full donut in hand, the only one eating.

"And that way no one has to eat an entire donut because, gross," a woman said.

I pulled it away from my mouth, prematurely swallowing a lump so I wouldn't still be chewing. I looked down at my feet, my mom's narrow flats causing flesh to bulge out the top, my prodigious foot veins green and angry.

"You know what's so wild," I said. "I can't look at a box of donuts without thinking of this crazy story." It had been a long time since I was inspired to change the temperature of the room by telling a story, but I needed to try. If I didn't try, what was I even doing here? I checked in to see if the group was still with me and launched in.

"Okay, so my hands are ziptied behind me and I'm sitting on this bus with, like, a hundred other people. However many people fit in a city bus. Muni bus. It's 1992. San Francisco." I thought I detected a small intake of air at the mention of the year, the sound of everyone collectively realizing they were in elementary school at the time. "I was fixing my bicycle on the sidewalk when the Rodney King riots broke out. You know the Rodney King riots?" A few heads nodded solemnly. Now they were afraid the story was going to be a downer, and they braced for it. "The verdict was read and they found the cops not guilty of beating him up, even though it was all captured on video and everyone had seen it. People went nuts. They filtered out onto the streets in this spontaneous protest. People were breaking windows, looting stores on Market Street. The cops were all over it and I got swept up in the dragnet. Moms out with their kids, drunks kicking it on the sidewalk, and legit protestors were all corralled together, wrists tied up with zipties, and marched onto buses that were waiting for us under the freeway on Duboce Street. The mayor at the time was this conservative asshole that everyone hated. Frank Jordan. Total pinched weasel face. Former police chief. The mere fact that he was in charge was an insult to anyone who identified as a freak, and San Francisco," I looked around at their faces, "used to be full of freaks."

"There are still a lot of freaky people there," a guy said. "A lot of homeless people."

Not wanting to lose my momentum, I ignored him.

"So we were driven down to the piers in the buses and we had to sit there all night, freezing our asses off in the fog. I had a wrench in my pocket, because I was fixing my bike."

"Wait," someone said. "A motorcycle?"

"No," I said, visibly annoyed, mostly at the fact that I never owned a motorcycle.

"A bike. A bicycle. And they confiscated my wrench and said I had a weapon. So we sang some songs, they gave us these disgusting bologna sandwiches, and then we were released in the morning. Never gave me my wrench back. But a few years later there was a lawsuit and everyone got a few thousand bucks so that was cool."

"What does this have to do with donuts?" a woman in the back said.

"Hold on, hold on. I'm getting to that." The caffeine rushing through my system had my head feeling like a pachinko game. "So then we heard that some of the buses had been driven all the way over to Alameda County and the people were booked at Santa Rita, a jail there. They were screwed for days. No phone calls, nothing. Totally illegal. Finally, the Board of Supervisors called for them to be released and they were finally let go. But everyone was so fucking pissed." I was talking faster, my teeth vibrating. My pits were really starting to sweat and I made a note to keep my arms down by my sides. "So the chief of police at the time's name was Richard Hongisto. Richard. Perfect, right?"

"Why is that perfect?" Dude in slip-on sneakers and baseball hat.

I shook my head a little too vigorously and chuckled like a game show host.

"Because, my friend, any time a guy is named Richard and the press doesn't like him, they call him Dick for short. You've heard of Tricky Dick, right? Richard Nixon?"

That was overkill. They all knew who Richard Nixon was.

"So anyway, the next week one of the alternative papers runs a cover story about him. There were a bunch of weekly newspapers back then. It was how we found out about all the shows and whatever was going on. Everyone read them. You didn't have the internet! It was one of the gay papers, which is amazing, right? That there were so many different papers that there were multiple gay papers. The cover had a photo of Hongisto's head attached to the body of some dyke activist wearing a cop uniform and holding a baton in front of her crotch. The headline above it said something like Dick's Hard Swing or Dick's Cool New Tool. Some classic dick thing that was juvenile and hilarious." My top was going dark under the armpits. Was I losing them, or would the dick talk get them back?

"Apparently, Dick retaliated, ordering the cops to gather up as many issues of the paper as they could find and bring them back to the station. They disappeared from news racks and cafes and stores all over the city. Eventually, around two thousand copies of the free papers were found in a storage closet at the Mission District police station. Can you believe that? Hiding in plain sight! Dick was publicly accused of ordering the confiscation as an attempt at censorship and he was fired. The funny thing is that Dick had been a gay rights advocate and had made sure that gay and lesbian deputies were hired on the police force." It was a bit of a sidebar, but it felt important. I looked around. I wasn't going over so well. "Hang tough here, I know this is getting long, but Hongisto had also tried to delay the eviction of residents of the International Hotel, which was this low-income apartment building where a bunch of Filipinos lived. That was really famous. You can look that up. Jim Jones from the Peoples' Temple—you know Jonestown—he also fought against the eviction. It was just a crazy time, but no one likes their free papers getting stolen by the police and cops don't like to be on the cover of a newspaper holding a baton out like an erect dick."

"I'm so sorry," the rollerblader said gently. "This is really great and everything, but I have to get back to work."

"Oh yeah. That's cool. Go ahead." He swanned out the door and I noticed two other people duck out with him.

"I should go too," the baseball hat guy said, "but I want to hear the donut part."

"The donut part! Getting to it! So the mayor, Jordan, tries to make good with the gays by showing up in the Castro by himself. No security. As he's walking around, shaking hands, a crowd gathers and they start to lift him up and move him through the people, not really in a heroic way, but just as some sort of strange but fairly peaceful protest. They move him along through the streets like he's crowd-surfing at a punk show and he's not really struggling. As he's being floated along, one of his brown loafers comes loose and some dude grabs it. Now suddenly the shoe is the star. Everyone is paying attention to the shoe! The mere fact of the mayor's shoe coming off made everyone giddy. Just seeing his socked foot, a tan dress sock with one of those reinforced odor strips. A guy was all, *I've got the mayor's loafer!* and everyone was cheering him on. They refused to give it back, they were playing keep-away with it, and the guy who grabbed it ran off into the neighborhood. Half the crowd stayed with the mayor and half the crowd followed the guy with the shoe." My coffee jitters were at the tipping point now. I had to wrap this up.

"Okay, here's the donut part. The next day an activist group called Bad Cop No Donut lined up hundreds of donuts on Castro Street, maybe thousands, I don't know, and I don't know where they got them all from, and they lined the donuts up from the movie theater up to Market Street. And at the end of the donut runway, there was a donut tower made of dozens more donuts. And at the top of the tower, was the mayor's shoe! A nun ran out..."

"A nun?"

"One of the Sisters of Perpetual Indulgence. Have you heard of them? They're rad." I was really taking these kids to school! "They're like activist drag nuns, they're still around and you should look them up, they do a fundraiser bingo night, and this nun poured gasoline all over the donut trail. And then they threw a match on it! Whoosh! The flames traveled down the line of donuts and up the tower, igniting the loafer, and the crowd went nuts. Can you believe that? Isn't that crazy? Could you imagine that happening now?" I paused for a moment, and then realized I was done. "So anyway," I mumbled. "That's what donuts remind me of."

There were three people remaining and they nodded and muttered their way out of the kitchen, leaving me standing alone with the rest of the donuts. I blotted the sweat off my face with a paper towel and went to go find Andrew. He had made it seem so simple when we talked at the party.

I peeked my head into his office. "I don't want to bother you, but I think I'm blowing it already."

He was sitting there at his desk, astoundingly nondescript in his white-collar white man drag. "Come on in. You all right? Were you shooting hoops or something?"

"I think I just alienated half of the office."

He seemed amused. "Just be yourself. It's fine."

"I mean, I think that's the problem. I think that's what went wrong."

"Well, what would you do if that happened at your bartending job?"

"I guess I would just suck it up and hope that tomorrow would be better."

"Great advice."

I plopped down in the chair across from him and kept my voice from going full-whine. "But I know that tomorrow will probably be like today."

Andrew tilted his head and smiled. He was handsome. Period.

Simply handsome in a symmetrical way that everyone would agree upon. "It happens to be my birthday tomorrow," he said, "so something exciting will happen."

I winced. "But what you're saying right now is like what I've heard about that TV show about the office. Isn't it why everybody likes that show so much? Because it's about working in a boring office and going through all these stupid rituals, like birthdays— not that your birthday is stupid—but dealing with all the personality types. Meetings. Copy machines. Office crushes. Etcetera." I was gesticulating too much, having forgotten to keep my arms down. I was now showcasing the damp rings under my armpits. "At least at the bar there would be a fight or someone famous would come in or you could listen to music."

"You can listen to music here. Everybody rocks their tunes."

I forced my closed lips into a polite smile.

"Here," he said, getting up from his desk, "if you want to do something exciting, you can use the new printer to print out some charts for me. And I can get someone to show you the program and then you can learn how to make the charts yourself." He pointed a finger gun at me and fired.

I fell to the floor and had a hard time getting up.

I WASN'T PLANNING ON returning to HydroCrunch on Monday. I had enough to do around the house. The doorbell rang and I sprang up, freaked that I had spaced an appointment with a fumigator or carpet cleaner, but when I opened the door it was Shirley Sklamberg. She had dolled herself up a little, still wearing the pink windpants from the other day and one of her "fun" T-shirts that showcased a smiling banana and strawberry doing a do-si-do. Her grey pageboy had been combed forward and she had affixed a yellow plastic barrette next to her temple. It was a child's barrette, shaped like a bow, and wasn't holding any of her hair back. A purely decorative touch. Her coral lipstick needled out around her mouth.

Shirley Sklamberg's eyes peered back into the living room. There were about fifty grocery bags of old stuff that I had planned on driving to a donation station any minute. I stepped outside and shut the door behind me. "I need you to help me," she said.

Shirley was nervous, talking double-speed, shifting around a lot. "I'm sorry about your mother." She stumbled as she tried to say something kind about her. "She was very private. And that's okay. I do feel like she was a good neighbor. She wasn't a bad neighbor and that's something. I'm here because I'm really desperate. I need somebody, anybody, any *body*, for Willow Glen Lifestyles this afternoon or I'm in deep yogurt with Ann Marie and the gang. You know Ann Marie. Her daughter Lisa was in your class at school."

"Oh, Mrs. Sklamberg." That sounded odd. "Shirley. Do you mind if I?" I crossed my arms in front of my braless boobs. "I have no idea what that is or what you're talking about, but I'm trying to pack and get a job and…"

Shirley's natural expression, sort of a tarpaulin of regret strapped over a flatbed of disappointment, changed for the worse. Here she was asking for help, and here I was turning her down.

I took a breath and tried to square Shirley off in a moment of direct eye contact. "Well, what is it? What is Willow Glen Lifestyles? Also Lisa Milner was always a bitch to me, such a snob. She made fun of how old my car was and told me my back was fat."

Shirley flinched momentarily, brightening. "It's only our biggest fundraiser of the year! All the proceeds go to benefit programs for low-income preschoolers. We get ten families in the neighborhood to open their homes and people get to buy tickets and go on home tours. There's a catered luncheon afterwards."

"I don't like a luncheon," I said. "Lunch is fine, but a luncheon is too much."

"And I apologize that Lisa Milner was a B, but some of these homes are real showplaces!" Her verbal roller coaster started up again. "You wouldn't believe it! These people have marble countertops and outdoor kitchens and state-of-the-art media rooms. And if you help us, you get to enjoy one of the homes on the tour for four hours."

"What do you mean by 'enjoy?'"

"Well, you get to stay in the house and greet the guests."

"What else?"

"You make sure they wear the paper booties over their shoes."

"What else?"

"And watch out that no one takes anything or knocks anything over."

I was quiet. I watched her downturned mouth and pleading

eyes. Scott had left a message about a painter coming this afternoon. I had a completely legit excuse.

"And you get a free box lunch and a goodie bag!" Shirley said.

This sounded like the worst deal I had been offered since the time I was asked to pick up a placenta from a birthing center in exchange for a gourmet meal that included the cooked placenta.

"I'd like to help you, but I don't know, Shirley. I think I'm too much of a jerk."

"I'm sure you're not a jerk, Paula. Ed Barbara at Furniture USA, now he's a jerk. Dr. Kornfeld who lived over on Quito Road and touched girls' privates while they were in the dentist chair. Jerk. You're a nice girl and it would be a huge help to me. And maybe I could give you a hand here packing boxes. Whatever you need!"

I missed my mom. I missed old people. I'd been stuck on a life raft with a crew of apathetic middle-aged cynics. And get a load of Shirley. Look how hard it was to be old. I didn't have anyone lined up to take care of me in the future. I didn't have any close friends with kids. I'd be like Shirley, putting on a colorful barrette to ring doorbells first thing in the morning.

"Okay," I said, putting a hand on her bony shoulder. "I'll do it."

Shirley didn't crack a smile at first, but her toes danced upon the suede insoles of her brown sandals. "I know you're going to love it!" She clapped three times with her hands right up in front of her face.

I put on a dress I found in the closet, a white shirtdress made out of an unappealing blend of cotton and polyester that pilled easily and featured red buttons and an elastic belt with a plastic closure. A red catamaran sailed across red waves on the breast pocket. The dress may have actually been amazing. I couldn't tell anymore.

"You look lovely," Shirley said when she picked me up. "Very smart."

For the afternoon I was paired with a retiree named Carl

(Lockheed Missiles and Space '65 – '91) at one of the open homes, an antiseptic McMansion built out on all ends to the property line. It was probably about 4,000 square feet and wedged in between two '40s bungalows.

"I think it will be nice for you to know some fun facts about the family that lives here," Carl said. He had mild case of what I call "cakevoice," which sounds like there's a dense chunk of poundcake permanently lodged in the throat, giving it a slight Kermit the Frog quality.

"That's okay," I replied.

"Three kids, a second home at the beach, Giants fans," he rattled off, waving his meaty, paw-like hands around the room. "And they like jet skiing and board games. Each summer they volunteer with their church at an orphanage in Zihuatanejo."

I cleared my throat, hoping he would subconsciously follow along. Or it was possible he had perma-cakevoice, an affliction that could never be cleared.

Carl barreled on, briefing me on the main rules. "Mandatory paper booties for everyone and absolutely no use of the restroom. If they've got to use the john, send 'em packing down the street to the Hurwitts."

I took a look around. It was nice enough, oversized and overstuffed with furniture. The rooms were decorated in a bold mishmash of styles that included rococo, contemporary New Jersey Mafia, and Malibu recovery center. Carl and I decided we would trade off stations. For the first two hours he would be manning the house and I would watch over the backyard with its koi pond, herb garden, and trampoline.

I sat on a wicker sectional in the outdoor kitchen, imagining the seemingly insurmountable logistics of hosting a dinner party. How could you possibly like enough people to invite? And what if they hated each other? How much food would you make? How would you know what time to start preparing everything so it was done when people arrived? What kind of food would you make that wasn't just hot dogs? I had never grilled a hamburger in my life. The most basic suburban gathering, the outdoor barbecue, was as vexing to me as dark matter in interstellar space.

Shirley had given me a name tag, but I decided against putting it on, in order to prevent anyone from mistaking me for someone official or asking questions I didn't know the answers to. I simply watched the people wander out into the yard, mostly older women, who all shared a similar trait. They were determined to keep their commentary upbeat, *beautiful brick work, the lavender smells lovely* but then they capped off their thoughts with a petty grumble. *Not a lot of room for kids, the yard is much smaller than I thought, where do they put the wicker when it rains.* I guess we're all the same. Humans love to complain.

After I moved inside for the remainder of my shift, I had a revelation. Expanding on the idea that early middle-age, like I was experiencing, was another kind of adolescence—you're awkward again, your hair's all wrong, you have problem skin, etc.—I started to notice that a lot of older women, north of sixty, transform back into babies. They wore lots of pastels, their pants had elasticized waistbands, and their T-shirts and sweaters were adorned with cute pictures of things like teddy bears and sandcastle building equipment. Shirley and her smiling fruit tee. They seemed to love dolls. Their socks had silly patterns. Their shoes had Velcro closures. I watched those women all day as they toddled around, heads lolling about, cooing at shiny objects, babbling in their own code. They traveled in packs, not unlike a home day care center out for a mid-morning stroll before diaper checks and a nap. It's harsh, but it was only a thought inside my head and I knew I was well on my way there too. If I made it that long. Of course there were exceptions. I had seen women flawlessly sail into their senior citizenry with gleaming silver hair and capes made from rich tapestries. They wore chic low-heeled boots and chunky statement jewelry. There were also the hippies with their long naturally gray hair, caftans and leather sandals. Ancient punks with their great old cartouche faces and dirty Converse. All of those were preferable to this peculiar brand of toddler-woman.

Towards the end of the day one of these toddler/crones (flushed cheeks, matching purple vest and pedal pushers) came in and padded straight for the half bathroom in her little paper booties. I had been fending off incontinent seniors with tiny tanks all day and it was exhausting.

"I'm sorry," I said. "We can't have you using the bathrooms here. There are bathrooms available at one of the homes just around the corner."

The woman looked like she was going to cry. "Oh, my stomach," she said.

I looked down the hall to see if anyone was watching.

"It's an emergency," she pleaded.

And then a wet farting sound oscillated through the hallway, ricocheting off the bamboo floors and vaulted ceiling, as she clenched her thighs tightly together and looked up. Now I felt like I was going to cry.

"Go ahead," I whispered. "Go on."

She scooted into the bathroom as if her ankles were bound. As more visitors came down the hall, I tried to distract them from the closed door, but on a home tour, bathrooms are fetishized as much as kitchens.

"I thought we weren't allowed to actually *use* the lavatories," a woman said when I shooed her away. "I would have loved to just march in here to tinkle."

I bit back. "I'm sorry but you're going to have to tinkle in another lavatory."

"I don't have to tinkle anymore," she announced. "That's the point. I just want to see the bathroom and I can't because someone is breaking the rules."

I could hear the woman inside unrolling a length of toilet paper, the faucet turning on and off, shifting her feet this way and that, shoe soles squeaking. I stood guard, plucking another pillow mint from the carved teak bowl in the entryway, and tried to remember the last time I had crapped my own pants. Early '90s. Double dose of ecstasy. Outdoor robot war.

When at last the woman emerged into the hall, I could see that she had been crying. Aging was so cruel. I put my arm around her and guided her toward the front door.

"Damn medication. It makes me furious!" She dabbed underneath her eye with the pad of her pinkie.

"I'm taking one thing that makes me all stopped up so they have to give me another thing and it swings the other way. It's all out of balance."

She pulled out her phone and started tapping on it but her hands were shaking.

"Can I help you at all?" I asked. "Do you want me to call someone for you?"

"For God's sake." She handed me her phone. "Would you mind texting my friend and telling her I won't be there for the luncheon? Because I have to go home and *change my pants*? Her name's Marsha. It's under Marsha N., not Marsha P."

I took the phone and looked at it. I tapped the screen a few times to try to figure out how to get the name to come up, but it was clear I had no idea what I was doing. Who was the incompetent baby now?

"I'll just call her from the car," the woman said, grabbing her phone back. "I can take care of myself."

Andrew called and asked me to dinner. I told him I'd go as long as he didn't bring up why I never went back to HydroCrunch. Was this a date? I wasn't sure. If it was, I was sincerely hoping for the best that there was hardship in his history. There was something repulsive about a person who seemed like they hadn't suffered. Especially if they looked like he did. Not that I wanted to date people with a lot of unresolved issues anymore, but I needed *something*. A manageable mental illness, mild self-loathing, a negligent mother. I hadn't sniffed anything out on him yet, but I was looking for a sign. I wanted to see a black thread inside the smile, a hook in a tooth attached to a line that would lead down their throats to a tight coil of misery at the pit inside them. Initially, I would be attracted to this thread, mostly for the pride I felt in detecting it. And then once I needed a reason why things had gone south, the secret black thread would explain everything away. This was probably another area I needed to work on.

Anywhere was cool to meet, I told him, preferably a low-key place. I was trying to avoid going to either a goony, expensive date restaurant or a popular new place that didn't take reservations, where everybody acted like they were engaged in very important sociocultural research as they waited forever for a table to open up while drinking modern cocktails that were as expensive as an entree. And then I panicked and specified that I couldn't go to an Applebee's or a Chili's in case he had misunderstood.

"How about Red Robin?" he asked.

"It's the same thing!" I blurted. "I can't go anywhere with trademarked fun names for the food like dippers or crispers or crunchers. And no place where the calorie count of each dish is listed next to it with a tiny Weight Watchers logo. I'm sorry, but no baby back ribs braised in Jack Daniels or Jim Beam either. No Tex-Mex unless we're in Texas, and no wraps. Is there anything sadder than a wrap? And the menu cannot have more than, like, twenty items total on it. Those restaurants where the menus are pages and pages, combining every item they have with every other item in a seemingly infinite number of dishes? Just, please, none of those places where the big Sysco semi-truck backs up and dumps off tubs of pesto and nacho cheese."

"Whoa there!" he laughed. "I was joking about Red Robin. But I would love to know what it is about me that made you think I would take you to Applebee's."

"If we could just go to a regular restaurant owned by regular people who live around here, that would be great."

"Roger that," he said. "Also, what did you say? Some kind of truck with tubs?"

"Sysco. Sysco! Have you never had a food service job or driven down the highway next to a Sysco truck or seen one parked outside a restaurant?" I had been obsessed with the industrial food supplier since God knows when. It helped me piece together an idea I had about the homogenization of America. And uptick in I.B.S. "They literally carry every type of food in an industrial tub and most regular restaurants get their food from them. That's why all that shit tastes the same. Like, do you think they're actually making marinara sauce or minestrone soup at these places?"

He paused to make sure I'd finished. "I never really thought about it. I'll be on the lookout."

The place he picked was located in shopping strip called Cedar Plaza, only a couple miles from the house. I told him I'd meet him there so I could walk and burn off some of my nervous energy. Maybe the exercise would make me less rude. Andrew stepped out of a shiny, new car just as I walked into the lot. I approached him with my hand extended so he wouldn't try to hug me.

"Hey!" He shook my hand, and then pulled me in for a hug anyway. "Where did you park?" Before I could answer, he figured it out. "Okay! Feels like you walked."

"Yes, sweating to the oldies." I dabbed at my forehead with the backs of my hands. "I'm a wonderful specimen of womanhood."

"So we get to sit on the floor at this place," he said. "I thought you'd like that, but I wasn't sure."

"No, that's great. Why would I not like that?"

"I don't know. Hundreds of restaurants with tables and I pick the one where you eat on the floor. Maybe you'd think I was trying too hard…to do something different."

Did he think sitting on the floor was romantic? It is in the movies, I suppose. A couple signs the lease on a new apartment, puts newspapers on the floor, and has a picnic of cracked crab and champagne before making love on the hardwood. Strawberries are sometimes involved.

I looked into his perfectly nice face, my head cocked. "What's wrong with that?"

"I was trying to get into your head and think about how you'd react. I don't know. I can't figure you out. Every time I say something, I'm not sure if I should duck and cover."

"I've never been to an Afghan restaurant before. I don't even know what kind of food it is."

"You mean I get to show you something new? I feel very cool right now."

Andrew held the door open and I walked in while trying to decide if I liked that or not. I figured it was okay, but if I were to ever hold the door open for him and he refused to go in before me, then there was something wrong with him. I definitely hated the pleats in his khaki pants and the way his belt was too tight so that the waistband got all all bunched up which made his shirt billow over the top. I was certain he was wearing his Good Shirt. Date Shirt. A bit too jazzy for the office.

The place was empty except for a family with two little kids, but it smelled good. It reminded me of Indian food, without as many competing aromas. Stripped-down, somehow. Fewer spices. Meaty. I felt open to it. A man in a suit and tie led us to a squat glass-topped table underneath the TV. I didn't comment on the TV. I was doing great.

"We have no liquor license here yet," he said. "But you can go next door and get some beer to bring in if you want."

"That's okay," I said. "I'm fine with water."

"You sure?" Andrew asked.

"I feel like I've already fulfilled my lifetime quota of brown-bagging beer at places where there's no beer."

Andrew laughed and then stopped abruptly. "Have you ever been to prison?"

"What? Because I've had a lot of beer in my life?"

"It just seemed like a good first-date question to ask you."

"Did you read that on a website? Sorry. You know what? I'm

going to sit on that one because it's fun to leave you guessing."

"So have you thought more about coming back to the office?"

"We're not going to talk about it, remember? If you mention it again, I walk." I said this last bit smiling, hoping we'd both relax a little.

We ordered dumplings and lamb kebabs, pomegranate-glazed eggplant and fresh yogurt with cardamom. Andrew talked throughout the meal, and I let him go on and on. It seemed like the less I said, the better. This way I could decide whether I liked him before he could decide whether he liked me.

North Carolina childhood. A younger sister and an older brother. Parents divorced. Soccer scholarship to UCLA. Sigma something. A few wild parties. Business degree. Job offer. Apartment. Tennis on weekends. Action movies. Recent ankle surgery. Health insurance.

I hadn't been on a lot of normal dates, but this is exactly what I was expecting. A rundown of one's personal statistics in a fairly boring getting-to-know-you monologue. He finally stopped, seeming satisfied with his performance. Just in time for the check.

The asphalt in the parking lot was still burning hot when we left. I had planned ahead to end the date here, just a quick dinner to get it off the table and out of the way, but I didn't want to say goodbye yet. The past few nights I'd felt bummed after the sun went down. Maybe having some company would be okay.

"Hey, you want to give me a lift home?" I said. "It's not too far. And I can show you the lamppost near my house where kids have been sticking their chewed-up gum for the last thirty years. It is so disgusting, it's great."

"How about I give you a ride home if you promise not to show me that?"

We got in his fancy silver car with leather seats. I sat there quietly, starting to feel a little nauseous, which I thought might be my heart opening up a little bit. When I looked at pictures of myself as a kid, I could see that I was wide open. Joyous, unguarded. Maybe if I tried, I could turn that back on.

"You're quiet," he said. "Food coma?"

"We should go swimming in my mom's pool."

"Your mom?"

"Well, my pool. The pool in the house I'm living in. I live in my mom's old house. For now. She's dead. She died."

"I'm so sorry. When did she die? There I was talking your ear off all night about soccer and my fraternity."

I explained the situation to him, about Scott fixing up the house, super-casual. Quickly so he wouldn't feel sorry for me.

"I really want to go, but I don't have a suit and I really don't think we should go skinny dipping."

"You wouldn't ever swim naked, anyway." Obviously a dare.

"Of course I would," he smiled. "Just not with you."

"Ouch. Well, why don't you come back and simply look at the cool, refreshing water of the swimming pool for a second?" We were parked in the driveway and I was moving into my low-key flirt mode. "Feast your eyes on the pool, at the end of this hot summer day, and then decide whether or not you would like to swim in it with me."

We walked through the back gate and the motion sensor light ticked on.

"You can wear your underwear if you think that would be more dignified," I proposed. "You in your droopy Hanes would really make my night."

He smiled. "Okay, this is embarrassing but, and I swear I'm not making this up. I didn't put on any underwear because I was in the middle of doing laundry and I was late."

"You can just tell me it's so hot that maybe your balls needed a break."

My words were like a wad of spit landing square on his face.

"Jeez! You like to be one of the guys, huh?"

Ugh. I let him take in my too-dramatic sigh. I know I needed to learn to go slow with people, to not blurt out everything I was thinking, but what was the point of amputating part of my personality? Then again, was that part of me, the part that would mention a man's balls to him on a first date, really so great? Maybe, like a gangrenous leg, I'd be better off without it. I'd try that approach later.

"One of the guys? You mean I'm not allowed to talk about sweaty balls? That's not a thing a woman does? Oh, okay. Duly noted! Don't mention balls to guys even though they talk about balls all the time. And what kind of adult waits to do laundry until all their underwear is dirty?"

That last part was flat-out stupid because *I was exactly that kind of adult*. I would go without underwear for days if I had to. Turn them inside out and back around again. I steamrolled on.

"And you didn't even have one ugly old pair to wear?" This seemed to rankle him for some reason. To be accused of not having a crap pair of underwear.

"Of course I do. I guarantee you that I have old underwear, but why would I wear those on a date?"

"So, wait! Ha! I got you. You thought there was the possibility that I might be seeing your underwear tonight!"

He jammed his hands in his pockets as his eyes darted around the yard. "Well, like right now, if we went swimming you would see my underwear."

I felt like I had caught him, *in what? In something!* and I couldn't let it go.

"But you didn't bring your swimsuit, which obviously means you would rather I see you with nothing on than your ratty old underwear."

I wasn't sure why I couldn't stop embarrassing him. I kept pushing and pushing, but he was starting to laugh, so I pushed on.

"So, here's what we do. Wear these." I grabbed my mom's old bikini bottoms that were drying over the back of a chair and tossed them his way. "It'll be like a Speedo. Like you're a Euro dude."

I quickly peeled down to my bra and underwear, flipped the pool light on, and jumped in.

The green glow made my body cast shadows on the fence and the side of the house. I watched them for a bit with my back to him. Man, I wanted a drink. This was a situation where it would be reassuring to have a margarita or a vodka tonic at the ready. I dove down to the bottom and came back up to find him draped over the sad noodle in the shallow end wearing the bikini bottoms.

"You're in! I can make you a drink. There's stuff in the liquor cabinet inside."

"I don't drink anyway."

"But back at the restaurant I thought you wanted to get beer?"

"I asked you if you wanted to get beer, but I wasn't going to have any."

"Oh. Are you in the program? I'm doing a no-drinking thing right now but I don't go to meetings."

"No, nothing like that. I just stopped drinking about six months ago. I was training for a triathlon. I haven't felt like going back to it."

"So, you're a dry drunk? Like George Bush?"

"I hope not."

"Inside you're really angry and frustrated that you can't drink and you're going to end up falling off the wagon and leading our country into a false war that kills hundreds of thousands of people, all for the profit of your rich friends?"

He said nothing, just sloshed out of the pool and started to dry off.

"Now you're mad? I was just kidding. Don't tell me you supported that bullshit war. Or that you're a Republican."

"No. I didn't support the war. This is getting really tiring. I thought you'd be a bit more, I don't know, fun. You're bumming me out."

"Well, I'm sorry that I can't ignore the daily assault of atrocities as we stare down the impending apocalypse."

"Apocalypse?" He buttoned up his too-long Date Shirt and

walked out the side gate to the driveway like that. Without his pants on.

"Nice forty-thousand-dollar car!" I yelled after him. "Or however much it was! Probably more! Probably way more! I don't even know what cars cost! You should be embarrassed to drive down the street in that."

"Goodbye, Edie," he said without turning around. "Your bathing suit is back here by the garbage cans. Good luck with it all."

Fucking tech industry bro-nerds. The nerd lobby has been working overtime for way too long. The last time nerds were cool was back when they had pocket protectors and taped-up glasses and felt happy when anyone was nice to them. Now look at this stupid valley. Jerks and boring people with no imagination thinking they can fix their stupid lives by joining the billionaire bro-nerd army. Has someone done their thesis dissertation on this horrible downturn for nerds? When non-nerds started calling themselves nerds, they gave themselves license to run roughshod over everything because they started believing their own hype. These fake nerds weren't oppressed. These fake nerds didn't deserve a thing.

I HAD NO MEMORY of entering the raffle, but when Beverly from the supermarket called to tell me I'd won, I went along with it. Four tickets to the minor league baseball game on Saturday, plus four hot dogs and four large drinks. Jonah couldn't come with me, which only left Shirley Sklamberg as a possible date. I was making progress on being open to more people, but I hadn't come that far yet. I would go by myself, ensuring I could escape as soon as I'd had enough.

Villianizing sports and jocks was a fairly common practice among people I knew. It wasn't very original and yet I too harbored an abiding hatred of them. Why? I was no longer certain. The twelve-year-old me, with purple hair and a thrift-store wardrobe, had picked a side early on and stuck with it, unexamined, for decades. It had something to do with men and beer and yelling and the asshole boys on the sports teams at my school. I couldn't get more specific than that and it made me squirm to think what else had I rejected that I didn't know anything about.

I spent the rest of the week slowly ticking off chores from Scott's to-do list, making runs to the dump and the donation station at the church. The more stuff I got rid of, the better I started to feel. I was still behind schedule, and perhaps I was procrastinating until I figured out my next move, but it was happening. I started to look forward to each day, swimming and cooking for myself, catching up on decades of sleep. Deirdre was trying to lure me up to a big party for the anniversary of the Rave Up on Sunday, but I couldn't commit. The more time I spent down here, the less inclined I was to re-enter my old world. I just needed a break, to decompress and see what shape I wound up in.

On Saturday, I took my seat in the stadium and waited for the game to start. It was an experiment. Unfortunately, when I got there my seat was facing directly into the sun and I hadn't brought a hat or sunscreen. I was still learning. I was wearing my old black jeans and a hoodie. Within minutes, my forehead and cheeks were burning. It had only been about five minutes and already I was trying to figure out how long I had to stay for it not to seem sad that I had gone to a ballgame alone. Two innings? Was that enough? How long was an inning?

A young woman came out onto the field to sing the national anthem. I stood up with everyone else, but couldn't find my voice, embarrassed to discover tears in my eyes. The singer wasn't very good, too pitchy and full of poorly controlled melismatic vocal flourishes, but she was going out on a limb, full-belt, and it was touching. At least she got all the words right, which counted for a lot. I wiped the corners of my eyes with my fingertips and forgot about the excruciating heat for a moment. I looked around. All my countrypeople, hailing from all over the world, many from families who endured untold hardship to arrive here, united in this moment with their love of the great American game. Or maybe they were too unimaginative to figure out something else to do with their friends and family on a weekend. I wasn't quite sure. Probably a little of both.

There was a brief announcement over the loudspeaker introducing the owner of a small chain of Italian restaurants, a squat man in a team windbreaker and hat, who threw out the first pitch. He did a big, overblown wind-up that got the crowd laughing and then lobbed the ball slowly across the plate. Applause. I went to cash in on a couple hot dogs and when I returned to my seat, it took a minute to figure out that the game had started. It was so slow and quiet. I watched one guy in the middle of the outfield and imagined what it would be like to be him, out there doing nothing, waiting for action. The ball didn't come to him for a long time and then the inning was over. That was it. He was there and waiting, technically doing his job, but nothing was happening for him. I heavily identified. The difference was that when he got the ball he would know what to do.

A man sat next to me. I refused to look over at him. What was the etiquette?

"Who are you rooting for?" he asked.

"The Giants, I guess. The San Jose Giants, right?"

"No, I'm talking about the race." He gestured to what remained of my hot dog. Looks like you're a mustard woman."

"Sorry?"

"It's starting," he pointed to the field. "The ketchup, mustard, and relish race. I always root for relish even though relish never wins. He's not as popular or as quick as the others."

I looked out at the field and saw three large foam hot dogs racing a lap around the stadium. Everyone was cheering for their favorite. "Relish!" the man yelled. "Run faster, relish! You can do this!" Alas, ketchup crossed the finish line first.

"It's because you didn't root for mustard," the guy said. "Do you mind if I stay sitting here? It's a much better seat than mine."

As I watched the players out on the diamond, hurling balls across the field at high speeds with absurd accuracy, diving horizontally through the air to catch line drives, sliding face-first in the dirt to tag a base, I realized I hadn't witnessed anything so physically dynamic in ages. My attentions had been focused elsewhere, on subcultures that required different types of agility, and I tended to knee-jerk reject anything that was mainstream without even bothering to investigate any of it. Not just sports, but: is a thing (any thing) popular? Then fuck it. Do people love it? Must be terrible. Are the tickets only available through a corporate ticket-ing agency? Has to suck. Is a major Hollywood star in that movie? Must be cheesy. Platinum record? Garbage.

And here I was sitting at a baseball game and kind of loving it. Sure, it was the minor leagues, so it had that underdog quality that was my stock and trade, but these were large men with muscles and bad haircuts and I was enjoying looking at them. What was next? Was I going to purchase a calendar of shirtless firefighters from the local firehouse? Get a poster of a barechested hunky dad holding a newborn? A Chippendales stripper hoisting a couple of tires over his head? Would I spend money on a large foam finger with my team's logo on it? Could going to one game qualify someone to claim a team as "theirs"?

At the seventh inning stretch, a man came out in a top hat and tuxedo tails with three kids from the stands. Two dudes rolled a junker car out by the third-base line and the kids were trying to smash a headlight by pitching a ball at it. I surprised myself by standing and cheering them on. Get it! I screamed. Go get it, guys!

The man next to me laughed. "I have a question for you," he said. "Would you like to see a game with me another time?" He introduced himself, giving his name as a two-syllable some-thing that I didn't quite catch. Addie? Adit? Was it Hadit with an H? I should have asked him to spell it right off the bat, which was a good thing to do when you couldn't understand some-one's name. It was a little embarrassing, but not as embarrassing as pretending you understood them the first time they said it. He told me he liked to duck out of work and come to the games when he could. Much more affordable than going to the major leagues and more fun too.

I was surprised. "Wow, what a question! I'm honestly not sure. I'm liking it okay and everything, but I'm so hot and sunburnt right now."

He held his arm up to block the sun from my face. "I'll give you my card and you can call me if you wish. That's the way to do it."

I looked at the card. Adit. Tech support. Silicon Valley Microelectronics.

"Thanks. It's really nice of you, I just...."

"What I've been thinking about lately," he said, adeptly letting me off the hook, "is how a sporting event is one of the only things left that you can watch and no one on earth knows how it's going to turn out."

"I never thought of it like that."

"With a movie or a book, there's someone out there who knows what's going to happen. With a game, like right now, anything can happen but you don't know what that is until it's happening. It's in a state of constantly being revealed to the universe."

I took my eyes off the field for a minute and looked right at him. "What are you, some kind of poet or philosopher or something?"

"I like how that sounds, but no. I'm just a man with various likes and dislikes."

I looked at his card again and then slipped it into my pocket. "Well, maybe I'll call you sometime to do something you like that's also something I like."

"Bowling?"

"Bowling is cool."

"Air hockey?"

"Yes."

"Rosicrucian Museum?"

"I went there every year on a field trip when I was growing up."

"Who doesn't like a mummy?" he said. "I'm a big fan of exploring my surroundings while I'm alive."

Back at home, there was a message on the machine from Scott. He wanted to know how the work on the master bathroom was progressing? Did the hole in the closet wall get patched? And how did the new coat of exterior paint look? Did the landscaper come and take out the rocks yet? What was the status on the grout? Did

I think there was a disgusting smell coming from underneath the refrigerator? Could I write a check to the pool guy? Why was I still not using the cell phone he bought for me? Would I call him back at my earliest convenience, which meant immediately?

"Listen," he said, signing off, "My work schedule is up in the air right now, but we have to talk about my next trip out. We're going to get this thing on the market soon and you have to be ready. I'm afraid you're not ready, P.J. Next time I come out, that's it." He paused for a second. "Love you, mean it."

He always ran it together like that because it was too awkward to say the real way. I love you. Too difficult. I didn't call back.

Adit and I settled on meeting up at a chili cook-off that took place in the parking lot of a country and western bar located in an industrial section of Fremont. The Saddle Rack. I had grown up hearing about the bar, mostly on the hard rock radio station KOME, where the deejays would say at station breaks: *Don't touch your knob. It has KOME on it.* This was on a regular commercial station listened to by hundreds of thousands of people. It has KOME on it? I asked my mom, Scott, and my babysitter, what did they mean by that? I never did get an answer, but what were they supposed to say? *Essentially it means that we should not switch stations because there is ejaculate, which you might someday discover is quite viscous, on the actual knob, knob being a slang term for the penis.* Man, the '70s were really wide open, weren't they? I decided not to tell Adit about it just yet.

I sat in the car and watched people stream in through the gates. Burly firefighters, little kids sucking on things, old veterans wearing special vests and pins, dessicated old ladies with meth face, mall goth teens in packs of five or six, young tech couples in microfleece. I saw Adit coming up the street and checked him out as if I'd never met him. He looked just the same as he looked at the baseball game, only without his work lanyard around his neck, but still the cell phone clipped to his belt. I hopped out of the wagon. At first his face crumpled when he saw me and then his eyes got wide as he put his hands in the air like he was seeing my name in lights.

"Miss Edie! Are you ready to do this thing?" He snapped twice with his arms above his head and then rubbed his palms together.

In the parking lot behind him, a lady in her sixties wearing a mustache and rainbow clown hair was doing a Charlie Chaplin walk to the delight of her friends.

"I'm ready, man. We're totally going to eat the shit out of some chili."

Adit frowned. "That is a disgusting combination of words, but I'm still glad you called me."

He was right and I apologized. "I'm sorry. Yes, I am ready, as you have indicated you are, to do this thing."

He handed me the booklet, which he said he had pre-purchased from his neighbor. "His name is Charles Barkley," he explained. "Before you get any ideas, he's not the basketball Hall of Famer, but still a great man."

In my mind was: Yes, Adit. I didn't think Charles Barkley lived a condo complex in Milpitas. I was making progress with pointless sarcasm.

"The way I like to do this is to get the lay of the land first," he said. "There are twenty-five different booths, but you only get six tastes with the booklet. When you see one you want to try, tear out a stub from the booklet and hand it to them."

"Okay. I see one I want to try."

"You can't try one yet," he said. "You have to walk around and see which ones look the best."

"Adit, are you micromanaging my chili cook-off experience?"

"And here we have the Rotary Club," he said, answering my question. "They had a pretty good one last year."

"Great. I'll try that one."

"No, not yet. Maybe we should divide and conquer. I mean, we should stick together, but share our tasters. I call them tasters, because they're really more of a taste than a full serving. That way we can try twelve different ones."

"I'm hungry!" I was enjoying being lightly annoyed by him. "I'm at a chili cook-off and I want to eat some fucking chili."

He surrendered. "Okay, why don't you go ahead and do the Rotary Club now."

"Thank you."

"But only because I know from experience that the quality is high."

I handed the woman my stub and got a small plastic cup in return. Like something they deliver your pills in in the hospital.

"This is the best chili in the whole place," the woman beamed, pointing to a sign near buckets of grated cheddar and sliced onions that said FIXINS. "If you vote for us, we'll let you ring our bell!"

"Great song, fun song!" Adit said, launching into the chorus of the '70s disco hit. She joined in. *Ring my be-e-ell, ring my bell! My bell!* As I watched them sway back and forth, I absorbed the full, trippy revelation of this bizarro world. This, too, existed as a way that people lived just a few miles outside of the place I'd been for years. I'd never even given it a single thought.

The woman was holding out an actual bell, sweet expectation on her face, hoping we would soon ring it. I spooned some in my mouth and Adit was on me immediately. How was it? What did I think? Was it good? Was it spicy? How would I rate it on a 1-10 scale? Could he try it?

I thought for a minute about spooning the chili into his mouth, but that was the kind of shit I used to do, when it didn't occur to me there were things called "signals" people all apparently "sent." I held out the cup and let him use his own spoon.

"Oh, yeah. This is good," he said. "I think last year it was a little smokier, but smokiness is overrated. This is better than last year's. Impressive."

I could feel myself starting to slowly disintegrate, as I listened to my date extol the virtues of the Rotary Club's entry in the

Fremont firefighters' chili cook-off as we stood under heavy rain clouds in the parking lot of the Saddle Rack with the hum of the 880 in the distance. I wanted to get on board, to get past how dorky it all was.

"So what did you think?" another woman in the booth said. "Want to ring my bell?" She also had a bell. She grabbed a hold of the fat rope tied to the clapper beneath it and jangled it around. "One ringy-dingy!" she laughed. Adit laughed too, though I doubted he knew she was imitating the voice of Lily Tomlin's operator character, an imitation my mother would also often do. So this was the wholesome fun I thought I might need to break out of my existential slump, but why was it so difficult?

We walked up and down the rows of chili stands. There was Disco Inferno from the nurses union, Voodoo from the car dealership, Bean Here Now from the non-denominational meditation center, and a booth from Hooters staffed by so many boobs dancing in front of it that to get a taste you had to squeeze yourself in between them. That was the idea anyway.

"Want a taste?" one of the women cooed in Adit's ear.

I could tell this made him feel embarrassed. He held up his palm to her plastic cup, politely, a gentle talk-to-the-hand gesture, eyes downcast. As we kept walking, he whispered, as if we were being followed. "The Hooters chili looks and smells subpar, which I could have predicted. We've made the right decision not to squander any of our tasters on them."

As David Lee Roth hit a damp crescendo from a battery-operated boom box nearby, I looked back at the booth, just as one of the girls tried to wipe a smear of syrupy beef juice off of her suntan nylons. Now that was the kind of thing I enjoyed. A moment of the sublime in a conventional landscape.

"Come on," Adit said. "Let's go get a seat for the demo. The firemen are going up. You'll love it."

We sat down on a wooden pallet and watched the fire chief take the microphone. He looked to be about sixty and had really bad mic technique. He held the microphone loosely at stomach level, as if his belly button were doing the talking.

"I'd like to start with a moment of silence for our brothers who were killed in Oakland last Tuesday."

Everyone bowed their heads except for me. Why? Why was it me and all the five-year-olds who were curious to see what a crowd of two hundred at a chili cook-off looked like with their heads bowed? The desire to watch the moment take place was bigger than my desire to share the moment with everyone else. The captain snapped to. "And with that, we're really sorry about whoever parked their car illegally in the lot over there. Yep, we've had to tow it over here and now we're going to put it to use in our demonstration. Sorry about that!"

Everyone laughed. Adit leaned over and said, "Hey, that's not your car, is it?"

I smiled, just as I heard the woman behind me say to her friend, "Is that your car, Jen?" They both laughed.

"Glad that's not my car," another guy said.

Two firefighters approached the black Celica with what looked like a giant pair of scissors.

"Those are the jaws of life," Adit said.

"I've always loved that name," I said. "Like, what could be more important?"

"They're very important," he said, without taking his eyes off the action.

The taller fireman stabbed the windshield with one firm jab and the whole thing shattered. Then they both reached in with gloved hands and started peeling out the glass. I was mesmerized by the way the windshield folded over on itself in small sheets, so quietly. Judging by all the hushed exchanges, a lot of other people enjoyed this too, watching an entire windshield being folded up like a dinner napkin. The captain continued narrating the proceedings, though he was largely inaudible. His mouth was opening and closing while the bulb of the mic rested comfortably against his belly, which was as tight and goblet-esque as a djembe drum. Everyone was straining to hear him. I wondered why none of his comrades tapped him on the shoulder and told him what was up. Why was no one in the crowd yelling, "Louder!" like someone always does. I was sure it was because he had a terrible temper. A mad dad type. Adit was laughing at me. Without realizing it, I was miming holding a microphone in front of my face like a newscaster would, and silently moving my lips, hoping the police chief would notice and step up his game. He blathered on and on until the firefighters stood on either side of the car and lifted the roof right of it like the lid of a can. Everyone clapped and cheered.

"Now it's a convertible," Adit said, laughing at his joke.

The chief pulled the mic up to his face and said, "And you've got yourself a convertible."

"Well, that's a funny way to make your car a convertible," a man next to us said.

"Mommy, they made it a convertible!" a kid shouted.

We wandered past a dunk tank where a pretty woman in a bikini was sitting on the metal platform yelling through the Plexiglas to a small boy with a ball. "Are you going to dunk Mommy? Throw it your hardest and see if you can make Mommy fall in the water." The boy threw his three balls and missed each time. "Isn't he adorable?" a woman said, maybe to me.

I turned around and saw a tall, handsome fireman in uniform bounding over from a climbing wall, shouting, *All right, honey! Here I come!* The woman squealed and writhed on the platform as he approached. He walked up and pushed the target in with his hand and the woman hit the water. She came up screaming while everyone cheered. He walked over, gave her a hand, and they kissed. And then with little effort she pulled him into the water while he pretended he didn't know what was going on.

"That is too much!" the woman who liked the baby said. "They are too cute!"

I went to look for Adit and found him cheers-ing someone else's plastic tasting cup with his. A chili toast. Were we done here?

I was starting to feel very done until a band called Full Throttle hit the stage. One glimpse of the lead singer with his cleanly-shaven bald head, deadpan goatee, and tight black T-shirt and I got a second wind. The bass player was a short guy with the classic cholo look, plaid shirt buttoned only at the top, white T-shirt, black Dickies, and a pair of brand new winos. The drummer looked like someone's software engineer dad. They probably met at a Guitar Center. If you found out they played AC/DC, Led Zeppelin, and the Rolling Stones, you could probably fill in the names of the other nine bands they covered, except for the wild card Lenny Kravitz song that harkened to the singer's softer side.

"I like this song," Adit said when they started to play it. "It reminds me of college and I partied all the time."

"Really? You were a big partier?"

"Well, at least every Friday night."

"Did you drink back then?"

"No. I didn't dance either, but I'm a very good dancer."

"Okay, let's go dancing sometime. I used to love to dance."

He grabbed my wrist and motioned toward a small spot on the concrete next to a corn-on-the-cob stand. We threaded through some recycling bins, and then he launched into a series of moves that I later demonstrated to Deirdre. He made choo-choo chugging motions leading with his shoulders, he bent his knees and jutted his butt out, he waved his arms in the air like he just didn't care. Wobbly chicken knees. Walking like a baby deer. Adit was into it! I mostly wanted to sit and watch him go at it, but instead I did a real mellow shuffle, keeping my eyes fixed on him as he smiled and laughed, made overly serious pouty faces, scrunched his eyes shut, and shook his head around like he was feeling long silken tresses grazing his back and shoulders. When the song ended, he doubled over from the waist and clapped his hands, a little out of breath.

"Yes!" he said. "The stuff of life!"

"You're so good! We have to do this again. Maybe somewhere a little darker," I teased.

"Let's hear it for those guys!" the lead singer said, motioning over to us. "They're going to Let Love Rule!" The singer then bowed down for an I'm-not-worthy.

Adit lifted his arms and double-pointed at the singer. "Thank you, sir!"

"Seems like we should leave," I said. "It's not going to get better than that."

We walked toward the gate and one of the young firemen tapped my arm and said, "You guys are too much! That was awesome."

"Thank you, my man!" Adit said. "We were inspired!"

I looked over at him, beaming with a giant smile on his face. I hadn't noticed earlier that his eyelids had a purplish tint. Deep and smoky. It was a color that seemed perfectly plausible in a landscape painting, even though you rarely saw it in nature. Or perhaps it was a color in nature I didn't recognize because I'd hardly ever been out in nature. Purple mountain majesties, like in the hymn.

Our goodbye on the street started with a handshake and morphed into us slightly holding each other's hands for a moment. I pulled my mine away to hold an invisible phone to my ear.

"Call me," I said. "I'll be around."

"Okay, but I'll be on my Bluetooth so it'll look more like this."

He pulled out a pretend headset and strapped it on for me, to make me laugh.

I CAVED AND SAID I'd go to the Rave Up anniversary party with Deirdre. In exchange, she'd come down to the house next week and help me cope. I still had at least a month before I hit the panic button, but was starting to feel a filament of anxiety adhering to my fascia.

I reached under her gate for the key to let myself in. The whole interior of her place had slowly changed over the years since I'd first come home with her the night of the Loma Prieta earthquake in '89.

There was still the familiar soggy newspaper smell in her hallway, but now Deirdre's kitchen looked straight out of a mid-century showroom. Aqua and black linoleum tiles that she had laid herself, refurbished wooden cabinets from the salvage yard to display her Fiestaware and Fire King treasures, and two ovens shipped from a private seller in North Platte, Nebraska. Even her refrigerator was one of those new models designed to look like it was a bulbous old one. Not many people would put that kind of money and effort into a rental, but she'd done a commendable job of manifesting her surroundings into a cohesive aesthetic that was occasionally photographed for interior design blogs. Deirdre, unlike me, had an incredibly disciplined approach to curating a lifestyle.

I liked to think I had some sort of philosophy about how I lived—improvisation, surprise, and randomness—but I could never commit to one thing. Was it at all disturbing to live in a place where every last detail was thought out? Possibly, but then I looked over and saw her luxurious cloud bed, shadows from the palm trees outside moving across the rose chenille bedspread, topped with six pillows of various sizes, foams, and feathers. That was exactly what I needed right now. The mattress was a recent purchase, handmade by a local company that had been in business since 1899, and cost just over $3,000. I climbed inside, gazing up at the giant saucer pendant lamp, and experienced a deep charge of pleasure that was quickly gilded with dismay. Now that I knew such a comfortable bed existed, how could I go on without one? Before I could give it a second thought, I was unconscious. Would I ever stop being so exhausted?

I woke to the sound of Deirdre puttering around in the kitchen. She popped in the bedroom wearing a flowery housecoat that zipped up the front. Her hair was pulled off her face with a peacock blue chiffon scarf.

"Hey, napper." She slipped into a pair of feathery kitten heels.

I stretched my fingers up to the ceiling. "Man, I slept so hard I feel like I just came back from another planet. Your bed is so comfy, it makes me want to cry."

"Cry away. It's worth crying over. I might take a little disco nap before we go out tonight, too." Deirdre was a champion sleeper and napped nearly every day, even after getting eight or nine hours at night.

"Is there a new term for disco nap yet?" I asked. "It seems like there should be by now."

"Come in here and talk to me. I'm making brownies."

I got up and followed her into the kitchen.

"I've been trying not to smoke weed because my bronchitis kicks in, even if I just have one hit, so I'm thinking about forming a new edible habit." She held up a beveled jelly jar with some buds in it. "I stopped at the apothecarium and bought this stuff I haven't tried yet."

I looked at the vibrant green buds, so appealing, so natural, so *healthy*-looking. They made me say something Deirdre had heard me say many times before. *Maybe I should try some?*

I had been attempting to become a marijuana enthusiast for nearly thirty years, with results that were either negligible (falling asleep within minutes, discomfited by people's faces and voices) to disastrous (extreme paranoia, racing heart, shortness of breath, paralysis.) Still, I would try it a few times a year to see if anything had changed. With the legalization of medicinal pot, I had high hopes that there would be a particular strain that worked well with my body chemistry. Some weed genius had to be out there wild-crafting a plant that would make things better in the exact way that I wanted them to be. Could a hit off a joint give me the two-valium-and-a-goblet-of-red wine feeling I desired? Pills, I had decided, had become undignified. Too commonly abused and they turned you into a gray zombie. A minor weed habit could be just the thing I needed.

Deirdre looked at me and smiled. She had witnessed many of my marijuana fails. "But you should probably just stick to alcohol. I don't think your wiry, spazzy body was made for THC. You can try some of this, but remember that we might find you drooling in the corner tonight." She put a Tito Puente record on the turntable and tied on a frilly polka-dot apron. The buds were tossed onto a baking sheet.

"I've heard it's even better, more potent, if you roast the weed first before you infuse it in the butter. My budtender told me that."

"Budtender."

"Oh, I know. Alert Merriam-Webster. I found some recipes online but they're all written by such stoner losers that I don't trust them. You get the feeling that these people have never read a recipe or cooked anything in their lives. You have to see the pictures of this guy's kitchen. Come here." She held out the laptop. "He has a poster of the Sydney Opera House taped, taped, to the wall. And a papasan chair." She scrolled further down. "Look. The mixing bowl he's using is this disgusting old tupperware that's probably leeching chemicals into everything."

"Well, what did you really expect?"

"I don't know. These shops try to be so high-end, and now that it's getting legalized and we got the white man taking over a job that black people are sitting in jail for, people are acting like weed is all fancy now. Designer."

"Right, the artisanal treatment."

"I just expected more from a lifestyle blog about cooking with weed. Maybe I should write a marijuana cookbook. With kind of a retro homemaker spin on it. That would probably sell."

She pulled out her grandmother's electric mixer and set it on her pink Formica table. While she beat the butter and sugar together, I melted flat chocolate disks over a double boiler. I loved making food with Deirdre. It was the only time I ever did it. She hosted a Sunday dinner party for years. Deirdre would prepare a pot roast or a casserole and I made the cocktails. Sometimes it turned into a pinochle tournament and other times a dance party. When new neighbors moved in and started to complain, some other friends took over the tradition. But they lived in Oakland so we never went. We always meant to, but the bridge was a whole thing.

The entire apartment was infused with the smell of weed and chocolate when there was a brief knock at the door followed by a regular mid-thirties dude wearing shorts and a shiny headband.

"Uh, hey you two. Wow. Baking some brownies, huh?" He extended his hand to me. "I'm Brian. I can trade you something for some, or pay you in bitcoins or a back rub."

"I'll bring something over before we go out, okay?" Deirdre said, kind of pushing him out the door.

"That was nice of you," I said after he left.

"He's okay. We had sex a couple times when he first moved in. I like him."

I let the envy register on my face. "How are you having sex with so many people still? I kind of don't want to have sex with anyone because I feel so rundown and what's the opposite of vibrant?"

"Rundown."

"Yeah, that's how I feel. I like the idea, but the reality just seems like, ugh, why."

I went into a long thing about how I felt like I had been really busy for the past twenty-five years, that I barely had a moment to myself, even though I knew it sounded ridiculous. I didn't have kids. I didn't have a full-time job. I hadn't had to take care of aging parents. "If you think about it what I've done," I said, "if you add it up and try to quantify it, it's basically zero. Goose egg!"

Deirdre's philosophy was that a lot of the stuff we witnessed, the parties and the music and the art, wouldn't have happened if we hadn't been there watching it happen.

"We altered things by being there," she said. "By showing up. We were everywhere. How could the San Francisco art scene have existed without us?"

It made me think about my failed attempts at singing and drawing, writing and dancing. I thought of the blur of bands and clubs and parties. Beach parties, house parties, art parties, street parties. "I didn't contribute anything," I said. "I was just *there*."

"We were important because we were making the scene," Deirdre said.

I thought of *making the scene* as meaning you were showing up. You were *making* it out of your house to see the band or *making* it to the party.

"But so did a lot of other people," I said. "We just as well couldn't have been there and it would have happened the same way."

"Or would it have?" She arched a brow. "I think it's like, by being there, we were *making* the scene. We were *making* it happen. It's not happening if there's no audience."

"So does that mean we're partially responsible for the tech boom? I mean, we were here when it happened."

"Totally," she said. "Things can't exist without their opposites."

"Remember that day when a bunch of us were at the park and we started talking about how people behave at a park? How funny they look when they're barbecuing or throwing a frisbee or getting a tan? Eating a popsicle? And then we kept going, pantomiming all of it for each other."

"Oh yeah!" Deirdre pretended to spike a volleyball.

"And Alex was there and he was really getting into it and then it became part of his standup act?"

"That was such a good day. We all worked like three days a week and could still pay our rent and buy beer."

"Like, we're not comedians but we helped him write that whole section of his act because we were there laughing about it. We kept going to his shows and helping him expand it. And then it became part of his comedy special. Now he lives in L.A. and owns a house and is on TV and shit. He must be a millionaire now. Maybe that's why I feel so empty and useless."

"Look, you've done your work around here," she said. "Not a lot of people can live in a dank warehouse with no heat for twenty years. You let people crash on your floor for weeks and it doesn't bother you. You barter things with alcohol at the bar. You can go with a flow like nobody. You don't even seem to notice the flow. You're in there and you're moving. You've been very important to San Francisco as we know it."

"Thanks for saying that. I feel like I've laissez-faired myself into a corner. Like I went with the flow and got washed ashore and I'm just sitting here drying up. Or like I'm one of those flotillas stacked high with garbage floating around the ocean."

"I'm not saying that means you never have to do anything different. If you ever do, you'll probably adapt to your surroundings very easily. You'd make such a good traveler. When you sell the house. Go to Iceland or Hong Kong or somewhere."

"But what do I come back to? I need money from the house to travel, but where will I keep all my stuff while I'm traveling?"

"Your new gross storage space, dummy. You don't have any stuff, anyway. I'm the one with stuff."

She was right. I didn't really own anything. "There's a chair I might want. A chair that was my grandfather's."

"Bring it over here while you're in Estonia. Next?"

"I think I'm going to eat a brownie."

Deirdre stepped back, lifted her arms up, and gave me a look like *not-my-problem-anymore.*

IT WAS THE KIND of night bound to go sideways. In between bands, trying to get another drink, I felt it. My legs went wobbly for a second and I grabbed the edge of the bar, briefly locking eyes with the woman next to me. Greta, maybe? Liesel? A German. The ex-girlfriend of the bass player in the next band. Deirdre's brother's old roommate. Cashier at the health food store. Used to make purses out of old Levi's. I knew all this, but had never spoken to her.

"You okay?" she asked. "You looked like you were about to go down for a second."

As soon as I started to speak I knew it was a mistake. My throat was dry, my voice a whisper. *I'm good.* I backed up against a stool and hoisted myself onto it. Lots of people in here. Lots of faces. Lots of hair. Lots of teeth. Lots of loose limbs. I'd get the bartender's attention and order a drink. No, I'd better wait. No, I'll order now. Maybe just a bitters and soda. Or a simple shot of tequila. I probably needed water. A tequila and soda. The soda would be good for me. Where was the bartender? Ignoring me. Probably for the best.

In a corner booth, Deirdre leaned back, her tattooed arms outstretched like colorful vines climbing a trellis. My goal was to make my way over there as quickly as I could without falling down or talking to anyone. First, I pivoted my hips with my hands planted on the back of the seat near my butt, and then I slowly slid my feet onto the floor, toes first. I started walking very carefully, hips tucked under, shuffling. Deirdre thought I was doing a bit.

"Oh, god. I love when she does this." She tapped the shoulder of the guy next to her. "This is exactly how a lot of old people walk if you check them out. It's like they're afraid of falling down, but instead of just walking slowly, they subconsciously pull everything in close, like they're curling up a tail underneath them."

"It could also be a back injury thing," the guy said, watching me approach. "I've fucked up my back before and totally walked like that. Is she okay?"

As I got to the final stretch, Deirdre egged me on. "Turn around! It looks so good from the back. You look like you don't even have an ass at all. Turn around!"

I kept coming toward them and slid in.

"Whoa. You are fucked up," Deirdre said. She pulled me in close. "It's not your drug, girl. Weed is not for you."

"Wait," the guy said. "That's from weed?"

I heard their voices making more sounds as I slumped into Deirdre's shoulder and tried to tune them out. I was now the fucked-up old person at the bar. The cautionary tale. Time to swirl down the toilet into self-loathing. Everyone was surely looking at me, talking about what a loser I was. How I was living in The Hose now. In my dead mom's house. How I left my job. How bad my skin looked.

"Help me get outside," I whispered to Deirdre. "I got to go walk."

She petted the back of my head. "You can't be walking around outside by yourself when you're like this. You're going to get raped. Or rolled like a bum."

Deirdre took me out to the sidewalk. The doorman was sitting on his stool with his arms folded across his chest smoking a cigarette.

"I need you to do us a favor, Gabe. Keep your eye on ol' Edes here, okay? She's kind of messed up. Slight edible overdose."

Gabe had been working the door for the past twenty years, but no one knew him very well. He was fiercely loyal to all the regulars, but never broke rank. He dutifully kicked an upturned bucket toward his stool. "She can sit here. I'll watch her."

"You sure you don't want to go home?" Deirdre asked.

I lowered myself onto the bucket. I never wanted to go home. Where was home? I'd be fine in a few minutes. I leaned back into the wall, newly dizzy when I closed my eyes. I wish I'd brought that cell phone so I could stare at it. A recent development was that if you sat somewhere with your head down, eyes on your phone, not engaging with the world, everyone assumed things were perfectly normal with you.

A few minutes or an hour later I went back inside the bar. The barback was someone I had slept with a few times when I was in my twenties. I couldn't remember why we eventually stopped doing it, but it probably had to do with both of us doing it with other people. Too much cross-fading all over one another back then. He came around to my side of the bar and gave me a big hug that lifted me off my feet.

"You look messed up," he said. "Are you okay?"

There were sirens coming down the street. A lot of sirens. Fire trucks, squad cars, ambulances.

Gabe came in, real low-key about it, and started telling small groups of people that the apartment building across the street was on fire. "Inside job," he said. "Fourth one to go up this summer."

Everyone from the bars spilled out onto the sidewalk. Firefighters were trying to get people to move, but it was nearly 1:30 a.m. and everyone was drunk and belligerent. Cops came over and told Matthew, the owner, that they wanted all the businesses on the street evacuated. Matthew handpicked a bunch of regulars, pulled us back inside, and shut off the lights.

I sat and the barback poured me a pint of water. I began to feel less neon.

"I have to show you something," Matthew said. He gestured to a kid, maybe about twenty-five or so, who came right over. "Okay, now give her the full show."

The guy put down his beer and stood in front of me like he was on stage. He slowly rolled up his left sleeve and pivoted to give me a good look. Gandhi tattoo. Then his right sleeve went up: Buddha tattoo. Left pant leg raised: Bob Dylan. Right pant leg: Matthew. Wait. This kid had a tattoo portrait of the fifty-three-year-old bar owner on his leg. It was actually a pretty decent rendering, but I wasn't quite sure what to say. He took his bows. Show was over.

"Don't you think he's cool?" the kid said. "Don't you think he's one of the coolest guys ever?"

Matthew sat there with one arm across his stomach, the other resting on it with his index finger hooked over the bridge of his nose, concealing a smile. "I told him it was a bad idea."

"Great idea," I said. "Legends."

Alert me when someone gets the face of a fifty-three-year-old woman tattooed on their body.

When I felt like I could walk again, I went into the back to see if Deirdre was still around. The dark room full of empty booths was too tempting and I passed out the minute I climbed into one. When I came to out of my blackbrained conk, it sounded like there were even more people in the bar. Another party had migrated over and I could smell smoke from the fire. The new bartender kept trying to shush everyone so that the neighbors didn't call the cops and it was clear that Deirdre had left. Probably with that guy she'd been having an off-and-on again thing with. I'd probably do the same, leave her here if she was passed out in a booth. Even though most people wouldn't understand, I thought it was a perfect example of what made our friendship work. We treated each other with respect. She knew I was safe. The bar had been like a second living room to us. She knew it was better that I sleep it off and walk out on my own rather than be carried out the door like an amateur. She had someplace else to be. The last thing I would ever want is to infringe on her freedom.

I peeled myself off the black vinyl and walked outside into

the wet, charred air. The sun had come up and I could see that the building across the street was toast. I looked both ways before I stepped out of the bar. The daywalkers were coming out. It was time for them to start their shift.

THE BOOZE HAZE, THE weed fog, the lack of sleep; none of it was helping. The wagon was gone. I walked around the block, up and down a couple alleys, retracing my steps as best I could. Nothing. I repeated the whole process three times, the third time saying out loud, *Not my car!* or *Nope!* every time I passed a vehicle that wasn't mine. Yes, the wagon was hard to miss, but it wasn't like I hadn't lost cars before.

What I did for years was buy a car for a few hundred bucks—real beaters, absolute shitboxes—and then lose them. Release them back into the wild. If you never had it registered or bought insurance, you could park anywhere you wanted, let it rack up a bunch of tickets, and then one day, its fate would be decided. You'd be walking down the street and there it would be, all locked up, jacked with the big yellow Denver Boot and you'd simply keep walking. Or sometimes the car wouldn't be there at all and you'd wonder whether it got towed, stolen, or you'd just been wasted and forgotten where you parked it.

I turned down a little alley I may or may not have parked on. Nothing. Dore Alley was a veritable laboratory of urine. Some old and dried, some canine, some feline, probably a little raccoon or opossum, but mostly it was fresh and human. Dried piss had this trick of transforming into invisible crystals that got lodged in your nose hairs. Once you smelled sun-drenched urine on a particular morning, it's nearly impossible to get through the rest of the day without being reminded of it.

I passed a yellow car and recalled the time a friend of mine rolled up to fetch me in an old yellow Datsun B210. It was *my* car. I'd only owned it for about six months and hadn't driven it in a few weeks, but it must have been hauled off by the city without me knowing. And there it was idling on the street with my friend behind the wheel. He said he bought it at the car auction out on Pier 70 a couple days before for $200. I laughed so hard.

The alley was quiet. I continued trudging past the cheaply built modern condos and waterlogged Victorians, all chipping and milky. I saw security cameras and electric garage doors and dead ferns plastered against windows. Each dwelling was the story of a historic battle, chaos masquerading as a formal explanation. There was the pornographer who had been there since the '70s. The shoemaker from Wisconsin who used to be a waitress. The music producer who made one popular record in 1994 and had a blue-felted pool table he never used. Lots of people with cancer. Women who no longer spoke to their sisters. An adult baby. The line cook who white-knuckled through his shift every night and then got trashed at the same bar before going home and falling asleep in front of the TV. The married couple who couldn't get pregnant. The party promoter with the bad back who secretly wore a girdle. The typesetter who died of AIDS. And who was there before them and before them and before them, going all the way back. Had anybody written down the stories from this particular block? Did anyone besides me care? Maybe once the mapping vehicles with the cameras on top were finished photographing every square-inch of the earth, they'll be free to circle back and vacuum all the stories. Was there a tech company already working on an app for stories of city alleys? Of course there was.

There were multiple specimens of human shit on the sidewalk and it all looked very unhealthy. I had the urge to yell, "You got a lot of tarry stool, San Francisco!" but I kept it to myself. There was an unspoken social contract between people on the street. If you do not need to let loose with the tornado inside your head, if you are capable of stopping yourself from crying and yelling in public, then by all means, you're required to do it. Keep it together for the good of society because we know the whole thing could unravel any moment.

On Harrison Street, walking zombie-slow, I wished that as I passed each address, it would disappear from my memory like a pencil illustration that could simply be erased. The leaden weight of so much history, all of it entirely unnecessary to move forward.

And then I couldn't hold it in. Just like that I became another disheveled woman dressed in black talking out loud to myself on the city streets.

I have pebbles in my shoes! I have rocks in my pockets! I yelled, and then checked to see if anyone was looking. I was in control and not in control. *There's liquid mercury in my veins!* I yelled up to the sliver of sky. I took a deep breath, lowered my voice, and started mumbling. *I'm a pile of ash. I'll seep into the ground and start over. Apricots and plums and the tennis balls found in juniper bushes and the moths in jars with blades of grass. It's gritty out there, people. It's a pretty gritty city. I've been dipped in the fog machine and rolled in the grit and that's part of me. I'm advertising it. It's not for sale. Joke's on you.*

People walked toward me, giving a wide berth as they passed, but I couldn't stop.

My coating of grit. My grit coat. I've been wearing it for a long time. A dirty mirror. A mirror reflects you back to you so you see you, not me. The better I am at it, the less I have to do.

I was crying. Walking through South of Market while talking nonsense and blubbering. A mess, a puddle. I stopped on a corner when a teenager asked if I was all right.

My answer: *This hologram may look shiny, but it isn't fooling anyone!*

His response: *You trippin'!*

I needed money to get on the train. I would ask someone. I would collect money from strangers as strangers had so often collected money from me. I approached a young white woman in a scuffed, tan leather jacket who also looked like she was finally heading home after a long and tricky night.

"Hey, can you help me out with a train ticket? I lost my wallet and..." But she was gone. Walked right past me like I hadn't even been there.

A skinny red guy with a body like a question mark sat in a nest of blankets and started talking to me from his corner perch. He'd been watching me pace around. "Hey, you! In the black! Blackie Onassis!"

I approached him slowly. His face was shiny, pockmarked, striated like shale. Corn kernel teeth. His voice sounded like he'd just chugged a pitcher of gravel.

"I'll give you a dollar if you go up to my friend over there and give him a message."

"That's it?" I asked. "Why don't you want to tell him?"

"Go tell him to suck the shit out of my ass."

"Hoo boy," I said. "I don't think I can right now."

"Do you want the dollar or not? All you gotta do is say, 'Laird says you can suck the shit out of his ass and walk away. It's easy. He's my friend. It's a joke. He's right over there."

I backed up so I wouldn't get another whiff of his breath, breath like someone had peeled back a can of dead mice fermented in malt liquor. I turned to where he had pointed. More or less a human mound tented by a yellow rain poncho. "Yeah? He won't freak out on me or anything?"

"No," Laird said. "His legs don't work so well. He could never stand up fast enough to come after you."

I walked over to the dude and cleared my throat. He squinted up at me, even though it wasn't sunny out, and I said it, employing the formal tone of a thespian butler. "Excuse me, sir. Sorry to bother you. Laird over there would like me to tell you that you can suck the shit out of his ass." It was hardly necessary, but I waited a moment to see if I could confirm receipt of the message. "Just a message from Laird," I said when he didn't respond. "If you want my opinion, I think that he's being very rude."

He lobbed a pathetic *Fuck You* my way and then yelled a louder one in Laird's general direction. I hoofed it back over, leveled my eyes at Laird, and held out my hand. He plunked down two warm quarters and some nickels and dimes.

"Oh, that was rich. That was worth it. Thank you. I'll pay you to do that anytime."

"Really? Well, I need some more money, so maybe there's someone else around you want me to provoke?"

"Don't get greedy. Jesus. All you bitches are alike." He laughed as if to show me that either it wasn't personal, or he hated all women. I couldn't tell.

I moved a few feet away and squatted down against the building. I asked passersby for change for a few minutes to see what it felt like. Not good. Too passive. Like I'd be stuck here all day. I tried approaching people to get used to what it felt like to be rejected over and over and over again. If I was going to start a new life, I should probably know. It was much too aggressive and I probably looked strung out. People dodged me or pretended to be talking on their phones. I did get a handful of pennies from someone who looked homeless. Why did the broke people give me money? Same thing at the bar. The poorest were the best tippers. Finally, I settled in to making myself look smaller, pitching my voice higher, and not overstating my case. "Do you have a quarter?" I said in a genteel, almost British lilt.

After about an hour, I had almost four dollars, but I was getting impatient.

I spotted a young black man, dressed in a slim, slate-blue suit. There were so few black people in San Francisco that maybe he would get a kick out of a down-and-out white person asking him for resources. "Sorry to bother you," I said. "I'm trying to get some money together for the train. I lost my wallet and my phone."

"That sucks. Maybe I can give you something." He pulled the wallet out of his inside jacket pocket. I saw a few twenties inside. "Shit. Sorry."

He started to walk away and then stopped and turned around. "You know what, why don't I just get you a ticket?"

I'm so glad I hadn't yelled something awful at him.

I walked beside him as he gave me a side-eye once-over, picking up speed as he approached the machine.

"Give me your address," I said, "and I will pay you back. I promise. I actually have almost four dollars right now, so I only need a little."

"It's no big deal," he said, putting his card in the machine. "What station?"

"Sunnyvale. That name sounds fake, huh? Sunny. Vale. Sunnyvale."

The machine spit my ticket out. He held it for a minute.

"Well, let's just say," he said before handing it over, "that I hope someone would do this for me if I ever had a night like you had. Or like it looks like you had."

A flush of shame washed over my face as I looked at the ticket in his hand. "Let me give you the money I have right now. I want to pay you back, though."

"It's okay. I mean, I guess you could Venmo me if you want."

"I've never done that before. Venmo."

"Paypal?"

"It's probably easiest if I send you cash in the mail."

"It's not easier, trust me."

"You can just write your address down and…"

"No one has ever sent me cash in the mail except my great-grandma. And then you'd have my home address and I don't really want to do that."

"Really?" I didn't want to blow it. "It must be hard to get made to feel uncomfortable so easily. Do I seem like I would be a stalker or something? Do you really think I'm going to show up at your house unannounced? I can barely remember my email address. You don't have to buy me a ticket if this is a big problem. Just forget it. This is getting stupid." I cut myself off and took a breath. "No, you're right. You know what? I'll just gift you this. Think of it as a paying you forward type thing. Did you see that movie?"

"No."

"The idea is just, like, do something nice for someone else…"

"Right."

"…and eventually it will come back around."

The next train was leaving soon. "Got the concept. Just didn't see the movie. Pay it forward," I said. "Heard of it. Thanks, again. I appreciate it."

I ran over to Laird's friend in the poncho and dropped the bills and change I'd received in his empty coffee cup. A few coins hit the pavement, startling him, and he looked up and shouted a final Fuck You. I ran down the platform and settled into a seat, the sun on my face. Made it.

The landscape changed quickly from the urban tangle of skyscrapers and apartment buildings to the homeless camps set up on the marshy flatlands next to the bay, and on to the soothing stretch of bus depots, pizza parlors, car washes, hardware and plumbing showrooms, with the brown hills in the distance on the east side and the green hills on the Pacific side. I tried to think about where I was going next, what I was going to do with whatever was left of my life, but my head hurt. It wouldn't let me hold on to an idea. My body ached, my heart was tired. I remembered a bumper sticker in a witchy pagan font I'd seen many times: *Exist.* Or *Co-exist.* Or there was one that said *Live Simply So That Others May Simply Live.* Was simply existing supposed to be some kind of life goal? Wasn't that what I'd been doing all along? Living one day at a time, living in the moment, in the present. Wasn't that the kind of advice lifestyle gurus were always going on about? So why did I feel like such a failure? Was it possible for a person to decide that they had been zen *retroactively* and feel chill about it? Maybe my problem wasn't that I'd been doing nothing, and that was just fine, but I'd been operating under the false impression that I'd accomplished something. I folded over on the seat next to me. It's fine not to be the eye or the light. I was a speck of dust from a distant star, one of billions of specks that had gotten caught up in the whirl. Maybe I had my own mini-glint. That sounded all right. I spent the rest of the ride practicing how it felt to believe that.

SUNNYVALE WAS ALREADY HOT and it would take me at least an hour to walk home. I imagined that the parking lots and the mini-golf course and the condos and the office park were orchards instead. The landscape as it was in the early twentieth century. Then, like a mirage, I thought I saw an actual orchard in the distance. Trees with gleaming dark red fruit dotting the lush branches like ornaments. I blinked, a wandering exile lost in the desert. Yes, it was a real orchard. Part of the old fruit stand, a place I'd passed in the car many times as a kid, but had never been. It was a hundred years old. Barely any businesses in this valley were that old.

I walked over, looking at the rows of fruit, wishing I had the guts to grab something.

"Have a cherry!" There was a woman behind me. I turned around, taking in the heavy lines on her face, her bright eyes, the vented bucket cap on her head. She motioned toward an overflowing basket and I plucked one out and looked at it in my palm, gleaming like it had been polished. I popped it behind my teeth, pulled out the stem, and tasted the sweet and sour of it.

"I would buy a whole basket if I hadn't just lost my wallet."

"Take a few," she said. "You look like you could use a little pick-me-up." A pick-me-up. Something my mom would have said.

I spit the pit into my hand and looked lost for a moment.

She pointed to a bowl with pits and used toothpicks in it. "Now take these."

I cupped my hands and the woman dropped a bunch of perfect cherries in them. "You're so nice. I'll come back and buy some. I've been meaning to for years, for my entire life."

"No problem. We're all on our own schedule."

I pictured what it must have looked like around here when I was born. Before I was born. There was a Native tribe I had learned about in elementary school. The Ohlone. At least I remembered the name, though all other details escaped me. In elementary school we only learned about natives in the context of Father Junipero Serra and the Missions, but I'd never bothered to find out what else there was to it.

I said thanks and continued home with my fistfuls of cherries, spitting the pits out through the pellet gun of my tongue. As I walked down the sidewalk looking at the houses, the older ones in browns and tans, the modern ones painted gunmetal and tangerine, my eyes fixated on the color they all had in common. Green. Garden hoses. Sources of water coiled up in front of every one. I hadn't drunk straight out of a hose in years and I suddenly craved that taste in my mouth. The warm, grassy, mineral taste of water from a hose.

I skittered up to a garage like some kind of hamstrung ninja, cranked on the spigot, and held the nozzle to my mouth. So warm and dirty. I glanced up and saw a granny looking straight down at me from inside. Busted. I scampered back to the sidewalk and tried to resume walking like I had done nothing wrong. One of the ways I consoled myself when I felt self-conscious was to remember that people weren't looking at me half as much as I thought, but that wasn't true of old people. I looked back and the old woman was out on her front step, hands on hips, shooing me away like an unwelcome goat. I smiled and waved. Another mile to go. Soon, I would collapse on my mom's bed. But then what? A nap, if my fried system would allow me to settle down enough. And then what? A swim before the onslaught of Scott's scheduled workmen? I could possibly call Adit.

As I headed down the final stretch home, I looked at the line of parked cars on the block. Someone was either having a big summer pool party or someone had died. Yellow and white balloons were tied to a sign of some kind, a sandwich board. A red and white realtor's sign. An open house. The address on the sign was mine. Ours. Our house. For sale.

I broke out running toward home just as a couple emerged from the atrium. I ran right past them and came through the front door, hair damp, face mottled red. I stopped in my tracks and my b.o. spread out around me like a gas. A couple with a baby was in the entryway with Ken, the realtor. I grabbed him by both shoulders.

"How the fuck is this happening now?"

Ken was tall and muscular with a thick neck and high-voltage smile.

"Whoa, whoa. Hello! Everything is fine."

The couple scooted out and it seemed like he was placating them more than me. His eyes flashed something that went from disgust to recognition, the smile remaining all the while. He steered me down the hallway by the shoulders, just as Scott opened the screen and came in from the backyard.

"What the fuck is going on?" I screamed. "What are you doing? How could you do this? You asshole!" He had a soft, light blue sweater knotted around his shoulders like a fucking maniac.

"I'm sorry. I really am," Scott said. "But I had to do it. I told you I was going to do it. We talked about this. I've been trying to get hold of you for the last two days and if you would just turn on the phone I gave you, you would have known I was coming."

"Why now? When did you get here?"

"This morning. I took the red-eye."

"You spent the night on a plane? Why do you look like you just stepped off a golf course? What is wrong with you?"

"Could you two do this somewhere else please?" Ken pleaded.

"I knew you weren't going to do it," Scott said.

"I was doing it! It was happening!"

"I had to make every call, manage every appointment, pay every bill. We have to rip off the Band-Aid."

"Where am I going to live? I have nowhere to live!" Ken patted him on the back, his head bowed. "What am I going to do?" I fumed on. "Someone is going to make an offer on it and then I'm going to be like, Oh, welcome to your new house! Let me just dump my things in a grocery sack and end up I don't know where!"

Ken turned and walked away with his phone to his ear.

"Come on, let's get out of here," Scott said. "There'll be a bunch of people coming in and out until four. Let's drive the wagon somewhere. Why are you so sweaty? You look terrible."

"It got stolen."

"What? Did you call the police?"

"No." I looked at the ground. "Or maybe it got towed."

"Or maybe it got towed?"

"My phone and my wallet also got stolen or I lost them or something."

"Of course." He lifted my chin with his hand and leveled his eyes on mine. "Answer me one last time. Are you a drug addict?"

"No!"

"Pills count as drugs. Are you on pills?"

"Shut up. The car was in pretty bad shape anyway. It was a pain."

He turned away and silent-screamed at the ceiling. "I can't believe you lost it. Hold on."

I followed him into the living room where a woman in a backless sundress was squatting down, opening a low drawer in the china cabinet.

"Oh, excuse me," she said, standing up and backing against it. "This is a beautiful piece of furniture. Is it part of the staging?"

We walked out of the room and then I quickly popped my head back in to see if I could catch her snooping again. There she was rolling open another drawer.

"You think you're a Kennedy?!" I shrieked. "Opening all the drawers! Ken, make sure that woman is not pocketing the pewter napkin rings!"

Ken speedwalked into the kitchen, blabbing on his Bluetooth. "Yeah, yeah. Little old lady situation. Everything really out of date." He looked over at us and mouthed a *Sorry*. "Cheryl, can I call you back?"

Scott put a hand on Ken's shoulder. "Bro, do you mind if we take your car to go get some food? We don't have wheels right now and it's probably better if we give you some space anyway."

I saw a flash of the high-school Ken. The guy who would breakdance in the quad at lunchtime and anointed himself with some kind of rapper name. It made me happy to remember it. How stupid and innocent.

"Ken, what was your rap name?" I said. "MC what was it?"

"You mean MC McDiddly?" He busted out a gangster pose and held it.

"Yes, yes. That was it."

Ken stayed frozen in the pose as Scott and I waited.

"Okay, you can stop doing that now," I said. "I remember."

He shook his limbs loose, but the memory of MC McDiddly had kindled something in him. "Do you remember the air jam contest? The one where me and Lopes did the Too $hort song?"

I did. I thought for a second about saying I didn't remember, in order not to give him the satisfaction, but the only point of that was cruelty.

"Yeah, yeah. I remember," I said. "And then when you won…"

"We didn't win!" he interrupted. He was wound up. "That's the thing. We *should* have won. Fucking Krista Lindow won with her Madonna bullshit."

I knew he hadn't won, but I wanted him to think people remembered him winning.

The door opened and Shirley Sklamberg suddenly came wandering through, looking embarrassed to be there, like she'd been caught breaking the rules. "I just wanted to say thanks again for Willow Glen Lifestyles. You'll have to help out again next year." She waved and walked out to the backyard.

"What's Willow Glen Lifestyles?" Scott asked. "Who was that?"

"And all the teachers and the administration were pissed off at me," Ken went on. "They said it was because of the language, but there Krista was, doing "Like A Virgin." It was really because I wasn't black and it was black music. The sheer definition of racism."

"Is that the definition of racism?" I said. "Don't answer that. Anyway, I remembered you winning so that's something. Did you ever go to France? To study clowning?"

"I can't believe you remember that."

"Well, it was memorable. It was the first time that I ever heard that word used as a verb."

Scott said impatiently. "So, the car? It's cool if we take it for a bit?"

MC McDiddly pulled the fob out of his breast pocket and tossed it across the counter. "You'll know which one it is, bro. You should take her out on Pierce Road and open her up. Zero to seventy in three-point-three seconds. Just watch out for the fuzz."

My hangover and lack of sleep was having a drug-like effect. I had gone from experiencing supreme betrayal to fond reminiscence to surrender in the space of five minutes.

"The fuzz!" I screamed.

Scott put his arm around me and held up Ken's car key. "Awesome. We got a Tesla for a few hours."

"How embarrassing," I said once we were outside. I plopped down into the matte grey electric sports car and looked around. "What do we know about Ken's penis?"

"It's very environmentally conscious," he said.

We took off toward the hills, staying silent for a few blocks.

"I'm sorry," Scott said softly. "But you know how you are."
I started to get mad again, until he followed up. "And you know
how I am."

Tears sprung to my eyes and my nose started to itch. "I know,
I know," I said, rubbing my nose furiously with the back of my
hand. "I'm sorry I haven't been the greatest. I tried to do what I
could to help, but I guess I was stalling."

"Because now you have to decide what's next."

I turned the radio to KFJC. Even seeing the call numbers of
the college radio station on the display soothed me a bit. "That's
weird, right?" I looked over at Scott as he adjusted his legs underneath the steering wheel. "Tears of a Clown just went right into
Cathy's Clown. Two clown songs in a row."

"Maybe they're onto MC McDiddly. Maybe they're doing an
all-clown set." He grabbed my nose and squeezed it while honking
the horn a couple times.

When the song ended, the deejay came on with his lazy surf
drawl. "Next up, it's a rad song from one of my favorite Elvises."
Scott and I looked at each other. *Clown Time Is Over.*

"I think a lot about clowns. About how necessary they are,
you know?" I said.

"Necessary?"

I tried harder than usual to articulate my thoughts. I talked
all throughout the song about how I thought clowns performed a
service to society. Whether they were funny or stupid or grotesque
or sad or scary, their job was to be a spectacle for you to project
your emotions onto. I thought so many people were scared of
clowns because they were scared of their feelings.

When confronted with my flimsy philosophizing, Scott usually
tore into me. This time he acted as if it wasn't happening. "Is this
Cocteau Twins?" he said when the next song came on. "What
language did this woman sing in anyway?"

"Let's call the deejay!"

Scott roared into the air, "Call KFJC!"

"Calling KFJC," said the car.

Scott looked over at me and smiled when the deejay answered. "Are you in the middle of an all-clown set?"

"That's right. All clowns, all day. Or until my slot ends at five."

"So what was that last one? Cocteau Twins, right?"

"Fifty-Fifty Clown. Off of *Heaven or Las Vegas*."

"Thanks, man! We're loving it."

"We love clowns!" I yelled at the windshield. "The world needs them!"

"Right on. I'll give you a shout out on air. What's your names?"

We gently rounded the corners, passing older ranch-style homes and new stucco palaces with circular driveways and wrought-iron gates. With each one, another wash of memory came over me. Driving for no reason. Driving to parties. Driving to crash someone's pool.

"Okay, are you ready?" Scott looked over at her. "I'm going to gun this thing."

"Take off your seatbelt!" I knew he wouldn't do it. I unfastened mine and put my feet up on the dash and folded my arms behind my head.

"Aw, don't do that. Come on."

"No, you come on. You know this road so well. Just open yourself up to the distinct possibility that we can drive fast for thirty seconds without crashing and dying."

"You might not be afraid of dying, but…"

"It's not even dying I'm afraid of, really. It's being maimed. The worst would be lying by the side of the road, punctured and bleeding. Slowly bleeding out until help comes. But maybe when that happens, your body goes into shock so you feel kind of great and spacey. We'll never know unless we try."

"I have a family. I have people who depend on me."

"Good one! Okay, go ahead. I'll keep my seatbelt off and you sit there like a safety conscious law-abiding citizen with yours on."

"And in doing so I'm clearly demonstrating that I'm not an idiot."

"Think about it. We're definitely not going to crash now because we just spent all this time talking about what if we crashed. That's how these things work."

Scott looked out his window for a second. He took a breath, looked over at me, and unlatched his seatbelt. Bracing himself, he punched the accelerator. I screamed. Houses and mailboxes were flying by on both sides. The car swerved around the bends, the yellow signs a different speed limit for each curve, 21 MPH, 19 MPH, 13 MPH, numbers that were designed to make you slow down and take notice. On one of the sharpest ones, the guard-rails came within a foot of the car. We flew past scrub oaks and redwoods and mountains of ivy.

"This thing is wound tight!" Scott yelled.

In the distance, I could see kids kicking a ball on the lawn in an unfenced front yard. I yelled in a voice like the narrator of a safety film. "Remember that a bouncing ball in the road is usually followed by a small child!"

"Stay there, children! Don't run out in the street!" Scott yelled.

"Honk the horn, honk the horn!"

Scott blasted the horn, racing past the children at about ninety. and let his foot off the accelerator. The needle on the speedometer started to drop. We were both laughing.

"Again, again, again!"

But we knew we wouldn't do it again. We were out of breath, cracking up. We passed a series of metal mailboxes that had obviously been pegged by a teenager holding a baseball bat out the passenger-side window.

"I remember that," Scott said. "Swinging bats at mailboxes and catching air off of Fruitvale Road."

He turned up the radio. The methodical drumming and tambourine of one of my all-time favorite songs.

"This was your favorite," Scott said.

"Until I heard it played way too much and it became everyone's favorite and they named a music festival after it."

"You should be happy you share the earth with other people who recognize it's a good song."

I put my feet back on the dash and clasped my hands across my belly. "I want to cry again."

"Just listen to it."

"And it has the word clown in the lyrics! Listen. *She'll turn once more to Sunday's clown.*"

We stopped talking as the song wound down and we reached the top of the road by the old Paul Masson winery. The place where I snuck in through the brush to see James Brown, Ella Fitzgerald, Ray Charles, Stan Getz, Dizzy Gillespie, Dave Brubeck, Willie Nelson, Diana Ross. The list went on. My greatest education to date was growing up near a winery that closed down and became an upscale concert venue with poor security.

Scott killed the engine and we got out, the whole valley spread out below us, its freeways and roads pumping cars all the way out to San Francisco and the Bay. Scott took out his phone. I waited for him to snap a picture of the view, but he put his arm around me, turned us around, and reversed the camera so the picture was us against the view. I threw my arm around him and smiled. My first selfie. A fiasco.

"You want to try?" Scott asked, offering me the key.

"I'll do it, but my adrenal system is all blown out. Fight or flight. Running from the proverbial bear."

"Yeah, just take it slow. You really don't want to fuck up Ken's car."

"He'd breakdance all over my face."

I got into the car and carefully adjusted the driver's seat and the mirrors. I clipped my seatbelt on and looked over my shoulder as I backed onto the road. The DJ was reading off the nightly entertainment calendar, new bands I'd never heard of and clubs I'd probably never go to.

"And here comes another clown song," he said. "I also wanna give a hey to Scott and Paula for calling in. They're, uh, really enjoying my whole clown thing. Right on."

We continued down the hill. At the first turn, I accidentally hit the wipers and quickly shut them off. Then I turned on the headlights when I meant to signal.

"Turn them back on," Scott said. "You should have them on right now."

"Look at that," I pointed up to a biplane dragging a banner across the sky. "What does it say?"

"It says, don't hit those squirrels!"

I jammed on the brakes and Scott pointed to two little buddies scampering across the road.

"And don't wreck the Tesla," he teased. "And come out and visit us sometime."

I accelerated slowly, coasting along at a steady speed, and then I turned my lights back on.

THANK YOU

Jami Attenberg

Anthony Bedard

Raquel Bedard

Alex Behr

Phyllis Berg

Alan Black

Michael Black

Jack Boulware

Susie Bright

Jibz Cameron

Marc Capelle

Leland Cheuk

Angela Coon

Eli Crews

Gus Crews

Ruth Curry

Arielle Eckstut

Dia Felix

Emily Gould

Jim Greer

Jonn Herschend

Pia Hinckle

Tara Jepsen

Jennifer Joseph

Chris Kehoe

Dan Kennedy

Christian Kiefer

Arline Klatte

Anne Lisick

Chris Lisick

Paul Lisick

Ron Lisick

Laura MacDonald

Lisa Margonelli

Jeff McDaniel

Chris Mittelstaedt

Randy Miles

Greg Milner

Joshua Mohr

Carrie Bradley Neves

Marc Neves

Marcy Norton

Aimee Page

Richard Panek

RADAR Productions

Jan Richman

Mary Roach

Zachary Ronan

Rowland Writers Retreat

Alena Rudolph

Samantha Schoech

Lora Schulson

Anna Seregina

Bucky Sinister

Matthew Specktor

Penelope Starr

Amy Sullivan

Amber Tamblyn

Michelle Tea

Kevin Thomson

ABOUT THE AUTHOR

Beth Lisick is a writer and actor from the San Francisco Bay Area, currently living in Brooklyn. She is the author of five previous books, including the *New York Times* bestseller Everybody Into the Pool, and co-founder of the Porchlight Storytelling Series. Beth has also worked as a baker, a promotional banana mascot, a background extra for TV and film, and an aide to people with developmental disabilities and dementia. This is her first novel.

7.13OOKS